THE TRIALS OF JACK KEMPER

LIBERTY ISLAND
Episode 1

JOHN BLAHUT & JOSEPH PUGH

THE TRIALS OF JACK KEMPER
Copyright © 2017 John Blahut and Joseph Pugh

All rights reserved.

No part of this publication may be reproduced, distributed, or transmitted in any form or by any means, including photocopying, recording, or other electronic or mechanical methods, without the prior written permission of the publisher, except in the case of brief quotations embodied in critical reviews and certain other noncommercial uses permitted by copyright law.

This book is a work of fiction. Names, characters, places and incidents are either products of the author's imagination or used fictitiously. Any resemblance to actual events, locales, or persons, living or dead, is entirely coincidental. All rights reserved. No part of this publication can be reproduced or transmitted in any form or by any means, electronic or mechanical, without permission from the authors.

Cover by Joseph Pugh
Print format by The Book Khaleesi

ISBN: 978-1-0722-3409-8

CHAPTER 1

The Bravo Colony Operations Center had seen its best days come and go. Long gone were the days of high polish, spotless floors and, for the most part, working command consoles. The hustling purpose of motivated people had slowly disappeared over the years. The large shifts of dutiful operators had devolved into shifts of a half dozen, somewhat lazy, state employees who occasionally monitored the few remaining radio, radar and environmental systems that still functioned.

The boney rear end of a clearly long and wiry man protruded from beneath a sensor console. A tool belt hung from the hips of his dirty and stained overalls. Two spanners, a screw-driver and a single roll of duct tape sat on the floor within reach. His voice called out, "Try it again!"

A man in uniform sitting on the other side of the console pressed a few buttons. He scratched his head, furrowed his brow and promptly smacked the top of the console causing a loud thump, "Nothing!" he said.

It always struck Jack as odd how the invention of integrated circuits actually added more parts to a machine being that the nature of the mechanism itself was to integrate parts. But as old parts get integrated, inevitably, so are new parts created. This created complexity that over the course of the past one hundred and ninety-seven years evolved in a way only great minds could actually comprehend. And if suffering in the absence of a great mind, Jack Kemper and a roll of duct tape were usually an adequate substitute.

A loud buzz and pop could be heard just seconds before a puff of smoke bellowed out of the console. It was followed by a thump on the underside, which, in turn, led to a barrage of shouting and cursing, "You stupid mother-fucking piece of shit bastard!" A few seconds later Jack crawled out from under the console rubbing the top of his head through his scraggy, short, blonde hair while shaking the feeling back into his other hand.

"I think it's dead, Jack." the uniformed man said.

Jack stared at his hand for a few seconds, flexing his fingers and giving it one last shake. He stared hard at Carl, the naturally brilliant blue of his eyes barely even noticeable through the bloodshot sclera that entangled them, "Carl, I don't know who was playing around down there but they've crossed a bunch of wires and I think it's even missing a board or two."

"Who would do that?" Carl asked.

THE TRIALS OF JACK KEMPER

Jack bent down and picked up his tools, "I don't have a clue, Carl. I'm an engineer not a detective."

"Do we need to report this?"

"Have at it," Jack said flatly as he turned and walked away while feeling for a bump on his head.

Bravo Colony was NASA's second attempt at a permanent orbital colony. While the wealthy elite were building private manmade island kingdoms back on Earth, the US govern-ment was more interested in distancing itself from the chaos and disease that was sweeping the planet.

The colony maintained an orbit of about eighty miles above the Earth. Many colonists held fast to the argument that this distance wasn't quite far enough. There had actually been a movement among them to have the colony orbit the moon. This idea was promptly voted down by a group far too sober to make such decisions. Jack Kemper was not a member of that group.

Jack spent the better part of a decade helping to design Bravo Colony although he grew quite disenchanted through the process. Sure they had accepted his plan for the water reclamation system and his air circulation and recycling system was once deemed "revolutionary" by Engineering Quarterly, however, his plans for a brewery and distillery had been soundly rejected. It was this setback that had kept him from joining the colony at the outset.

Jack had also played a role in Bravo Colony's aesthetic appeal. It was largely the result of taking the lead architect out to a series of bars on a Tuesday night. It was at bar four and on drink number seventeen that Jack recounted his grandfather's wonderful tale of the 2072 Kansas City Chiefs victory in Super Bowl CVI. He mentioned how he felt the colony should be shaped like a football. Its spinning motion would be like a perfect spiral endlessly floating through space. At first the architect wondered what would be so unique about a spherical colony. It took Jack no less than three more drinks to explain, to the Brit, the nuance of American football and the shape of its balls.

Bravo Colony was now fifteen years old. Its population had peaked a decade ago at the original target of twenty-five thousand citizens, however, the strain of maintaining that high of a population proved to be too difficult. Food and supply shortages were common. Power outages were frequent.

The outlook of most colonists had waned in synchronicity with the civilization they had left below. It became all too apparent to everyone involved that there would be no shiny future. So as one would expect, the population began to naturally reduce itself over time. After all, what sane person could justify bringing a child into this situation?

Jack Kemper was a very frustrated man. As a Mechanical Engineer for Bravo Colony he was expected to keep the place in orbit and habitable. This meant he was essentially tasked to do the impossible. So he drank a lot of alcohol and he drank it quite frequently, but he never drank it on the job. That's not to say he never drank it in between jobs. He had thought about stopping for a drink on the way back from his morning work order and as he stood in the office of his supervisor, Sam Dillinger, he had a difficult time remembering why he hadn't done so.

The overhead light flickered erratically as he soberly discussed the results of his morning work order, "Sam, I don't know who would do that to the sensor array but it was quite properly screwed in all the right places."

A firmly built man with a halo of graying brown hair, Sam was ten years Jack's senior and at fifty-five his wit had aged like a fine, dry wine. He sat behind his desk without looking at Jack and shuffled some papers, "Sounds like someone that knew what they were doing."

"Even if that were the case, why would anyone do it?"

An exasperated Sam looked up at Jack, "I have no idea," he said as he pulled a work order out of the stack.

"Right, but do we need to be concerned."

"Sure, we're pretty much flying blind right now. I'm just not sure what we can do about it. We don't have the parts to fix it." He held the paper out for Jack.

Jack grabbed the paper and looked down at it, "Scrubber 6? That scrubber is shot, Sam."

Sam leaned back clasping his hands behind his head and put his feet up on his desk, "You say that every time."

"Right, I do say it every time. Look, if you can't get us the parts we need we're all going to die anyway. What's the point?"

Sam shook his head with a wry smile on his lips. He was all too familiar with Jack's doom and gloom prognostications, "Sure. Sure, Jack. I'll just wave my hands around and produce the parts out of thin air!"

Jack's sarcasm was a therapeutic response to imminent death. Well, sarcasm and alcohol. Unfortunately, due primarily to poor decision making on his part, he barely had a buzz going so sarcasm would have to suffice, "Maybe you could try it with a wand in one hand?"

Sam was the only boss Jack had ever known. He had recruited Jack straight out of MIT to work on Bravo Colony. Jack understood Sam's position. And Sam understood the futility of their predicament, "I could try a wand. I could also put Malinda in a slinky dress and have her prance across a stage. Sadly, not even 'The Great Samdini' can make the parts appear. They don't exist! They're not coming! You need to come up with an in-house solution."

Malinda was a close friend to Sam and Jack and a frequent overnight guest at Jack's living quarters. She had long black hair and a very sultry build. Sam waited impatiently for Jack's reply.

"Sorry, you lost me. I was picturing Malinda in a slinky dress. She didn't have it on long." Jack winked.

It was apparent from Sam's expression that he was quickly growing tired of a conversation that was going nowhere. It couldn't go anywhere. The resupply vessels stopped arriving two years ago when the US Government dissolved, "Fix the damn C02 scrubber Jack!"

"Can I borrow your wand?" Jack quipped.

Sam conceded, "Sure, if I had one."

Jack's short lived jovial manner faded, "But in all seriousness Sam, do you have some duct tape? I'm working on my last roll and this scrubber is going to use most, if not all, of it."

Sam pointed to the supply cabinet, "We always have duct tape, but we're down to the pink and green."

Jack was not amused, "Fuck me!" He walked over to the cabinet and picked up two rolls of pink duct tape, "I also need something I can use for the tubing; about an eighth of an inch in diameter and roughly six inches long."

Sam shrugged and shook his head, "I don't have anything that small."

Jack resigned himself to another dodgy patch job, "I guess I can stop by the Mess Hall and pick up a straw. It should get the thing working again but I'm not sure how long it's going to last."

Sam tried to buoy Jack's spirits, "Jack, just keep things patched together until the Texas Republic gets their resupply on its way." But they both knew Texas was falling apart with the rest of the world.

Jack put the duct tape in his belt, turned around and started out of the office, "I stopped holding my breath for that last year. I kept passing out. I honestly can't believe you still think it's going to happen." he said dismissively.

"What else is there? Accept our fate? We might as well jump into the escape pods now and head back down to hell... I mean Earth," his voice rising as Jack disappeared out the door.

Harry Tang was a small, thin man with thick glasses. He was always quite personable however he could often come across as a bit of an odd duck. The son of a wealthy Chinese businessman, he didn't suffer through the food lines, riots and near starvation that afflicted
many of his peers.

He had attended Stanford University and focused on microbiology for several years, but unfortunately the university system collapsed just before he could complete his PhD. This left Harry at somewhat of a disadvantage in the field and filled him with a deep-seated resentment. It was this resentment that now motivated him.

Harry was currently one of Bravo Colony's finest laboratory technicians whose primary area of expertise was the restructuring of waste proteins into useful and tasteful forms of sustenance. He was quite a fan of the more exotic proteins as they offered the greatest potential for new flavor profiles. The search for such proteins often led him through the bowels of the colony where he was able to collect samples prior to treatment. His dedication to the craft allowed him special access to the more industrial areas.

The water reclamation area was located on Subdeck "C". It was a large and noisy area that was unusually moist for those accustomed to the low humidity of the colony. A myriad of large pipes ran like a maze along the walls and over the ceiling. Smaller pipes branched off the larger ones leading in and out of a staggering number of filters and processors. The air had the heavy scent of sewage and that smell usually found its way into the clothing of those that spent any amount of time here.

Harry stood among this labyrinth of engineering on this day, not as a lab technician searching for new proteins, but as a pragmatist. He might argue that it was patriotism, but he'd be lying to himself. Looking at all the pipes and intricate valves before him he wondered; exactly how drunk was Jack when he came up with this design?

It took Harry several minutes to find the one particular part that he was looking for. It was the single point of failure that would cause the entire water reclamation system to breakdown. Jack would later reflect on this and argue that he had pointed that fact out to Sam, but Sam assured him that failure of the part was highly unlikely and the budget wouldn't… Jack lost interest in the conversation at that point.

Harry slid an overstuffed backpack from his shoulder and let it drop to the floor. It landed with a muted clang, but his back screamed at him at a much higher volume after being relieved of the heavy load. He straightened himself, almost as a reflex, and fixed his attention on the flow governor.

The flow governor was solidly affixed to the pipe by six rather large bolts. After thoroughly examining the situation, Harry knelt next to the pack and began burrowing through its contents. He retrieved tool after tool, testing each one against the bolts that held the flow governor in place. Mechanical aptitude was not one of his strengths. He quickly became frustrated and started tossing the tools aside when they proved to be the wrong one. The floor around the pack became littered with those that he had discarded. Eventually, after sorting through everything he had brought with him, he found two spanners that would work.

Removing the nuts proved rather easy, but when Harry tried to pull the first bolt out from the mount it wouldn't budge. It had seized in place. He tried prying it out with one of the screwdrivers he brought, but the attempt was unsuccessful. Luckily, he had also packed a rubber mallet. He attempted to hammer the bolt out but the mallet missed the target altogether. The momentum of the wild swing caused him to bang his knuckles against the adjacent pipes. In a fit of rage and pain, he threw the rubber mallet against the wall where it ricocheted off the pipes and hit him squarely in his bollocks. A series of searing pains, bolts of lightning sent by what must have been Thor's hammer radiated from his groin; doubling him over.

Harry staggered in pain for a few moments waiting for it to subside. He glared at the flow governor. All of this strenuous activity was quickly tiring him out and the lingering pain certainly helped to exacerbate his mounting frustration. He walked back over to where the mallet had landed, cursed at it and picked it up. Turning toward the governor in a fit of rage he swung at the bolt. With his first swing he knocked the bolt out. His second swing came in quick succession and took out another. The swings kept coming until, he was breathless, his rage had subsided and all six bolts were scattered on the ground.

Harry tossed the mallet towards his pack and sat down on the floor to regain his composure. There was no doubt in his mind that Jack was to blame and these tribulations were all directly related to Jack's terrible design. Sam would have agreed with that assertion, but only in an effort to mess with Jack.

After a few moments of rest and having regained some of his composure, Harry stood up and began his effort to remove the flow governor from the mount. He tried to pull it free, but much to nobody's surprise it wouldn't budge. Placing one foot on the piping to the right side of the governor he pulled once again. He grasped onto it and lifted his left foot onto the piping putting the entire weight of his small body into the effort. With one final momentous pull the infernal device sprang free from its mount with a burst of water.

The sudden release of the part sent him flying backwards. He had a quick sensation of weightlessness for just a split second before it was rudely interrupted by impact with the floor. The jolt knocked the wind out of him, leaving him dazed. It took a few seconds for him to regain his sense of awareness. Water was pouring out of the hole. The floor of the subdeck, as well as Harry himself, was quickly being covered with quite offensively smelling water and it was rising far more rapidly than he had expected. He quickly stood up and grabbed his backpack. He tossed the flow governor into it, hurriedly rounded up the scattered tools and began to head towards to the lift.

Harry cautiously poked his head out through the access panel to see if anyone was around before stepping out into the main corridor of Subdeck "C". It was clear. He stepped out in to the corridor and the access panel quickly slid shut behind him. He slung his backpack over his shoulder as he walked down to the end of the corridor and calmly entered the lift.

Jack exited the lift on Subdeck "C" with a thick white straw in hand and packing three rolls of duct tape. Enough material for any engineer worth their salt to bitch, piss and moan for thirty minutes while fixing a myriad of problems.

As Jack stepped down from the lift deck he was greeted with wet feet. He had landed in a pool of water. The result, he thought, of a small but consistent leak in the water reclamation system. This did nothing to improve his mood. He angrily muttered, "That's a lot of water."

Jack considered himself a pragmatist. There were times though, like this one, where he thought through all of his options and even included the remotest of possibilities. This usually occurred when the solution

THE TRIALS OF JACK KEMPER

could involve a lot of work. For instance, he felt he should investigate the source of the water and at least verify it was just a small leak that had been going on for some time, however, there was the possibility that this was something much larger. It might require the better part of his afternoon to repair. And his work order was for a quick scrubber repair job. He reasoned he could be at the bar in less than two hours if he stuck to his work order. He might, then, be in just the right mental state he'd need to be in when Sam called him in the middle of the night to fix the issue, if in fact, it was a more serious issue.

Jack resigned himself to figure out what was going on after several minutes of internal debate. He rarely took the initiative these days. He walked down the corridor, a few feet, to the maintenance access panel. He punched in his code and entered the water reclamation area. He could hear the water flowing immediately. He walked past a couple of large containment vats and the sight he was greeted with forced him to whimsically mutter, "That's odd. When did we put a fountain here?" Unfortunately, there was nobody around to appreciate the sarcasm. He really couldn't believe what he saw. It made about as much sense to him as someone removing boards from a sensor array.

Jack walked over to the communications panel on the wall. He pressed a few buttons. A familiar voice came over the speaker, "Engineering, Sam speaking."

"Hey Sam, you won't believe this shit." he said.

"What now, Jack?"

"It looks like somebody removed the flow governor on the water reclamation system."

"Well, that makes about as much sense as removing a couple boards from a sensor array."

"That's exactly what I thought!"

"Well we can't leave it like that."

"Right, could you bring down the backup?"

"I'm on it."

The Hog and Dog was a small, dirty, pub with poor lighting, cheap drinks and patrons that cared less about the taste of a cocktail than they did the strength of it. On the lower end of the seedy side, it had just seven tables, four bar stools and, for some reason, a tarnished stripper pole directly in the center of the room. Jack Kemper called it his second home and the regulars considered him family.

Jack's drinking buddies were already there waiting for him at their favorite table. Well, it was the only table in the place that didn't have a wobble. Ricky was the first to see Jack enter, "Hey! There he is! Jack Kemper, the guy that keeps us all alive!" Ricky was a professional drunkard with a promising paper shuffling career in the administration's red tape department. Jack admired him.

"Hey Fellas," it always felt good to get home, "actually, the guy responsible for keeping us all alive is a woman. Her name was Vesta Stoudt," he said as he sat down next to Ricky.

That piqued Darrel's interest, "And who's that

then?" Darrel was a surgeon. He spent his days in an operating room performing open heart surgery. More precisely, he spent his days operating a robot that performed the surgery.

"She invented duct tape about 200 years ago. This colony is held together by about 2 million rolls of the stuff." Jack really wished he was exaggerating.

Ricky slurred, "That's amazing!"

Jack put his arm around Ricky and smiled, "Amazing, ridiculous, scary; take your pick. So who's buying?"

Darrel piped up, "This round is on me." He looked toward the bar, held up three fingers and called out, "Three more over here Jim!" Jim, the bartender, nodded back.

"Darrel, you're a good man; a good man indeed!" Ricky slurred, "We'd be in a miserable spot if it weren't for liquor and duct tape."

"We would my friend! We really would!" Jack smirked. He pulled out a roll of pink duct tape and slammed it down on the table. The sight of the bright pink wonder tool caused an eruption of laughter from the group.

The laughter settled as Jim arrived with the drinks, "Here they are guys; three more casualties of the cause," he said as he set the drinks on the table.

Ricky slurred, "Jim, you're a good man; a good man indeed!" And he immediately consumed half of his drink.

"Thanks Ricky, so how are you doing tonight

Jack?" Jim asked.

Jack conceded, "It's been one of those days, Jim. My socks are wet, my feet are clammy and I went through three rolls of duct tape applying advanced engineering techniques to our water reclamation system. So, you just keep lining them up and we'll keep shooting them down."

"I hear ya Jack. I'm hearing that a lot these days," Jim nodded and continued, "It smells like you were working with Harry today as well?"

"Harry the lab tech?"

"Yeah, you two are sporting the same fragrance."

"I haven't seen Harry for a few weeks."

"Well, that's odd. How about Carl? Do you know Carl in Operations?"

Jack replied, "I do in fact, yes, I do."

"Carl came in with Harry just after lunch. They spent most of the afternoon here, actually, and he was saying they lost the exterior sensors this morning."

Jack sighed, "Yeah, this whole damn place is falling apart faster than I can tape it back together."

"I guess you do what you can."

"Indeed. Has anyone seen Malinda today?" Jack asked.

Ricky slurred, "She was here with me earlier. She ran back to her place to change out of her work clothes."

Darrel nudged Jack and nodded to a table in the corner, "Hey Jack, look who it is." Darrel had noticed Marie, a flirtatious nurse he worked with, was having some drinks with a female friend.

Marie was a tall brunette with olive skin and brown eyes. Darrel liked her because she seemed fit. Like she had the stamina it took to keep a man happy. It helped that she was al-ways friendly with him. He liked her more than he would admit.

Her friend was a vivacious redhead with green eyes; Curvy in all the right places. She caught Jack's eye immediately, "Is that Marie?" Jack asked, "Who's that she's with?"

Darrel sensed his opportunity had finally arrived, "It is. Let's go find out!" Darrel and Jack hopped up out of their seats

"See ya Ricky!," Jack said as he straightened his shirt. He turned back to Darrel, "Hey, do you smell wet socks?"

Darrel had a chuckle, "Nah, you're good."

The pair walked over towards Marie's table. She saw Darrel approaching and smiled, clearly happy to have been noticed. Jack's the smooth one. He was al-ways the ice breaker. As they got to the table Jack smiled, leaned over and gave Marie a friendly hug, "It's been awhile cutie."

Marie seemed charmed, "It's great to see you. It's been too long. Jack." She stood up to acknowledge Darrel, "Hi there, you two want to join us?" she said while greeting him with a slightly more intimate hug.

Darrel quickly agreed, "We'd love to." Darrel sat down next to Marie and Jack sat down next to her friend.

Marie made the introduction, "This is my friend Sarah. She works in the "A" Deck spa."

Darrel, always the consummate wingman, tried his best to give Jack some flare, "Sarah, it's so nice to meet you. This is the best friend I have, Jack Kemper – Space Engineer!"

Sarah couldn't help but laugh, "Space Engineer?"

"There's nobody better with a roll of duct tape." Darrel joked.

Jack replied, "That's not true. Sam makes the cutest little finger puppets. Gives them real personality."

Sarah replied, "It's important that they have personality. You have to care or it's just not entertaining."

"That's what Sam says!"

Marie looked toward Darrel, "I'm starting to understand why this place is falling apart."

"Sarah, this might be the alcohol talking but you kind of remind me of my mother."

Marie rolled her eyes, "Oh, Jack. That is not what a woman wants to hear. I thought you were smoother than that but finger puppets and now your mother?"

Sarah interjected, "Well, wait Marie. I am curious. How exactly do I remind you of your mother?"

Jack continued, "She was a tall redhead with translucent skin."

"Oh, was her family from Ireland like mine?"

"Nope, she was Nigerian."

"Nigerian? Pardon me but you don't look like a person whose parents were African."

THE TRIALS OF JACK KEMPER

"Well my father was a pasty little white guy from Southern Kansas."

"And your mother was Nigerian?"

"Yep, she was born there. She was also an albino."

"An albino? I thought you said she had red hair?"

"She had to dye her hair to avoid the albino hunters."

"Seriously? Albino hunters?"

"Yeah, you see in Africa they think albinos are magic. So they hunt them down and cut off pieces of them for spiritual protection."

"Wow! That sounds horrific."

"In fact, for the longest time my mother couldn't count past 7."

"That's weird."

"Not really. She only had 7 fingers."

"Holy shit!"

"Holy fingers is more like it. For years some crazy Nigerian was running around with a necklace made out of my mom's finger bones."

"That's so crazy."

Jack reached into his pocket, "I know, right. When I finally hunted him down he kept holding them up and pointing at me like they were going to shoot out some magic to protect him." he quickly pulled out the thick white straw and gave his drink a stir, "Of course, they aren't much good for protection, but they do make a fine drink stir."

Marie and Sarah were aghast. Their mind played tricks. To them, the quick glance they had at the straw made it look like a small finger bone. In unison they recoiled and said, "Oh my fucking God!"

Darrel burst out laughing. He couldn't hold it in any longer, "Your fucking mom's fingers! Awe, man that was good. That's my new favorite. You are one fucked up individual Jack Kemper!"

The foursome was on a roll when Ricky stumbled over to their table. "Hey Jack, I think someone is looking for you!" He teased as he pointed toward the entrance.

Malinda! Standing in the entrance wearing only three strategically placed strips of duct tape! And she was giving Jack the eye.

Malinda was the kind of girl that gave bad girls a good reputation. She wasn't shy. She knew what she wanted and she usually got it. She was Jack's best friend. A real buddy if you will. She was always there to carry him home at the end of the night or vice versa.

Jack and Malinda weren't a couple. People in the colony didn't believe in that sort of arrangement. Life was too short. There may not be a tomorrow. Why make it complicated? They did, however, quite frequently manage to wake up naked next to each other.

Malinda pointed over to Jim at the bar. She gave him a smile. He turned around and flipped a few switches on the wall. The lights dimmed and the music started. Malinda ran towards the stripper pole, leaping in what could only be considered a very dangerous manner landing half way up; pole lodged firmly between her thighs. She spun a few times, her long black hair whipping behind her and landed on one knee. Her blue eyes burned a hole right through Jack.

And Jack approved. Jack approved very much. He was enthralled. This was something new.

Malinda continued; Pulsating, bouncing and licking her fingers. She was eating up the attention. She pranced over to Jack's table, flung her hair at the girls, and proceeded to give Jack a very indecent lap dance.

Ricky loved it. Darrel loved it. Everyone loved it; even the ladies! But Jack loved it most of all. A fact that was QUITE apparent! As the song wound down, Malinda looked him in the eye and said, "I hear you're the duct tape master and I seem to have gotten some stuck on me!"

This prompted Ricky to raise his glass and slur very loudly, "To Vesta Stoudt!" To which Darrel had a great laugh.

Malinda grabbed Jack by his shirt and began to escort him out of the establishment.

Ricky smiled at Sarah, sat down next to her and slurred, "That Malinda, she's a good woman; A good woman indeed!"

Sarah was a bit disappointed that Jack left, but being ever the optimist, she smiled at Ricky and straightly asked, "Who is Vesta Stoudt?" And again Darrel had a great laugh.

Malinda rolled over to the side of Jack; Out of breath and fully satisfied, she laid her arm across his chest. That's when she noticed the tape and chuckled.

She pulled the piece off of Jack's chest and said, "You certainly are a master, Jack Kemper."

"I see you were paying attention when I demonstrated the proper technique for painless duct tape removal. It took me years to perfect that." he said proudly.

"Job well done." she whispered.

Jack laid there in the afterglow, quite proud of his work but far too clear minded, "That worked up quite a thirst. Have anything decent to drink?"

"I do," she replied and began to crawl over Jack to get out of bed.

Jack always enjoyed watching Malinda move. He enjoyed it more when she was naked. He appreciated her grace. She was a real beauty. He saw an opportunity and gave her a playful pinch on her ass.

"Ow!" she smiled coyly. "Careful there fella or you might have to wait another thirty minutes for your drink."

Malinda paraded across the room. She had a small apartment. It might be called a studio apartment if not for it being so small. It was just big enough for a bed, bedside table, chair, a kitchen/bathroom type area with a sink, waste receptacle and a few storage cubbies. She reached into a cubby and pulled out a bottle and two glasses. She turned around with a smile, "This is the real deal; Aged Tennessee Whiskey."

She began to walk back toward Jack but suddenly came to a stop, "Damn this duct tape!" She reached down and pulled a piece off of her foot. She flicked it to the side and continued back to bed.

Jack sat up as Malinda handed him a glass, "It's actually Whiskey?"

Malinda winked, "I won't tell you what I had to do to get it." She sat down on the edge of the bed, opened the bottle and poured a little into each glass.

Jack sloshed his drink around. He raised his glass to her with a nod, "Cheers gorgeous."

CHAPTER 2

Jack snapped awake. The fog of alcohol distorted his vision as he looked around. The room was slow to come into focus, but it was as he remembered. Malinda was draped over him like a blanket and that smell, "Fuck, that smell!" He whispered to himself, "I'm going to have to burn those damn socks."

Jack noticed the half full bottle of Whiskey resting on the bedside table and began to extricate himself. He tried to gently move Malinda to the side, but she started to stir. He sat up on the edge of the bed and reached for the bottle.

"Pour me one too, Honey." she groggily said.

Jack twisted off the cap and topped off the two glasses from the previous night. He turned to hand Malinda her glass and said, "Well, you can't say I never made you breakfast in bed."

"Always the romantic, Jack," she smiled as she took a drink.

Jack gulped his down, "Ah! Damn, this might be

the best breakfast I've ever had. So, how'd you manage to get a hold of real Whiskey?" he had to ask.

"A woman has her ways Jack." she said slyly.

"And you have ways most women don't!" He felt he should give credit where due.

She started to explain, "Well, Jim had been sitting on this bottle for a while. He actually tried to lure me in with it a few years back."

Jack reasoned, "Makes sense. It's not like anyone up here has the credits to make it worth his while to sell."

Malinda responded quite frankly, "Well, blowjobs are worth more than money to a lot of guys."

Suddenly, the entire room shook violently. The bottle of Whiskey was knocked to the floor. They looked at each other very concerned. Not for the Whiskey.

"What the hell was that?" Malinda asked.

"I can't imagine," Jack replied, "whatever it is, it's not good!" Jack jumped to his feet, "We need to get dressed." He saw one of Malinda's dresses draped across a chair. He bolted to-wards it, picked it up and tossed it to her, "Fast!" He picked his pants up off the floor and started putting them on with haste. He had one leg in when the room violently shook again. This one knocked him to the floor. He landed face first and nose deep in his socks, "Fuck me!" He cursed. It was not the start to his day that he had hoped for. He decided it was best just to continue getting dressed while on the floor.

An alarm began to shriek across the intercom, "Emergency Alert! Emergency Alert! Please report to disaster stations! This is a level 1 Alert!" The alarm began to repeat itself but cut off halfway through its message.

Metal on metal screeching could be heard, a loud, piercing sound that forced Jack and Malinda to cover their ears. It lasted about thirty seconds.

"What the fuck was that!?" Malinda asked.

Jack replied, "Well it's not the best remedy for a hangover, that much is certain," as he shook the ringing out of his head.

"It sounded close Jack." Malinda's voice grew concerned.

"We need to go doll." he said in a very serious tone. He put on his shoes, picked up his shirt and grabbed Malinda by the arm. He pulled her with some force behind him as he headed out the door.

The corridor outside of Malinda's room was buzzing with activity. People were running. Civil Defense was barking orders. "Get to your stations! This is a level 1 event!"

"Where's your station?" Jack asked Malinda.

"Jack, I'm a facilitator. I don't have a station for something like this," she said looking scared and lost.

Jack took control, "You're staying with me then. Let's move."

Malinda liked this Jack. She rarely saw him so serious. He was the wise ass; the joke cracker. She really enjoyed that side of him, but this Jack she could trust.

THE TRIALS OF JACK KEMPER

She knew her life was in his hands now. And somehow she knew they'd be okay.

"Let's get to the lift!" Jack barked.

They ran down the corridor as they became a part of the chaos. The lights were flickering. Smoke was starting to fill the air with the smell of burnt plastic. As they passed one of her neighbor's rooms Malinda overheard, "It's lost. That room is lost. Check the next."

"What did that mean? Lost?" She thought to herself.

They got to the lift and were greeted by a man in his Civil Defense vest. "Where's your station?" he barked.

"Engineering," Jack replied, "She doesn't have one."

"Deck 2 is still active. You're good to go. Best of luck," the man said as the lift door slid open.

The Chinese Troop Carrier had to force its way into the Bravo Colony docking bay. What were the few remaining colonial shuttle crafts were now nothing more than twisted and crushed metal brazenly pushed aside by the larger Chinese ship.

Chinese soldiers poured out of the carrier and began to form into their predesignated squads. Harry stood apart from the squads in front of Commander Seng at attention. The Commander looked him up and down approving of his work, "Mr. Tang, it's not often that I find the work of a civilian to be done to such high standards, but you've done a great work for your people."

"Thank you, Commander Seng, you honor me."

"We need to seize the engineering deck as quickly as possible. Dragon Squad will be your escort and help you take control of the key systems."

"Yes sir!"

Commander Seng turned toward one of the squads that was lined up in front of him, "Dragon Squad, Mr. Tang is here to help us with our mission. He will lead you to the engineering deck. Secure it and hold it until you receive further instruction."

In unison the squad responded, "Yes sir, for New Dawn!"

The morning's chaotic awakening left Darrel with only enough time to find a pair of pants. Ricky was deftly attired in a long sleeved button down shirt and his tighty whities. And while Marie managed to find her dress, poor Sarah, she could only find a pair of underwear - and much to her dismay it was Marie's thong!

They stumbled out of Darrel's room into a throng of frantic Bravo Colony residents and joined the flow of humanity towards the lift deck. Every few minutes the station would shake erratically causing Darrel, Marie and Sarah to bounce off the walls, each other and various others as they walked. Ricky, however, moved with the grace of a gazelle. He had a life-time of drunken stumbling experience, after all, that just had to pay off eventually.

The group approached the lift deck and was promptly greeted by a Civil Defense Officer who was dutifully directing people into the lift as orderly as possible. She approached Sarah and asked, "Where's your station?"

"The spa?"

"Okay, you can go with this group to the evacuation deck."

Marie stepped forward and spoke up, "She's with Dr. Thomas and me."

"And you are?"

"Marie Perez, Med Tech Grade 2 and we need to get to the Infirmary," her voice rose with a sense of urgency as she spoke.

"Right!" the CDO turned and began pushing people to the side, "Alright people, make way for medical staff." and gave the group priority to the lift.

The lift arrived and when the doors slid open an acrid smoke bellowed out. It became quite evident that the lift wasn't empty as the smoke cleared. Much to the horror of the residents of deck four there were two fresh corpses in the lift and the walls were covered in blood.

Darrel quickly sprang into action and Marie followed without hesitation as they entered the lift to check for vitals, "I've got nothing." Darrel stated.

Marie looked at him, "Same here. They're lost."

"Marie, these are bullet wounds."

"What the hell is going on here Darrel?"

"Nothing good."

"We need to get moving. If there's more wounded…"

"Right," Darrel turned to the CDO and said, "get these bodies out of here."

The CDO motioned to a couple Civil Defense members who rushed over and began to pull the bodies out of the lift. The residents quickly parted to make a path as the bodies were carried off. Everyone was properly mortified by the horrid scene as blood poured from the bullet wounds and covered the floor.

Ricky turned to Sarah and put his arms around her in a feeble attempt to shield her from the sight. "So, you'll protect me right, because I'm really more of a drinker than a fighter."

"I got your back Ricky."

"I'd rather you take the front."

"Of course you would."

As the last body was removed Darrel motioned to Sarah and Ricky, "Come on guys let's get going."

Jack and Malinda's lift arrived at deck two. They were immediately met by a large group of boisterous technicians franticly trying to push their way into the lift. Jack, with Malinda still firmly in hand, pushed through the group quite bluntly while taking note of the conversations going on around him as people tried to justify their priority on the lift.

"I need to get to the docking bay. Pressure sensors registered a breach." one tech shouted.

Another group of techs was loudly demanding a lift to the Operations Center. "We need to get to the emergency control system."

THE TRIALS OF JACK KEMPER

Jack continued to pull Malinda through the chaos and move swiftly towards Sam's office. The corridors lights were still on, but Civil Defense seemed absent on this level. Just outside of Sam's office they found a group of radio engineers that seemed to be in the middle of a very serious discussion. Jack knew one of them. He hoped to get a status update, "Hey Thomas, what have you heard?" he asked.

Thomas replied, "Jack, glad to see you're on the job. Comm's are down. We've been trying to reroute through a backup circuit but it's like the
damn thing doesn't exist."

"Has Sam made it yet?" Jack asked.

"Yeah, he's in his office. It's not looking good, Jack."

Jack burst into Sam's office with Malinda still firmly in hand. He had been holding on so long and so tightly that he had almost forgotten she was there.

"Jack! Thank the Gods!" Sam exclaimed.

Jack nodded to Sam, "Reporting for duty, Sam, catch me up."

"Jack, we're royally fucked. Communications are down. We've lost power to 80% of the colony. It's like we hit something or something hit us. Before our circuits started going down it looked like we were losing pressure on several decks."

"Where do we start Sam?" Jack pleaded for direction.

"Jack, I really don't know. I see you brought Malinda. Let me dig up a wand and see if I can work some magic." Sam quipped.

"Shit, it's that bad?" Jack fell momentarily into a state of shock.

Jack and Sam remained silent for a minute, maybe two. It was odd that one of them wasn't being sarcastic or hopeless. Malinda could see that they were being consumed by an overwhelming situation, "Is this it? Is it done?" she asked.

Sam snapped out of it, "If it were just one or two things, sure, we could probably manage. But, this is a cascade of events that I don't think we can recover from."

Jack let go of Malinda's arm and instinctively walked over to one of the supply cabinets. He grabbed a tool belt and loaded it with screwdrivers, spanners and a couple rolls of duct tape. He noticed a humongous wrench. He'd always wondered what it could possibly be used for. He thought, "Why not?" and picked it up.

Jack turned around and looked at Sam, "I'm going to try to get the sensors back online first. That should give us some clue as to what's really going on."

"We don't have those boards, Jack."

"I'll go down to the Subdeck and see if I can redirect some of the data to a control terminal. We might not have full functionality but at least we'll have something."

Malinda didn't believe in love. She was attracted to Jack. She enjoyed his company very much. But, as she stood there watching him, as she observed his be-

THE TRIALS OF JACK KEMPER

havior over the last hour, she wondered if this feeling was love. It was a new feeling that caught her off guard. She felt for this man. She felt with this man. She had somehow become inexplicably tied to this man. And in the midst of all the chaos and in the face of possible death, she felt absolutely okay with that.

Sam continued to pull through his hopelessness, "Okay, right Jack. I'll head up to the Operations Center and see what I can do with the communications circuit. You'll probably need another set of hands down there. Take Thomas, he has quite a bit of knowledge about the sensors." Sam shouted, "Thomas, get in here!" Thomas quickly joined them in the office, "Go with Jack and see what you can do with the sensor array," Sam started moving toward the door.

Thomas nodded, "We'll do what we can, Sam."

Jack reached into the storage cabinet and threw a tool belt, two rolls of green duct tape and two spanners in Thomas' direction, "Subdeck "A" sensor room. I guess that's where we start." Jack said matter-of-factly.

Thomas fastened the belt around his waist and tucked the tape and spanners into the pouches. A man with a mission, he turned on
his heel and headed out the door immediately.

Jack and Malinda started to follow but as Thomas walked through the doorway into the corridor, the side of his head exploded into a red mist. Jack instinctively pushed Malinda up against the wall and covered her mouth. The terror in her eyes seemed to give him a strength he'd never known he had.

JOHN BLAHUT & JOSEPH PUGH

As they were standing in the office with their backs against the wall, Jack let go of Malinda. He clenched that giant wrench. He saw the barrel come through the doorway first. He recognized it immediately as a gun. He lifted his wrench, spun around the corner of the door, locked eyes with what appeared to be an Asian fellow and swung as hard and as fast as he could. He brained him. That's what that wrench was for.

He ducked back in the office. His thoughts started racing, examining the events that had just transpired, "Did I see any others? Was that a Chinese guy?" He thought.

Something clicked in Malinda. She moved around Jack before he could stop her. She reached down and started pulling on the gun. The strap was wrapped around the body. She knelt down, unclipped it, slid the strap out, re-attached it and slung it around her body before Jack had come to terms with what he had done. This was fight or flight time. There was no flight in Malinda. There never was! "This bitch is a fighter!" she thought to herself.

Malinda loaded the chamber, did a combat roll out of the room and let loose a volley of bullets in the direction the Asian fellow had come from. Jack's thoughts screamed, "HOLY FUCK! AM I REALLY WITNESSING THIS?" He was.

The shooting stopped. Jack was afraid of what he might find as he looked out the doorway. What he saw was Malinda, alive, and with a look of gratification that he had never seen before.

THE TRIALS OF JACK KEMPER

Malinda pointed to a group of dead Chinese soldiers, "Grab one of their guns!" She barked at Jack, "And ammo. Grab all of their ammo!"

Jack complied. He darted down the corridor where he found three dead soldiers. He picked up one of their rifles and slung it over his shoulder. He grabbed pistols from two of them and stuck them in his waistband. He then gathered several magazines of ammo and put them in his work belt.

Malinda had moved down the corridor to where it intersected with the main causeway of the deck. She kept watch from there while Jack was scavenging.

Jack returned and took up a position on the opposite side of the corridor from Malinda, "This is one amazing woman," he thought to himself, "There isn't an ounce of fear in her." He couldn't help but think that this might be the sexiest woman he'd ever seen. Malinda was also the sexiest woman he had seen prior to these events, but, damn, this wasn't even fair. If he could only take her then and there!

Malinda glanced across at Jack and saw him staring at her, awestruck. She reciprocated with a smile, "Yeah, I know that feeling, babe. Are you with me?"

Jack shook it off and refocused, "We need to move."

"It's clear. Let's go." she said.

Just as they started to move Jack noticed some motion down the corridor near Sam's office. He refocused. "Wait up, is that Harry?"

Malinda took a look, "Yeah, what's he doing in Engineering?"

Harry shouted, "Jack Kemper! I knew you'd be down here trying to put out the fires."

Malinda continued to stand sentry for any encroaching soldiers while Jack eased up, "Hey Harry, you can't be running around down here," Jack motioned to the dead soldiers, "those guys just killed Thomas. You should probably head to the Evac Deck."

"Well, you see Jack; we're here to secure this deck," as Harry spoke two soldiers appeared around the corner and took up position on either side of him.

Jack raised his gun, "What do you mean? Who's we?" he asked.

"The people of the New Dawn. Didn't you think it a bit coincidental that you lose sensors and communications just before soldiers show up?"

"So you're with them? I just want to make sure I have this straight before I shoot you."

"Jack, you don't want to shoot me."

"I'm pretty sure I do, Harry."

"Jack, I'm not here to do you any harm. We need people like you. Besides, If you shoot me who's going to keep these soldiers from shooting you?"

"She will."

Harry laughed, "Jack, that's a lot of faith to put in a whore."

Malinda tensed and took aim at Harry.

Jack noticed Malinda's change in posture, "Woah, babe."

"And we don't need her. We only need those with

skills."

"Trust me, she has skills."

"Not the type of skills we're interested in, Jack."

"While she is skilled in that area those weren't the skills I was referencing." Jack turned to Malinda, "On you."

Without a second passing Malinda had dropped the soldier to the left of Harry. Jack started spraying shots toward Harry and the other soldier. Harry ducked into Sam's office while the soldier took cover and returned fire. Two more soldiers appeared from around the corner and began to fire on their position.

Malinda shouted, "Let's move!"

The two moved quickly down the causeway toward the lift deck keeping a constant spray of bullets on their previous position just in case any soldiers tried to come around the corner.

The ride for Darrel, Marie, Sarah, and Ricky was endured with a somewhat stunned silence. The alcohol from the night before hadn't entirely worn off and their abrupt awakening this morning left them all shoeless and standing in a pool of blood. The caustic smell of gunpowder and the blood spatter on the walls of the lift didn't help their psyche much, however, every few seconds the lift would shutter and Ricky noticed that Sarah had a nice jiggle about her. That helped his psyche just a little bit, although, not quite as much as a beer would have.

The lift came to a stop and the doors slid open. Darrell poked his head out of the lift and quickly peered in both directions. The hallway was barely lit and empty. He took a careful step out of the lift and motioned for the others to follow. The group began to cautiously make their way towards the infirmary.

"I guess I'll be the first to ask. What the hell is going on?" Sarah asked as she followed closely behind Marie.

"Maybe the colony was struck by space debris? I was pretty lit last night but I do believe Jack mentioned an issue with the sensor array." Ricky said from behind her.

"Space debris doesn't cause bullet wounds." Marie contested flatly.

The group approached the entrance to the infirmary. They could see light streaming through the open door. Darrel thought that was a bit strange. The door should have been closed. He put up his hand to slow their approach. They could hear voices coming from within the room. They were men's voices speaking a foreign language, "Is that Mandarin?" Darrel wondered to himself.

Darrel spoke softly, "Wait here." and slowly continued toward the doorway. The voices inside the room seemed quite agitated. He turned and took a step through the doorway and saw four Chinese soldiers rifling through the storage cabinets and desks.

"What the ...?" His question was cut short as the soldiers turned and leveled their guns at him. He stopped in the doorway and instinctively raised his hands. The soldiers began to yell at him and from the tone of their voices he knew it wasn't good. He quickly hit the emergency close button, mounted on the wall next to the door, and dove back into the corridor.

The soldiers opened fire. Their bullets riddled the doorframe and wall. Their footsteps could be heard as they rushed toward the door. It wouldn't hold them long. He knew that much. He jumped back to his feet, grabbed Marie's hand and began to run back down the corridor towards the lift.

Sarah had already grabbed Ricky and began running. Even with the head start the other two blew past her like she was dragging dead weight. She took a quick glance behind her just to verify that Ricky was indeed still standing. He was there - huffing and drooling.

Darrel had reached the lift a few steps ahead of the other three. He frantically pressed the button to call the lift. The others looked back down the corridor, holding their breath while time seemed to pass ever more slowly, as they waited for the lift to arrive. They could hear the soldiers shouting and the sound of boots striking the deck as they ran toward them.

Darrell growled through clenched teeth, "Where is this fucking thing?" he continued to press the button as if repeatedly pressing it would make the lift come faster.

The group looked on with utter terror as the soldiers came into view. Darrel moved Marie behind him putting her between himself and the lift. Sarah did the same with Ricky. Although they were unarmed it seemed like the right thing to do. Luckily, it didn't come to that. The lift doors slid open and Marie and Ricky pulled them into the lift.

The soldiers opened fire just as the doors to the lift closed. The lift was on its way. Darrel bent over and put his hands on his knees. He took a deep breath, looked at Marie and said, "Holy shit."

Sam entered the Operations Center and immediately found his technicians hard at work on several systems while the operations staff was doing what they could to get reports from across the station processed through to the correct authority. Sam walked to the center of the room and commanded, "Techs, I need updates."

One tech poked his head up from under a console, "I have power back on decks G through K"

"Great job, keep at it."

Another tech leaned around from behind a cabinet, "Inertial Stabilizers are back online."

"Excellent, I was tired of being knocked to my ass." Sam continued, "Give me an update on Communications."

A muffled response came from within one of the larger console tables, "External Communications are back online but internal systems are still down."

Sam dove under the console table, "Where are we on the internal system."

Jessica, one of Sam's best techs, was in the midst of soldering a board, "Well Sam, I'm trying to reroute the backup circuit through some of the old maintenance circuits but the damn thing is fighting me at every turn."

"I like where you're heading, but those old maintenance circuits weren't built for comms transfer between outside sources. They require varying security codes. You'll need to add that data to the stream at each relay depending on where it's going next."

"Right, how would I go about doing that exactly?"

"We'll need to access each relay individually and add it at the machine level."

Jessica finished her last bit of soldering, gave the board a quick blow to cool it and slid it back into its slot, "Okay that should do it. We should be able to get to the maintenance relays now."

"Excellent work Jessica."

Sam crawled out from under the console table with Jessica and sat down at the console. He hit a few keys and the screen began to boot, "Looking good so far."

"Fingers Crossed."

The screen came up. It showed external communications online but a fault with the internal communications just as it should have.

Sam hit a few keys and explained his actions to Jessica, "I'll need to log in at the administrator level to have access the system console prompt." Sam typed in his credentials and continued, "Okay, so the maintenance systems all operate on an old IP network. So to get to each relay we'll need the IP address for the switch."

Jessica interceded, "We have a script for that. It's

in the tech bin."

"IP discover?" Sam asked

"That's the one. Execute that. It will produce a list of all IP's on that network and give a description. We should be able to note which ones are the relays from there."

Sam executed the script and the console returned several pages of data. He scrolled through it a couple of times. He pointed to a group of about a dozen IP Addresses, "I think these are what we're looking for. The .172 references that domain."

Jessica nodded in agreement with Sam as he switched back to the command prompt and started to key in commands, "See what I did there?"

"Yeah, seems pretty straight forward."

Sam stood up, "Okay do that for the entire list. You'll need to work them in sequential order. You won't be able to get to the 3rd one without doing the 2nd one first. And so on. It should only take you a few minutes. Understand?"

Jessica sat down and continued the work, "Yep, I'll let you know when it's completed."

A tech walked up to Sam, "Sam, we have a serious problem."

"What is it?"

"We have the security network back online and the camera's..." he stuttered, "well, come take a look for yourself."

Sam and the tech walked over to the security command console. They looked at the security monitors and Sam, a naturally pale man, turned at least three shades whiter, "Are those soldiers?"

"We've closed all security doors. They've already blown through four of them. One more and they'll be in here."

"Well that won't take them but a minute." He turned to Jessica, "Encrypt that network!"

And, almost as if on cue, the door to the Operations Center blew. Soldiers rushed in screaming commands in heavily accented English while Jessica furiously typed, "Everyone to the floor!" they yelled.

She continued typing until a soldier ran over to her and grabbed her around the neck. He ripped her away from the console and threw her down, "Everyone to the floor," he repeated as he pointed a gun at her head.

It took the soldiers less than a minute to subdue the Operations Center. These people weren't soldiers. They weren't going to fight. Everyone but Jessica had complied immediately.

A soldier stood in the middle of the room and began to speak, "I am Sergeant Chiu. Please be calm. We are not here to hurt you." He gave a couple orders in Mandarin to his men then continued in English, "Please stand and form 2 lines here in the center."

The colonists slowly began to stand and wondered what would come next. Sam looked over to Jessica who gave him a quick nod. They all moved to the center of the room and fell into two lines.

"Private Wang and Private Cheung, here, will ask each of you a series of questions. Do not lie. They will be verifying the information you give with our data. We will know if you attempt to deceive us."

Sgt. Chiu gave a loud order to his men and several of them sat down at consoles and began typing.

Pvt.'s Wang and Cheung began to ask questions to the first people in each of the lines. Sam was first in Cheung's line, "What is your name?" he asked.

"Sam Dillinger."

"What position do you hold?"

"Technical Maintenance Supervisor."

"How many people report to you?"

"14."

Pvt. Cheung handed him a tablet, "Please list them here," he then moved on to the next person in line.

Jack and Malinda approached the corridor that led to the lift. They had kept a nice pace to stay ahead of Harry and his cohorts when Jack decided to try doing a combat-roll himself. He made it about half way across the corridor toward the lift. It took him a few seconds to get back to his feet. By the time he had regained his footing Malinda was laughing hysterically.

Jack fumbled for an excuse, "My belt shifted. Shut it!"

Malinda tried to regain her composure, "It looks clear. Come on!" she said, still laughing a little.

They approached the lift deck. Malinda kept watch behind them while Jack entered a maintenance code to bring the lift to them quickly. Gunfire rang out in the main causeway, "Where the fuck is this thing?" Jack mumbled, "Come on. Come on," as he grew ever more impatient.

A group of soldiers came around the corner just as the lift arrived. Malinda opened fire immediately. Jack spun around and launched a volley of shots catching one with a headshot. Malinda crippled another. The soldiers pulled their comrade around the corner to regroup. Malinda and Jack continued firing down the corridor as they backed into the lift. The door closed in front of them just as they heard something metallic bouncing down the corridor.

CHAPTER 3

Jack and Malinda lowered their rifles after the lift door closed and soon realized they weren't alone. They both swung around simultaneously to see who else was in the lift.

Ricky, who was ducking for cover with the others, dared to look up and saw his friend, "Jack?"

Darrel sprung to his feet, "Oh thank the Gods!" He grabbed Jack and squeezed him tighter than any man should squeeze another.

The lift had just begun its descent when an explosion hit. It blew the door ajar and knocked the lift off its track. It began falling. Everyone shrieked in terror. Darrel's grip on Jack grew even tighter as they were flung against the wall pinning Malinda. Sarah and Marie fell to the floor. Sarah landed on her back with Marie's face buried squarely in her tits. Ricky curled up into a fetal position in the corner.

The door wedged between the wall of the shaft and the lift causing their descent to slowly grind to a halt while showering the interior with sparks. The screaming subsided. Well, most of it. Loud cursing could be heard coming from Sarah, "Thanks for the motherfucking wedgie, Marie!"

As Marie worked to get her hands untangled from Sarah's thong, she lifted her head and couldn't help but laugh, "And thank you for the soft landing."

Ricky poked his head up and quickly focused on the two, "Oh damn! What did I miss?"

Marie extricated herself from Sarah's thong, stood up and helped Sarah to her feet.

Jack found it hard to breathe, "Hey, you can let go now."

"Oh! Uh, yeah." Darrel released his grip.

Malinda rested her hands on her knees and tried to catch her breath, "Damn it, I think I might have cracked a rib."

Darrel turned toward Malinda, "Let me take a look," he straightened her posture, "Can you lift your arms up over your head?"

Malinda slowly raised her arms above her head, "Yes." she said with a grimace.

"Can you take a deep breath?" he asked as he began feeling her ribs. Malinda winced as he pressed on a couple of them, "Looks like you may have bruised one or two but I don't feel anything that would indicate a break." He stated.

While Darrel checked out Malinda, Jack helped Ricky to his feet, "What, no tie?"

"It's still tied to Marie's headboard. A story for another time."

"Right."

Commander Seng and his Lieutenants strutted into the Operations Center as if they had just conquered all of Asia. His Lieutenants quickly moved to ascertain information from their various subordinates who had taken control of the command consoles.

Sam watched closely as one by one the Lieutenants reported back to Commander Seng. After a few minutes of discussion the commander moved towards the Colonists and began to speak, "Let me start by reassuring all of you that, if you cooperate, no harm will come to you. You are all integral to the continued operations of this facility, however, if you take any action in an attempt to circumvent our takeover of this facility, let it be understood that we will put you in an airlock and let you float back to Earth." Commander Seng turned away and took another briefing from one of his Lieutenants. He nodded and turned back to the Colonists, "Will the technicians please step forward?"

Sam stepped forward immediately in an attempt to show his people they needed to cooperate. His main goal now was to keep anyone from being killed unnecessarily. As the last of them stepped forward he spoke up, "These are all the techs, sir."

The Commander looked at his pad, "And you must be Sam Dillinger? Is that correct?"

"Yes, sir."

"Excellent, Mr. Dillinger, I need you and your people to return to the engineering deck and report to

THE TRIALS OF JACK KEMPER

Harry Tang."

"Harry?"

"He will be in charge of you going forward."

Sam was a bit confused by this, "What did Harry have to do with anything?" he wondered.

The impatient Commander prodded for a response, "Understood?"

"Yes, sir. Harry's in charge now. Understood."

"Good. We'll need one of your techs to stay behind and work on internal communications. It's my understanding that we're seeing a fault with that system."

Sam turned toward Jessica and gave her a quick wink, "Jessica, stay here and get internal communications working."

"Yes, sir." she replied.

Commander Seng turned to Sgt. Chiu, "Sgt. Chiu, escort these individuals to the engineering deck. Stay there and provide support as necessary."

Sgt. Chiu saluted the Commander, "Yes, Sir," and turned to his squad to issue his command. His soldiers quickly moved into escort positions. He turned to the Colonists, "You will follow me." He ordered.

All things considered, Jack was a happy man. His best friends were alive and well and now they were all in one place. He pulled a roll of pink duct tape out of his tool belt as he turned to Darrel and asked, "So how did you all end up here?"

"Well, all the shaking and alarms woke us up."

Marie interjected, "Scared the shit out of us really."

Jack tore off a piece of duct tape and moved toward

Sarah.

Darrel continued, "So we grabbed what we could and ran toward the lift. You know? Natural instinct really."

Jack nodded, "Yep, same here," as he applied the small piece of duct tape to one of Sarah's nipples.

Ricky said, "Oh, duct tape pasties. I think you started a trend Malinda."

Malinda was rubbing her ribs. She wanted to chuckle but it hurt too much, "I knew I should have gone with pink."

Jack tore off another small piece of duct tape and applied it to Sarah's other nipple, "There ya go. Now I can concentrate."

"Thank you, Jack." Sarah flashed an appreciative smile.

Darrel continued, "So when we got to the lift we found a couple of residents that had been shot dead."

Jack motioned to his gun, "Yeah, soldiers from New Dawn. They were trying to put some bullets in us too."

"New Dawn? The Chinese Colony? Really?"

"Yeah, apparently they're to that point."

Darrel paused for a moment to let that information settle in, "So, Marie and I figured we better get down to the Infirmary in case there were more wounded."

"Is that where you were heading? You might be right. We should head that way."

Marie jumped in, "No, we got there. And that's

where we were running from. We were heading for the evacuation deck when the lift changed course on us."

Jack smirked, "Ah yeah, that was me. I used the maintenance override. Sorry."

Marie was not amused, "Well we need to get off this thing. So I hope you have a plan."

"I think you guys had the right idea. We need to get to the Evac Deck."

Malinda noticed that Jack had dropped a few magazines and a pistol during the blast. She picked up one of the magazines and reloaded her rifle. She then picked up the other magazine and the pistol but realized she had no place to put them. Her dress just wasn't suitable for the occasion.

Jack noticed her predicament and produced two rolls of duct tape, "Pink or Green?"

Malinda looked puzzled, "What?"

"You need something to carry those in. Would you like pink or green?" he replied.

"Pink." She answered.

"Odd, I always pictured you as a green."

"What? And clash with Sarah?"

"Team Pink it is," Jack tore off a few strips and began fashioning a bandoleer for her. It took him all of sixty seconds, "Here, this should work."

Darrel looked toward Sarah, "See, Space Engineer!"

Sarah nodded, "So what's the plan, Space Engineer?"

Jack took that as an invitation to take command,

"Well first things first. We need to get out of this lift. Darrel, Ricky; Give me a boost. We should be able to get the emergency hatch open." The two slowly boosted Jack up to the ceiling. Jack took a spanner out of his belt and started removing the bolts. After all of the bolts were removed he looked down to the guys and said, "Okay, hold steady I need to lift this hatch off!"

Jack struggled to move the hatch but it wouldn't budge, "I think it's jammed." He let out a grunt that only Malinda could appreciate as he started slamming his forearm and shoulder against the hatch, "I can feel it moving," he hit it a few more times and it finally popped free, "Alright, I'm going to slide this thing to the side and see what we have to work with."

Ricky was struggling to keep Jack up, "Enough with the commentary already just move the damn thing."

Jack chuckled a bit, "Okay, ladies, cover your heads. There might be debris."

Marie and Sarah moved next to Malinda who still stood toward the side of the lift and covered their heads. Jack slid the hatch to the side slowly, popped his head through and looked over the situation. There was no debris, "Okay, bring me down guys."

Jack had a plan, "Okay, we've come to rest just beneath a service tunnel. It's pretty easy to get to from here. Luckily, I know every inch of these tunnels and barring any collapses or similar catastrophes, we should be able to take them all the way to the evacuation deck. And, even better still, I doubt we'll be running into any soldiers in them."

Jack and Ricky lifted Darrel out first. Then all three men helped the ladies get out as graceful as possible. It all went rather smoothly, but when they were lifting Malinda out Jack realized, "Ah, panties. I should have tossed her some panties." Ricky didn't mind. It wasn't anything he hadn't seen a thousand times. They were all friends after all.

Jack was the last to come up. He took a brief look around, "Okay, follow me. The service tunnel is just up this ladder." He wasted no time as he started to climb the ladder. He stepped off and crawled into the tunnel. He moved in a few feet and waited to make sure everyone made it in all right before continuing.

Harry settled in behind his new desk in Sam's office. He began thumbing through the work orders, but saw nothing of importance. The keyboard was hanging off to the side of the desk as if Sam had pushed it aside hurriedly or perhaps out of frustration. Harry grabbed it and struck a key to activate the system.

The system prompted Harry for a password. He pulled a small device out of his pocket and plugged it into a port on the keyboard. It had several little lights on it all of which were red. Within just a few seconds the first one turned green. A few seconds later the second one turned green. This continued for about three minutes until all the lights were green. The password prompt went away. The system was his.

Harry quickly brought up a status screen to see

what systems were functioning and which ones were showing faults. Most of the faults were his handy work, but some were the result of the assault. Even with the number of system faults displayed, he was pleased that the damage to the station was mostly superficial and that all primary systems were still functioning.

Sam walked in, followed closely by Sgt. Chiu, "Making yourself comfortable, Harry?" Sam asked.

"Sam." Harry said looking up from the terminal and smiling, "Commander Seng told me you were on the way," he looked at the Sergeant, "thank you Sgt. Chiu. Have your men relieve Dragon Squad. They're to report to their Lieutenant." Sgt. Chiu nodded and turned to leave.

Harry leaned back in the chair propping his feet up on the desk, "Sorry about all the extra headaches the last few days. Orders. You know."

"It's all forgotten with a drink or two, right?"

"Of course, once everything settles back into the routine, they're on me."

"Have you seen Jack?"

"I did. It didn't go well."

"Did you expect it to?"

"Well in retrospect it probably would have went better if Thomas hadn't been shot."

"Why did you go and do that?"

"Well, I didn't. You know. Soldiers. It's what they do."

"Yeah, I suspect that made him a tad touchy."

THE TRIALS OF JACK KEMPER

"We'll work it all out. It's a long way back to Earth without a shuttle after all."

"You might want to let me try to talk him down."

"I'll take that into consideration."

Harry took his feet off the desk, scooted his chair up and began to shuffle through the work orders on Sam's desk as if it were back to business as usual. He pulled out the work order for the sensor array, "I see Jack couldn't get this one completed."

"We didn't have the parts."

Harry looked toward the door and called out, "Private!"

A soldier walked in and presented Harry with a couple circuit boards, "Sir, the equipment you requested."

"There are your parts Sam. Head up to the Operations Center and get that fixed. The Private here will be your escort."

"Sure Harry," Sam grabbed the circuit boards. He started to turn and walk out the door then stopped. He looked back at Harry, "Well played, Harry."

The Operations Center hadn't seen this much activity in years. After all, it had probably been several years since the Bravo Colony Leadership had even been there. Yet there they stood the President and highest ranking members of the Council, Seng's new trophies. Lined up and ready to take direction from their new master.

Jessica kept her head down and peered intently at the terminal screen in front of her. She knew she didn't have much more time to get the internal communications working. She could feel Commander Seng's stare. His impatience was palpable. She felt like it was burning into her very nerves. It caused her fingers to go numb, but with a final set of commands - relief. The fault was cleared.

"Commander Seng, internal communications have been restored," her voice trembled as she made her report.

"Thank you, Miss…" Seng paused.

"Latimer, Jessica Latimer."

"Thank you, Miss Latimer," the cordial tone of his words tried hard to mask the sadist within, but only served the purpose of sending an icy chill down her spine, "Do we have video?"

"Yes, sir. Video is up."

"Excellent. Open a channel for public address. Broadcast throughout the colony."

Jessica turned back to the terminal. She typed in a few commands, a slight crackle from the station's speakers indicated that the public address system was active. One of the screens mounted along the wall of the Operations Center flickered on displaying the image of Commander Seng standing in front of the Bravo Colony leadership.

"Citizens of Bravo Colony," Commander Seng began, "I am Hueng Seng. Commander of the New Dawn Liberation Forces. Many years ago, our two sister colonies were founded with a purpose, a directive, to live beyond the turmoil of the world below while working toward its salvation and as that world fell ever further into the darkness of war, disease, and famine the citizens of New Dawn never wavered from that mission. Even when the leadership of Bravo Colony turned their backs on their brothers and sisters, we remained ever vigilant. We continued to persevere in the face of constant hardship. But, even the most dutiful siblings will reach a point where they can no longer stand for the inaction of their brothers and sisters. We could not sit idly by and watch as that inaction becomes a systemic malfunction that damns our world to a hellish reality."

He turned to the leadership of Bravo Colony, "It is with deep regret that we must take such action. But, while these elitists feel themselves above the turmoil's and tribulations of our plight, we feel it is our duty, no, our divine mandate to restore the covenant that bonded our peoples in righteous purpose." He paused to let his words reverberate through the station.

Commander Seng gestured for the President of Bravo Colony to step forward, "Citizens of Bravo Colony, it is with much sadness that I must step aside. I have failed you. I have failed the people of New Dawn. I have allowed us to lose our way. I have allowed the purpose of our cause to be forgotten. Please return to your stations and cooperate fully with the new leadership."

"Thank you, Mr. President," Commander Seng added as he stepped forward again, "I look forward to bringing our purpose back into focus. Thank you, Citizens of Bravo Colony," and with a slight nod towards Jessica the transmission ended.

Commander Seng turned to face the former leadership, "Lieutenant Wei, take them to a holding cell. Minimum rations." There was no protest as Lieutenant Wei and his men pushed them towards the door.

Sam rounded the corner to walk into the Operations Center and ran right into the President. He apologized, "Sorry Sir," and stepped to the side as the soldiers and council members also passed by. The events of the day had caught him off guard but he had never even dreamed he would run into the President. Quite literally.

Jessica was still sitting at the communications console too intimidated to move. The shame she felt overwhelmed her. Her thoughts were spinning into a whirlpool of remorse when a surprising tap on her shoulder caused her to jump and snap out of it.

Sam and his escort stood behind her, "Jessica, I need your assistance with the sensor console."

Jessica was relieved to see a friendly face but she wasn't sure of the protocol. Could she leave the console? Was she expected to sit there and act like a comms operator? She looked to the soldier and asked, "May, I assist Sam with fixing the sensor console?"

A terse nod was returned by the soldier with a heavily accented, "Quickly."

Sam led Jessica over to the sensor console and of course the escort followed. Sam set his tools and the boards down on top of it and said, "Good to see you're okay, Jess."

"Thanks, Sam."

He gave a quick wink, "Let's get inside this console and get to work."

Jessica promptly whipped a spanner out of her tool belt, kneeled down and in just a few seconds had removed the access panel. She slid in on her back, leaving enough room for Sam to slide in beside her while the escort turned his attention elsewhere.

Sam grabbed the circuit boards off the top of the console and made his way inside the console table, "Did you get those maintenance channels encrypted?"

"I did, barely."

"Excellent," he handed her the first circuit board, "Compliments of Harry Tang."

She sarcastically replied, "Well that was nice of him."

Sam pointed, "Slide that into the far slot over there."

"What are we going to do, Sam?"

"Well, I'm playing along for now."

"We can't just let them take over."

"I'm not sure we have much of an option, Jess."

"Well we have the maintenance channels. We could get something organized."

"We'd need to program some communicators to use those."

"That wouldn't be hard."

"No, but I doubt it would go unnoticed if a bunch of communicators go missing."

"What about the ones in the graveyard?"

"We might be able to get a couple of them working but they're in there for a reason."

"A couple is better than none."

Sam handed her the second board and pointed to another slot, "Put this one in the slot marked 30ao."

"We could also grab a couple working ones."

"Yeah, I doubt anyone would question us needing use of them."

"Have you seen Jack?"

"I haven't. Harry said they didn't part on good terms."

"That's concerning."

"I know right. Get a few drinks in that guy and there's no telling what he'll do."

"So where do you think he is?"

"If I know Jack, and I do quite well, he's crawling around somewhere nobody will ever find him."

"Well that's good then. If we can get him a communicator from the graveyard we'll have someone that doesn't have eyes on them."

As the second board slid into place the console buzzed for a brief second then stopped. Jessica jiggled the board and it began to buzz. She removed her hand and it stopped. She turned toward Sam, "I think they busted this slot when they yanked the board out."

Sam reached down to where his duct tape roll hung from his tool belt and tore off a piece, "Hold it in place."

Jessica held the board in place and Sam applied the fix all. The console buzzed to life. It was just then Sam and Jessica felt someone kicking at their feet. Their time was up. Sam slid out first to find the soldier standing over him, "Hey, we just got the boards put in place." Jessica slid herself out and they both stood up. The soldier backed off but kept his eyes firmly on the pair.

Sam sat down at the console, "Okay, let's run some diagnostics." Sam typed in a few commands and flipped through several screens, "See anything?"

"It all looks good."

"Alright, I'll let Seng know he has sensors once again."

"What should I do?"

Sam gave her another quick wink, "Keep fighting those bugs at comms."

"Understood," she said and promptly returned to her post at the communications console.

Sam turned to his escort, "Please let Commander Seng know that the sensor array is back online."

The soldier nodded and walked over to one of the officers standing near Commander Seng. They had a brief discussion and the officer turned to the Commander. Sam could see that the information was being relayed. Commander Seng began to walk toward Sam. The other two men fell in behind him.

Commander Seng spoke, "Mr. Dillinger, I commend you on your diligence with this matter. I must say I am quite impressed with your adaptability and that of your technicians."

"We aim to please, Sir."

"And Ms. Latimer, she has proven to be quite skilled in

her duties."

"Yeah, it hasn't been easy for her. She's running into quite a few faults with that system."

"Well, much to her credit we haven't been affected by those. I can see she's got her undivided attention on that matter now. Please, walk me through the sensor controls."

"Um, yeah sure." Sam pulled out the chair at the console and sat down. He began to scroll through pages on the screen, "Okay, well this is the basic display. It will show you that the sensors are operational. If any faults are registered you'll find them here. Of course that's when you call me." He tried hard to be cordial. The Commander and his officer nodded their understanding.

"There are two sets of sensors, the external sensors and the internal sensors. They're both controlled through this array," Sam selected the external sensor information, "This is where you'll see the external sensor data. We don't usually see much on here. Most of the satellites have gone down over the years. There's still a few out there but they're well out of our orbit. Not much to see really."

Commander Seng's interests lied elsewhere, "That's wonderful, Mr. Dillinger could you please bring up the internal sensor data?"

"Right, this menu will bring you to the internal sensor display. And if you flip over to this page you'll start to see the actual sensor output. This is page is high level. It will show you how many people are on each deck and such. You can drill down like this," He put his hands to the display and made a few gestures, "And as you can see it brings things into a room by room view."

Commander Seng nodded his approval, "What area is that?"

Sam had just picked the area randomly. He had to look closer at the display, "That would be the evacuation deck, Commander."

The Commander pointed to the screen, "And I am correct that what I am seeing here are people?"

Sam replied, "That would be correct. I'd say there's close to 100 people in that area. I don't know what they're planning on doing down there though; it shows all the escape pods as being offline"

"Yes, we have disabled that system." The officer replied.

Commander Seng spoke, "Lieutenant, send a couple squads down there to resolve that situation."

The officer snapped his heels and saluted, "Yes, Sir!"

"Good work Mr. Dillinger. You can return to Engineering."

"Thank you, Commander Seng." Sam couldn't help but wonder how it would be "resolved".

Jack helped his friends out of the tunnel one by one and into the main causeway of the evacuation deck. Malinda was the last one to step out and she was greeted with a kiss, "Baby, I think we got this." He reassured her.

"Good job, Space Engineer." she said with a smile.

The main causeway of the evacuation deck was a very large and open area designed to stage an orderly evacuation of the colony. There was a sturdy looking hatch every twenty feet along both sides of the causeway and behind each hatch was a bay with an escape pod ready to go. The pods were designed to carry up to ten people and as one pod jettisoned from the hatch another pod would load into the bay to take its place.

This was a very complicated part of the colony designed with many very important moving parts. Jack had spent countless hours here performing maintenance on the pods, pod bays, mechanical loaders and hatch seals. And, as he pondered the amount of duct tape holding it all together, he marveled that anyone was actually relying on it all to work.

The deck was full of colonists doing as they were told. They were waiting for the hatches to open so they could begin their evacuation. Their chatter was quite deafening. They had heard Commander Seng's speech over the PA system and the overwhelming opinion was that he clearly couldn't be trusted.

Word had already spread through the crowd of encounters with soldiers and killings. Tensions were high and a sense of panic had set in. There was talk of blocking the lift deck. Some even suggested disabling the lift somehow to keep the intruders out.

Jack looked over the situation, "Something's wrong. The pod bays aren't running."

Darrel asked, "How can you tell?" as he looked

over Jack's shoulder and followed his gaze through the crowded causeway.

"We'd hear them. And people would be moving."

"Can you get them going?"

Jack's jaw muscles tensed as he thought of a solution, "I need to get to a control terminal. Stay with me." He grabbed Malinda's hand and began to weave his way through the crowd pulling her behind him once again. Malinda in turn grabbed Marie who held on to Darrel. With his other hand, Darrel held on to Sarah who towed Ricky behind her.

It took them several minutes to work their way down the causeway to a terminal and much to Jack's dismay, when they finally got to it, the damn thing didn't appear to be functioning, "You have got to be fucking kidding me!" he shouted in disgust as he punched it, "Nothing is going to be easy today I guess!"

He pulled a spanner out of his tool belt and started ripping bolts out of the access panel that was just beneath the terminal. He tore off the panel, venting all his frustration as he tossed it aside. He quickly started yanking apart wires. Jack pulled a utility blade out of his pocket and began slicing and stripping wires with a fascinating coordination that looked like little more than organized chaos to the untrained eye.

Darrel marveled at his skill with a blade, "You could have been a surgeon in another life, Jack." Jack didn't have time to respond. He whipped out his duct tape and started splicing wires together.

As Jack worked, there was an agitated movement in the crowd that surrounded the group. The noise level of the colonists started to rise like a cacophonous wave that washed over the group from the direction of the lifts. "Soldiers!" one man shouted.

Seng's soldiers had arrived to "resolve" the situation. Surprisingly, it appeared that they were trying to do it peacefully. They began by ordering the colonists back to their quarters; however, the colonists were having none of it. They had only two things in mind; Spitting at Chinese soldiers and getting the hell off the colony.

Jack pulled one last cord out of the terminal and spliced it directly into the power coupling. The lights and display of the terminal flickered on. He frantically swiped the screen and tore through command sequences. And, with one final poke of the screen, the machinery of the deck rumbled into action.

The sudden activation of the pod bay systems startled the soldiers. They had orders. No one was to leave. A couple soldiers began to fire over the crowd in an attempt to gain control over the colonists. This, of course, had the opposite effect.

The colonists turned and ran. They pushed their way toward the now functioning escape pods. The lucky few directly near the pod bays were able to get in and trigger their launch sequence. Pods began to jettison.

Jack and the others were quickly overwhelmed by a sea of humanity. He didn't even have time to grab onto Malinda. He lost sight of her as she was swallowed up by the surging mass. He screamed out for her, "MALINDA!" but he could hardly hear his own voice.

Explosions began to go off that triggered blinding flashes meant to disorient and incapacitate the colonists. They were accompanied by a sweet smelling smoke that began to fill the causeway. Within a few seconds there was silence.

Jack had been carried across the causeway by the current of the people. Using all of the strength he could muster he wrestled free of the bodies that now lay on top of him. He felt empty. Spent. He laid there for a few seconds trying to regain his senses. He could barely focus his eyes through the lingering smoke. He thought he noticed the service tunnel just to his left. He squinted to bring things into focus and began to crawl. Well, he tried to crawl. His legs wouldn't move. He continued trying to drag his limp body toward the tunnel while gasping for oxygen. He pulled himself as far as he could until the lights started to dance in his eyes. Lights that made his head tingle. The tunnel grew long and dark.

CHAPTER 4

The Engineering deck had virtually returned to the normal ebb and flow of daily routine by the time Sam and his escort returned. Had it not been for the presence of Chinese soldiers and bullet holes in the walls, it would have been very difficult to tell that a hostile takeover had just occurred.

Bravo Colony was not a military installation. With the exception of a few security troops, that for the most part only provided security for the elite, there was simply no military presence. After all, who would want the place? It was slowly falling apart despite Sam and Jack's best efforts.

The change in leadership meant little to most citizens. They, much like Sam, were more concerned with their own status and that of their friends. Obviously the Chinese were here for a reason. Even more obvious was the fact that it had little to do with the topic of Commander Seng's speech. And the whole thing was all completely out of their control anyway, so, most of the techs just carried on with the task at hand. It really didn't matter to them who handed out the work orders.

Sam walked into his old office and threw the completed work order on the desk, "Sensors are fixed, Harry."

Harry grinned, picked it up and put it on top of a stack of papers, "Still remember how it's done eh, Sam?"

"I think you'll soon find out that you won't be sitting in that desk as much as you'd like to be."

"And how's that?"

"If you want something done right."

"Oh, I see. The thing is I'm not an engineer, Sam. I want things done right and me stepping in to do them is not the answer."

"I wish you the best of luck then."

"It's not about luck, Sam. It's about motivation. For instance," Harry picked up another work order, stood up and walked around his desk to hand it to Sam, "I tell you to go fix," he looked at the work order, "scrubber 6," and handed it to him, "and you go fix scrubber 6."

"And what if we don't have the parts."

"I hear ingenuity grows with hunger."

"Gotcha."

Harry got serious, "So, go fix scrubber 6."

"I'll need to go to the graveyard to do a little refabrication for that one."

"That's fine. Just get it done."

Sam gave Harry a half assed salute, "Right, boss."

His words dripped with sarcasm. He turned to walk out but stopped. He didn't want to leave with tension between them. He turned back to Harry. "Oh hey, you mentioned something about drinks earlier. Are you doing anything later?"

"We should be done at a decent hour. Remarkable as that may be."

"Do you think the Hog and Dog will be open tonight?"

"I'll have Jim get on it. I could use a few drinks."

"Sounds like a plan," Sam turned to walk out the door, "I should have scrubber 6 up in time for happy hour."

"Good. That's what I like to hear."

Marie woke up with a vicious headache. She opened her eyes and instantly regretted it. Wherever she was it sure was brightly lit. She held one of her hands up to shield herself from the light and tried to open her eyes again. As she struggled to blink things into focus it became apparent to her that she had been put in a holding cell. Judging by the kink in her back she reckoned she had been lying there for a few hours. The cold hard metal slab that constituted her bed was clearly meant more for utility than comfort.

She rolled over and attempted to sit up. The movement met with a searing pain in her head. She winced but wouldn't let the pain stop her. Her feet fell towards the floor. They were still somewhat numb. She paused to give her body time to adjust and looked around the cell. Her eyes were still a bit blurry but she could make out Sarah and Malinda each lying on their own bed slabs. Both were still unconscious. She also noticed a sink, toilet and a door with a small window in it; all standard fare for a holding cell.

She slowly stood up using the bed slab to balance herself. Her legs tingled as blood rushed into them. She tried to take a step toward the door but it seemed her legs only partially worked. Whatever it was that the soldiers had gassed them with, it hadn't fully worn off. She forced herself forward and managed to stumble all the way to the door. She tried to stand on the tips of her toes to look out the window. She couldn't feel her toes, but she rose just enough to get a look, so, apparently they worked. What she saw was a plain corridor with similar doors evenly spaced along the opposite wall in each direction. It was quite underwhelming. She lowered herself and turned to lean against the door when she noticed that Sarah had begun to stir.

"Ow!" Sarah grunted as she tried to lift her head up.

"Easy Sarah, go slow." Marie spoke barely above a whisper as if she were talking to someone with bad hangover.

"Where are we?"

"A holding cell."

Sarah groggily looked herself over. She noticed she was no longer sporting only a thong. Someone had dressed her in sweatpants and a t-shirt, "Did you put these on me?"

"No, I've only just woke up myself."

Sarah pulled her shirt out a bit and looked down the front of it, "Whoever it was took my duct tape pasties." she said with mock disappointment. She reached around her backside and gave a tug, "At least they were kind enough to leave the thong."

Malinda sat up and moaned, "Ugh, I prefer bikinis. Wedgies suck..."

Marie turned her attention to Malinda, "How are you feeling?"

"Like I drank too much of Jim's homebrewed sink Whiskey. See anything out there?"

"Nope. Just doors."

Ricky opened his eyes and instinctively wiped the drool from his mouth. It was a habit he had developed after years of regularly waking up on the floor. He took a deep breath and saw what his hazy vision would allow him to see. He tried not to move much. It could be dangerous to do otherwise; after all, he had woken up in some very precarious places in the past. He could see Darrel lying unconscious on the bed slab across from him, he muttered, "Darrel." There was no reaction. He upped the volume a bit for more emphasis, "Hey, Darrel!" and he regretted it immediately.

Darrel's eyes opened and he began to stir. Eventually he squinted across the room to Ricky, "Where are we?" he croaked.

"The drunk tank. They should let us out after we sober up."

Darrel propped himself up on his elbow and surveyed the room, "This isn't a drunken blackout,

THE TRIALS OF JACK KEMPER

Ricky." His head throbbed which almost caused him to lie back down.

"Ah... well you can't blame me for assuming."

"Where's Jack?"

"Well, I figured he was at Malinda's, but as I'm starting to remember things, I'm not so sure." Darrel staggered to his feet and reached for anything that he could steady himself with. Ricky could see him wobble, "You gotta pace yourself."

Darrel lurched to the door and looked out into the corridor, "Yep, we're in a holding cell."

"Anything going on out there?" Ricky asked as he slowly sat up.

"Nothing, just a bunch of cell doors."

Ricky noticed he had on sweatpants, "Wasn't that nice of them. They gave me pants." he mused.

"They don't really go with the shirt," Darrel said as he continued to look out the window wondering where the others might be.

"You're right, maybe we should trade."

"I think we have bigger concerns my friend," he said as he started to pound his fist on the door and yelled, "Marie!" This caused Ricky to cover his ears and shoot him a most disgruntled look. It was entirely too early in the hangover process for that amount of noise, "Malinda? Sarah? Jack?" he continued. Ricky winced with every yell.

A muffled voice from the corridor broke the silence in the ladies' holding cell. Marie pressed her ear against the window to try and make out what the voice was saying. The voice called out again, "I think it's Darrel" she informed her cell mates. "Darrel?" she yelled in response. The others cringed in pain.

"Marie?" he replied.

"Darrel, are you okay? Are Jack and Ricky with you?" The questions spat out rapid fire.

"Ricky is here, but Jack isn't."

Marie turned to Malinda, "Jack's not with them."

Malinda turned slightly and hung her head at the news.

Darrel continued, "Are you okay? Who's with you?"

"Malinda and Sarah are with me. Everyone is okay given the circumstances."

Darrel let himself relax a bit when he heard that at least the three ladies were okay. He turned to Ricky who was looking at him expectantly, "It's the girls. They're all together and okay."

"That's good news. Do they know where Jack is?"

"It doesn't sound like it."

Ricky hung his head at the news. The door to the cell opened and two Chinese soldiers stormed through yelling something in Chinese. One soldier forced Darrel to the back of the cell and pinned him against the wall while the other soldier pointed his gun at Ricky, "YOU!" he barked.

"Me?" was the meek response.

"Come!" The soldier's accent was thick. It was obvious that he had reached the limits of his English.

"But…" Ricky started to reply, hesitant to go with

THE TRIALS OF JACK KEMPER

the soldiers.

That was all it took. The soldier grabbed Ricky by the shoulder and threw him towards the door. The force of the movement sent Ricky sprawling to the floor as he slid into the corridor outside. The assaulting soldier followed behind him.

"Hey!" Darrel valiantly tried to object to the rough treatment of his friend, but his protest was promptly stopped by a rifle stock to the gut. The unexpected blow sent to him to the floor gasping for breath. He laid there helpless as the second soldier exited the cell and the door slid shut.

Marie could see the soldiers manhandling Ricky in the corridor. She wasn't having it. She yelled through the window, "Hey stop it assholes!" and punched at the door. The soldiers didn't seem to care.

The soldiers screamed at Ricky, "Up! Up!" as they continued to push him.

Ricky finally managed to stagger to his feet, "Alright! Alright! Just tell me what you want."

The soldier pointed down the corridor, "Go!"

One soldier followed Ricky while the other jumped ahead of him. They turned the corner and left the cellblock behind. Ricky started to worry that he might not ever see his friends again.

The soldiers escorted him into an interrogation room, "Sit! Wait!" they snarled.

The first thing Ricky noticed about the room was the temperature. They must have had the heat turned up. He began sweating almost immediately. It was also unusually quiet. He didn't hear the normal background noise. There were two chairs. Ricky sat in one.

A small Chinese man walked in dressed head to toe in black. His eyes had a reptilian, almost cross-eyed, quality to them and he was chewing on a straw. Ricky noticed he was also carrying a computer pad.

He looked at the pad, "You are Ricky Montopolis." There was no question. "You are the Senior Project Manager for Bravo Colony."

Ricky nodded, "Yes."

The man poked at the pad and turned it to show Ricky, "You know this man?"

Ricky looked at the pad. It was a picture of Jack, "I've seen him around on occasion."

His response was met with a slap, "Do not lie," he paused and the question turned into more of a statement, "you do know this man."

Ricky turned away. He couldn't even look at the picture of Jack, "Yes, I know him."

"Tell me where he is."

"I really don't know."

This response was also met with a slap, "Tell me where to find him!"

"Look, I would if I had any idea. He knows every inch of this colony. He could be anywhere. Please, slapping me isn't going to give me clairvoyance."

The Chinese man stared at Ricky. His eyes didn't move. He didn't blink.

"The last time I saw him was on the evacuation deck. I figured he got rounded up with the rest of us."

THE TRIALS OF JACK KEMPER

Ricky couldn't help but notice that, while he was sweating profusely, his interrogator wasn't perspiring at all.

"Of course we have him."

Ricky looked puzzled, "I don't understand."

"I wanted to know what kind of man you are." he grinned devilishly. "How fast you hand over your friends."

Ricky felt ashamed. He knew he would have given him the information if in fact he knew where Jack was. This made Ricky mad. How could he be so weak? Jack was his friend. He was his best friend. And he would have given him up. This wasn't who he was. The thought changed him; instantly. It was one of life's moments. He started to play the game right back, "Sure, you have Jack."

Activities in the Operations Center churned along. The Commander had left and put one of his Lieutenants in charge of the room. He seemed like an affable fellow, at least, he didn't threaten anyone. When informed of a problem he calmly let the operators work it and always kindly thanked them when it was corrected. He had been well schooled.

Carl stood up from the sensor console. He stretched and picked up his cup of coffee. He slowly meandered over towards the communications console where Jessica had been sitting for the better part of the day. He noticed the Lieutenant watching him so he started with small talk, "Hey Jessica, are you our new comms person?"

"It's these damn glitches. I fix one and another pops up a few minutes later."

"That's not good. Makes for a long day."

"It doesn't seem to end."

Carl leaned forward and set his cup down on the console table. He pointed at the screen to make it appear he was trying to help her. He lowered his voice, "Hey, I noticed a large number of people gathering near the waste ejection room. Have you heard any chatter?"

"Something big is about to happen. It's all high level. Tight security protocols."

"Can't crack it?"

"Not without being noticed."

"Do we have eyes down there?"

"There's probably a security camera or two."

"Can we get a look?"

Jessica scrolled through a few screens until she found the security camera feeds in that area. She turned to the Lieutenant, "Sir, I'm showing some feedback on circuit 130-a. It's a security camera. Permission to run some diagnostics on it?"

The number meant nothing to the Lieutenant. He only heard security camera and diagnostics, "That's fine." He had no idea. It was time for a coffee break anyway. He turned and walked into a small break room.

Jessica selected the security camera and brought it up on one of the larger displays. Everyone in the room could see it. And it immediately caught everyone's attention.

"Is that the President?" Jessica asked.

"It looks like the Council is there as well." Carl replied.

"What are they doing down there?"

"It looks like they're all just standing there."

"Do you think that's where they're being held?"

"No, they were being held in the cellblock."

They then witnessed something none of them would ever forget. A couple of the operators actually screamed. Jessica and Carl could only gasp. They were left speechless as the waste ejection airlock opened. The leadership of Bravo Colony exploded out into space. Cast off like unwanted garbage.

The Lieutenant heard the commotion and ran back into the room. Everyone was just standing there. Mouths agape, sickly pale and transfixed by the display. He had no idea what had just happened. There was nothing to see. It was just an empty room, "Turn that off. Get back to work." he ordered.

Darrel leaned up against the door of his cell as he tried to rub the pain from his ribs. It had been several minutes since the soldiers had taken Ricky away. He imagined the worst. Terrible thoughts raced through his head. He stood there alone, dejected.

Marie yelled, "What are we going to do Darrel?"

"What can we do?" He felt helpless and hopeless.

"Why Ricky?"

"I don't know."

The door to Marie's cell slid open and a soldier entered. The three ladies naturally moved as far away as they could. The soldier looked them over and pointed to Marie, "Come."

Sarah looked him dead in the eyes, "Asshole."

Malinda yelled, "What did you do with Ricky?"

The soldier didn't respond. He simply pulled Marie out of the cell into the corridor where another soldier was waiting. The cell door slid closed behind them and the other soldier pointed down the hall and pushed her, "Go.'

They got to as far as Darrel's cell. When he saw they had Marie he went bat shit crazy. He kicked the door and screamed, "Come back in here motherfucker. I'll stick that gun right up your ass this time!"

The soldiers stopped. They turned to Darrel's cell and much to Darrel's horror, the door slid open. Marie got ready for a fight, "Come." the soldier ordered.

Darrel was hesitant. He wondered what kind of game this was. Marie stared at the soldier and she looked quite intense. Her expression even scared Darrel a little. He stepped out of his cell prepared for a fight. He figured he had better odds in a fight with Marie in his corner than he did with Ricky. Marie could be downright mean! Ricky was more of a "take a dive in an early round for a paycheck" kind of fighter.

The soldier pointed down the hall, "Go."

The two of them began walking down the hall as the soldiers prodded with their rifles. They pair was led to the same room where Ricky was interrogated. The small Chinese interrogator sat across from two

THE TRIALS OF JACK KEMPER

empty chairs. Without looking up from his tablet he gestured for them to sit. The three of them sat in silence for a few moments as their captor poked and swiped at the tablet. He paused and looked up at Marie, "Med Tech Grade 2, Marie Perez and," he shifted his gaze, "Dr. Darrel Thomas."

Darrel spoke first, "That's correct."

Marie gave him the evil eye. "Tell me what you did with Ricky!"

"Ricky Montopolis?"

"Yeah, he's our friend."

"Of course he was. He was important to you?"

This response caught Marie off guard. Was? She nervously swallowed.

"I'm afraid Mr. Montopolis didn't find our terms agreeable and has decided to join your friend Jack Kemper."

Darrel angrily asked, "What do you mean? Where's Jack?"

"The two are on their way back to Earth as we speak. Unfortunately we couldn't spare a shuttle. You understand."

Their hearts sank. Darrel's mouth dropped open in shock. Marie turned white. They didn't want to fight anymore. They couldn't fight. They were paralyzed with grief,

"So, I sincerely hope that the two of you find our terms a little more palatable than your friends did."

Darrel quietly spoke in monotone, "What are your terms?"

"Our terms for you are that you will return to your duties."

"That's it?" Marie asked.

"Yes. That is all we ask. Do you agree?"

Darrel asked, "What about Malinda and Sarah?"

"All will be sorted within the next day or two. Do you agree?"

Marie spoke up, "We agree."

The door slid open. "We will be watching both of you very closely. You may go."

Darrel stood up while grabbing Marie by the hand. He didn't care if this was some sort of cruel joke. He was leaving. He was taking her with him. And he wasn't dignifying this man with a response. They walked through the door into the corridor and immediately headed for the pub. It was time to drink their grief away.

Sam walked into the room that was affectionately called the graveyard. It was, by far, the largest room on the engineering deck. It was warehouse like; laid out with aisle after aisle of industrial grade shelving. The shelves were tall, too, with several tiers rising all the way up to the ceiling. It took a ladder to get anything past the second tier. Old parts were stored here with the hope that one day they could be re-fabricated into something useful once again.

There were so many old parts creatively stacked, crammed really, into every possible space that the entire place had become quite precarious. Originally there was a filing system, but over the years it had grown beyond any capacity for organization. In fact, it was really just dumb luck that anyone ever found what they were looking for.

Sam turned to his escort and pointed up above, "You might want to stay here at the entrance. People have been known to get hurt by falling objects in here."

The soldier took a look around. Sam hadn't caused any trouble so he didn't see any reason to stick his neck out here, "Be quick."

Sam knew exactly where he was going. Aisle Thirty-two - Tier Eight - Bin Nineteen - Dead communicators. However, it took him a few minutes to find the ladder. Someone left it over on Aisle Nine. They left a mess there too!

He retrieved the bin and carried it to the nearest workbench at a good pace. He didn't know how long it would be before his escort would soldier up and come to look for him. He figured he had twenty to thirty minutes before that happened. He added another fifteen minutes of search time.

He was a little dismayed at what he pulled out of the bin, "Well, I guess they're here for a reason." He muttered. There were dozens of communicators but most of them were in pretty bad shape. One looked like it had been chewed on by some sort of animal but he couldn't recall there ever being animals on the colony, "Must have been a hell of a night." he thought.

After several minutes of scrounging he found three communicators that he thought might be salvageable. They smelled like burnt wires not burnt circuits. Over the years he learned to differentiate the subtle difference in scents. Burnt wiring had a hint of plastic. Burnt circuits smelled like fire.

He picked up a flathead screwdriver from the workbench and pried them open. They were just as he had hoped. Each one had shorted out wiring. He started to pry open the communicators that smelled like fire to look for usable wiring. After about ten minutes he had found what he was looking for. He grabbed the soldering iron and began the repairs.

It must have been about that time. The soldier was yelling his name, "Sam!"

Sam quickly finished the repairs, threw the unusable communicators back in the bin, and slid it under the workbench. He stuffed the three repaired communicators into his work belt. He quickly reached for the roll of duct tape on his belt and began to tape his fingers.

The soldier finally found the right aisle. He marched toward Sam with some pace expecting to find him up to something nefarious. What he found was Sam leaned up against the workbench acting out a scene with duct tape finger puppets.

Sam held his hands out in front of him. He wiggled a finger. "Was always kinda partial to Roy Rogers actually. I really like those sequined shirts."

He wiggled a finger on his other hand, "Do you really think you have a chance against us, Mr. Cowboy?" he said as he attempted a strong German accent.

He wiggled the first finger again, "Yippee-ki-yay,

motherfucker!"

The soldier let him end the performance, "What's taking so long?"

"This damn place. I can't find shit. Maybe a straw from the mess hall will do it?"

The soldier's patience was wearing thin, "Okay, let's go then."

Harry was standing in the corridor near the door to the graveyard. He saw Sam and his escort as they walked out and approached, "Sam, did you find what you need?"

"I found a few parts but I need to run by the mess hall and grab a straw."

"A straw?"

"It's a plastic tube, Harry."

"Right, well I guess you know what you're doing."

"Somewhat."

"Hey," Harry pointed to the soldier and continued, "I'm going to reassign your escort here. I think you'll be fine on your own."

"Yeah, probably be easier to get shit done without someone staring at me."

Harry turned to the soldier, "Take a break." and then turned back to Sam.

"The Commander has asked me to look at the docking bay. Apparently they had a rough entry this morning and the damage will make it hard to bring new arrivals on board."

"Sounds like a project."

"He said it was tore up pretty bad."

"You'll want to get Ricky Montopolis to head that up."

"That's what I was thinking but he's currently being held."

"Held?"

"Yeah, there was a big debacle on the evacuation deck earlier. They picked up him and a few of his friends."

"Well, he's really the only one that has the skills to coordinate something that big. Was Jack with him?"

"Unfortunately no. Malinda was though, so, at least I'll be able to sleep tonight. Darrel and Marie were with him too. I'll see if I can get those three released. I want your attention focused on fixing things not on missing friends."

"That would be great Harry."

It was four in the afternoon and Jim stood behind the bar of an empty establishment as Darrel and Marie walked through the door. The pair looked quite sullen. They sat down at Jack's favorite table and Marie began to quietly sob.

Jim brought over three drinks and set them down on the table, "They're on me."

"Thanks Jim." replied Darrel.

Jim asked, "Did you lose somebody today, Marie?"

She couldn't stop sobbing so Darrel answered for her, "Jack and Ricky," then he took a big swig of his drink.

Jim started to reply, "Ricky? He's in the..." when the door to the restroom opened and Ricky stumbled out with toilet paper hanging from his backside, "shitter."

Ricky immediately saw them and slurred, "You're free!"

Darrel was so shocked to see Ricky that he spit his drink out and jumped to his feet.

Jim looked at him, "C'mon it ain't that bad. I just made it in the sink this morning!"

Darrel rushed over to Ricky and gave him a bear hug, "Damn it man. They told us they floated you!"

Marie stopped sobbing. Her grief turned to pure joy. Her joy then turned into seething anger. These must be the three stages of vengeance.

"Floated me?" Ricky replied.

"Yeah, they said they put you and Jack out the airlock!"

"That little slimy bastard."

Marie interjected, "I'm going to kill that son of a bitch."

Darrel agreed, "If it's the last thing we do."

"Hey, I'm all right guys. And you're free!" He reached down for the last drink and gulped it down.

Jack had the wires pulled out from under the maintenance terminal in the scrubber room on Sub Deck "C". He was on a mission to locate his friends. He had been trying, unsuccessfully, to reroute sensor data through the maintenance network. He wasn't aware that the entire network was now encrypted. His attempts had not gone unnoticed.

A console message appeared on the terminal, "The

maintenance network is currently unavailable. JL"

Jack brought up a command prompt and typed, "SENDMSG JL this is JK."

Another message appeared. "HNDSHK PUBKEY 94527421825ddd4b4af99af402a"

Jack immediately understood. The network had been encrypted, "That's one smart lady." he said and set to work feverishly entering commands.

First, he generated his own encryption key so he could open a secure channel. The commands were input rapid fire.

"> CRT SECKEY"
"ENTER HASH ALG >"
"RA512"
"ENTER SEED >"

Jack thought for a moment, there was only one thing suitable, "VESTASTOUDT" he smiled a bit after typing it.

"> VESTASTOUDT:9a255e0dc5bcd12a7eb962ce"

Pulling up the communication console he sent the information for the newly created key, "HNDSHK PUBKEY 9a255e0dc5bcd12a7eb962ce."

The cursor flashed for a few moments. The response came, "ACCEPT ENC CHNL REQUEST 94527421825ddd4b4af99af402a." She had received his information.

He confirmed the request by entering his key information and waited again.

"CHNL ENC SUCCESS" Finally, something was going right today.

THE TRIALS OF JACK KEMPER

He typed, "Please send alcohol!"
"So it is you!"
"It is. Status?"
"Leadership floated."
"Shit. Sam?"
"Look behind you."

The access panel to the scrubber room slid open and Sam walked through. He stopped dead in his tracks. His eyes lit up, "I knew you'd turn up!"

Jack typed in one last message, "Thanks Jess," closed the channel and turned back to Sam, "So where are we?"

Sam pulled a communicator out of his tool belt, "Encrypted and keyed for the maintenance network."

Jack grabbed the communicator out of Sam's hand, "Nice fucking work Sam!"

"Jessica's idea really."

"That's one hell of a girl Sam."

"You know, I never noticed but when she bent down to get under the communications console. Holy hell! That ass!"

"I was talking about her other assets." Jack replied with a wink.

"Right, right. Quite the thinker she is."

"Jack, Harry just told me they're holding Malinda, Ricky, Darrel and Marie."

"Damn it. We got separated on the Evac Deck. They fucking gassed us man."

"Well, at least they didn't shoot you."

"They'll regret that. What about Sarah?"

"Who's that?"

"A friend of Marie's that was with us."

"I have no idea about her, but Harry said he'll see about getting Ricky, Darrel and Marie released. He's scared of Malinda for some reason."

Jack had to chuckle, "He should be. So what's this about the leadership being floated?"

"Yeah, that's a new development. Jessica just filled me in on that."

"You know it won't be long until they start floating the people they don't find useful."

Right, we need a plan."

"We need a plan, some good intel and I need a damn drink."

"Jessica can help us with the intel, but unless you feel like strolling into the bar that drink is a bit tougher."

"I've got a plan for that. I just need to adjust the sensors around Malinda's quarters first."

"I was here to work on Scrubber 6 but someone told me that it would be an exercise in futility. Let's fuck with some sensors!"

The clock had just struck happy hour, but there weren't a whole lot of happy faces at the Hog and Dog. While elated that Ricky was alive and well, Darrel was still quite concerned about Malinda and Sarah, "It's been an hour. They'd come here, right? If they could?" he asked.

Marie replied, "I would think so."

"It's happy hour. They never miss happy hour."

Ricky slurred.

"So we have to assume they're not going to be released." said Darrel.

Marie asked, "What about Jack?"

"I don't think they caught him. I think that asshole was feeding us a line of bullshit, just like with Ricky."

"I hope you're right."

"I just have a feeling," Darrel looked toward the bar, "Jim, three more please."

Ricky put his arm around Darrel and slurred into his ear, "Did, did, I ever tell you you're a good man?"

"Yes Ricky."

Jim was filling three more glasses when Harry walked in, "Hey Harry."

"Mind pouring me one of those while you're at it?"

"Sure thing."

Ricky raised his voice a little too loud, "Hey look! It's Poo Man Chu!"

Harry approached the table, "Mind if I join you?"

"Please, grab a seat Harry." Marie responded, happy to see another familiar face.

Jim brought the drinks over and set them down on the table. Jim said, "Thanks for getting the bar opened, Harry"

"It's the least I could do."

"How'd you get the bar opened, Harry?" Darrel asked.

"The same way I got Ricky released. I asked Commander Seng."

Marie started to turn a little red, "Wait, you're working with them?"

Darrel felt she had it under control and sat this one out.

"In case you couldn't tell by my facial features and skin tone, I am them, Marie."

"What the fuck Harry?"

"Calm down Marie. You're all safe. You're here doing what you always do."

"Oh yeah, of course, that makes it okay."

"Doesn't it? Life goes on."

"What about Malinda and Sarah?"

Darrel chimed in, "And Jack."

"Oh and Jack!" Marie was upset with herself for forgetting Jack.

"Look, if it will make you happy I'll put in a word for Sarah. I'm afraid Jack and Malinda are beyond my reach."

Darrel asked, "Why's that?"

"Well, they took out a couple of Seng's soldiers. I'm afraid he'll demand they answer for that."

"What the hell were they supposed to do?" Marie asked.

"The same thing everyone else did. Watch it happen."

Sam came strolling into the bar with a big smile on his face. He was whistling an Irish drinking song when he saw the group at the table. He walked up to the table, pulled two socks out of his tool belt and laid them over Harry's shoulders.

Harry recoiled, "Oh my god that smell!" He quickly brushed them off to the floor.

"Your handy work I believe."

"Maybe I should give those to the New Dawn Protectorate; they could use them for a new interrogation apparatus." Harry smiled at his own quick witted response.

"Thanks for dropping that escort."

"You did a good job Sam."

"I really did! I believe you owe me a drink or ten."

Harry turned to Jim, "Keep them coming Jim. Let's make them doubles."

Ricky was drunk. He was usually quite a charming drunk, but every once-in-a-while it turned on him, "You're a real asshole Harry. A big asshole indeed."

Darrel couldn't help but laugh, "Damn Ricky."

Marie rubbed Ricky on the back, "My sentiments exactly."

"I'll admit it. What I did could be seen that way. But honestly it was going to happen regardless of anything I did."

Sam tried to calm things down. After all, he knew Jack was fine and working on a plan to rectify the situation, "Hey Harry, why don't you go pick up those drinks from Jim. Ricky always loves the guy that brings the drinks."

Ricky seethed.

"Sure Sam." Harry stood up and walked over to the bar.

"You and Harry are real chums now, eh Sam?" Marie sneered.

Sam leaned in, ignoring the accusation, "Look, we only have a minute. Jack is okay. He's working on a plan. We're in contact." He pulled a communicator out of his tool belt and handed it to Darrel under the table.

Darrel turned to Marie and smiled, "Space Engineer."

Harry turned from the bar with five drinks in hand. All doubles. He set them on the table and waited for Ricky's usual gratitude.

"Nope, Nope I'm afraid you're still an asshole."

Feigning offense, "Really, I guess I'll have to double my efforts," Harry continued, "Jim, another five if you will."

Harry could almost walk with his arm draped around Sam; almost. Sam thought about dumping him down a trash chute. It seemed like a fair response to the events of the day, but he had already put in the work to gain his trust. And if Harry didn't show up for work tomorrow it would certainly be noticed. Besides, Sam knew Harry would get what was coming to him soon enough. Well, as soon as he could get Malinda free.

Sam grudgingly carried Harry back to his room. He fished the access card out of Harry's pocket and opened the door. He tossed Harry down on his bed, punched him in the face a few times and snarled, "Welcome to the party, Pal!"

CHAPTER 5

Jack crawled his way through the ventilation system. He and Sam had lowered the sensor sensitivity for a few key spots in the colony and the metal ductwork would now conceal his whereabouts.

The main ventilation ducts ran above the ceiling of each deck and made it rather easy for him to move around while also allowing him to avoid being seen. These ducts were rather large and weren't that difficult to maneuver through. Every ten feet there would be a smaller duct that would run into a room.

The ducts that ran into each room were much smaller, but they wouldn't be that great of a challenge for Jack to get through. He wasn't much more than bones. Malinda's room was the sixth one on the right so he counted as he went past five and figured the next one would lead to her room.

He was proven wrong. He must have miscounted. Malinda's pudgy neighbor was naked and working on his downward dog, "I can't un-see that," he thought and quickly backed up into the main shaft once again. He realized he had come up one room short and made his way to the next duct. His eyes widened and he started to drool as he peered through the vent.

There it was still lying on the floor. It was all alone. He hoped it didn't feel unwanted. Did it have feelings? He wasn't sure. He knew it had a purpose. And that purpose was to be drunk. And he knew his feelings. He felt like a drink. It was a match predestined by fate.

He unscrewed the vent cover and carefully lowered himself out and into the room. He walked over and picked the bottle of Whiskey up off of the floor, took another step, picked up a glass off of the floor, sat down on the edge of the bed, unscrewed the top off of the bottle, poured until his glass was full, lifted the glass to his lips and downed the entire drink. He took a deep breath, grimaced, wiped his mouth on his sleeve and said, "Fuck it smells in here."

Jack walked over to the kitchenette area and found a pair of tongs. He gingerly picked up his socks and held them as far away from himself as he could while he walked them over to the door. He cracked the door open and with one swing of his arm tossed his stinky socks down the hall as far as he could.

Now he could get on to the serious matters at hand without further distraction. He poured himself another glass of Whiskey and began to run through several scenarios. Getting the girls out of the cellblock wouldn't be hard. It was remaining free that would be the difficult part.

THE TRIALS OF JACK KEMPER

Bravo Colony was only so large and while it had plenty of hiding spots that made it easy for one man to avoid getting caught, it wouldn't be so easy to maintain such a fluid lifestyle with two ladies in tow. And keeping them satisfied? Was that even a possibility? The answer that quickly returned to him was, no, he definitely needed a workable solution.

Jack took another drink just as his left pocket started to vibrate. Had he been hanging left he might have just let it vibrate for a while, but since he was hanging right and only a couple people would be trying to contact him, at this time, he felt it might be important to answer. He fished the communicator out of his pocket, "This is Jack."

"Jack, it's Darrel."

"That was fast."

"I ran into Sam at the pub."

"Are Marie and Ricky with you?"

"Both safe for now."

"Good," he took a drink and repeated. "Good."

"I trust you got a plan to get Sarah and Malinda?"

"Trying to work something out. Getting them out isn't tough. Getting free is problematic."

"There's a lot of soldiers, Jack."

"Any ideas?"

"Not without a lot of soldiers of our own."

"Well we don't have any." Jack continued, "So, they just let you walk?"

"Yeah, we're all supposed to report as normal tomorrow. They're looking for you though. Something about you and Malinda taking out a few soldiers."

"I figured as much."

"Harry's working with them."

"Yeah, ran into him earlier. I probably should have played that a little differently."

"Nah, we can't have everyone just roll over."

There was a long pause. Jack finished off his second glass and said, "Darrel, I'm going to polish off this bottle and pass out for a while. Everyone is safe for now. Just do your thing and we'll get it all sorted soon. We aren't giving them our colony."

"Damn straight we aren't."

The next morning Jessica was back to work at the communications console. Sleep had not come easy for her after having watched the leadership get floated. The previous day had left her exhausted and on the verge of becoming mentally unhinged. She had no idea what today had in store for her but she had a dark feeling that gnawed at her and kept her nerves on edge.

It wouldn't take long, though, for the day to declare its true intentions. Startled by a powerful tap on the shoulder she turned to find Carl's face far too close to hers, "There's another large group of people in the waste ejection system." he said.

"What?"

"Yeah, there's close to 50 people crammed in there."

Jessica brought up the security feed on her local

THE TRIALS OF JACK KEMPER

display. Her response was immediate, "There's children in there."

A few seconds later the children and the parents who accompanied them were gone; ejected heartlessly into the vacuum of space. Jessica's eyes teared up. She gasped. Her body was paralyzed by grief.

Carl stood there silently. A minute passed. Two minutes passed, "It's not the first group." He whispered.

It became abhorrently clear what the purpose of the Chinese takeover was; space for their population to grow. It was a mission of genocide.

"How long has this been going on?" Jessica fearfully asked.

"Once an hour. All night." he replied.

"That's..." she stammered, "That's... around 400 people."

Jessica quickly did the gruesome math in her head. At this pace, all non-essential personnel would be floated within five days. She looked at Carl, "I've got to do something," she said as she stood up and turned to the Lieutenant, "Permission to use the lavatory sir?"

The Lieutenant nodded back, "Quickly."

Jessica walked as fast as she could without raising concern. She went down the corridor to the ladies room and pulled a communicator out of her pocket. She wanted to contact Sam but didn't know if it was safe. She decided that Jack was the only person she could contact safely. She dialed up his communicator.

A groggy voice responded, "This is Jack."

"Jack, it's Jess." Her voice trembled.

Jack could immediately tell something was wrong, "What is it Jess?"

"They're floating groups of people."

"What!?!"

"Groups of people. Children too!"

A scream came through from Jack's end, "Those motherfuckers! Those goddamned motherfuckers!"

"It's been going on all night."

The screaming continued, "I'm going to kill every last one of them!"

"Jack..." she tried to get him to regain his composure. "Jack, what are we going to do?"

"Go back to comms. Initiate a distress call."

"They'll see that."

"There are people on the ground that need to know what's about to happen."

"What do I say?"

"Tell them Bravo Colony is being evacuated."

"Okay, Jack. I'll do that immediately."

"And don't worry about the floats, Jess. I'm going to put a stop to that."

Jessica realized that bad things were going to happen to her the minute she put out a distress call. She unzipped her pants. She spread her legs and reached down between them with the communicator. When her hand was removed from her pants the communicator was gone. She pulled her up her pants, zipped them and steadied herself to do the most dangerous thing she had ever done in her life.

THE TRIALS OF JACK KEMPER

It took all of Jessica's bravery to walk back into the Operations Center. And as she walked to the communications console she gave Carl a look. It left little doubt with him that things were about to go sideways.

She sat down at the console, put on a headset and opened all broadcast channels, "This is a general distress call. Bravo Colony has been invaded by armed forces of the New Dawn Colony. Their leadership is perpetrating genocide on the Bravo Colony residents. Evacuation is imminent." A recording of her announcement repeated itself. She set it to repeat continuously.

Almost immediately an incoming transmission was received, "This is Liberty Island. We have received your distress call. Preparations are being made..."

That's all Jessica was able to hear before she was yanked backwards out of her chair. The blows began to land on her face and chest. She no longer had control of her body. She managed to stay conscious for the next fifteen seconds, but soon it had all gone dark. Her last vision was that of angry Chinese men and their boots. She didn't know if she would ever open her eyes again, but she knew she did the right thing.

Ricky stood in the docking bay dressed neatly in a freshly pressed suit and tie. It was standard attire for his work day. There were no signs of a hangover; after all, he was a professional. He looked over the carnage caused by the Chinese troop carrier while he sipped his morning cup of coffee.

Sam had met Ricky at the docks promptly at 8AM,

but oddly, there was no sign of Harry. Sam also had a cup of coffee in hand. He took a sip, "Quite a lot of damage." he said.

"It's like they didn't even try to find a good place to dock." Ricky replied.

"I think they wanted to destroy the shuttles."

Ricky took another drink and sighed, "Well, they accomplished that."

"What do you think?"

"Months."

"They're not going to like that."

Ricky pulled a flask out of his pocket and poured something into his coffee. He offered a pour to Sam. Sam graciously accepted. Ricky said, "Fuck'em."

Harry finally showed up a few minutes later. He walked up to Sam and Ricky and said, "Hey, sorry I'm late."

Ricky looked at Harry and noticed his face was all bruised up, "Rough night, Harry?"

"I don't even remember going back to my room."

Sam replied, "Looks like you took a spill."

"It feels like someone kicked me in the face."

Ricky laughed, "Well, that's understandable."

Harry didn't tell them about the giant shit he found in his sink. Or that his bed was moist and smelled of piss. He wasn't sure what happened and it very well could have been his own work.

Sam knew exactly what had happened. And he had a hard time hiding his grin. He was about to burst with laughter when he felt his communicator vibrate.

THE TRIALS OF JACK KEMPER

He pulled it out of his pocket, turned to Harry and said, "Hey, I need to take this. I'll be right back."

He walked until he had some relative privacy, "This is Sam."

"Sam, it's Jack. Jessica just contacted me with some pretty bad news."

"Really?"

"They're floating people Sam. Families. Kids."

"HOLY SHIT!" Sam exclaimed, immediately realizing he had yelled. He looked over his shoulder to see if Harry had noticed, "Holy shit! Are you serious?" this time a bit quieter.

"Look, I told her to initiate a distress signal. I'm on my way to the drone bay."

"What are you going to do there?"

"I'm going to do some reprogramming. I could use your help."

"Right, I'm on my way."

Sam returned to Harry and Ricky, "Hey, Harry, that was the Operations Center. That damn sensor array is glitching out. I should probably get up there."

"Yeah okay, get on that. Tell Carl he's buying tonight."

Sam turned to leave, "Right, will do."

Sarah was lying on her bed slab staring at the ceiling, "They keep taking people. When do you think they'll get to us?"

Malinda looked out the window of the cell, "I'm not too sure that I want them to."

"Anything is better than this."

"Sarah, I killed some of their men. I don't think this ends well for me."

"I don't think this ends well for anyone but staring at this ceiling is getting old. I just wish whatever is going to happen would happen so we can get on with it already."

"Well you might get your wish." Malinda could hear footsteps coming down the corridor. As they got closer she could see two soldiers dragging a limp body.

"They're dragging someone." The disheveled hair prevented Malinda from seeing who it was.

"Who is it?"

"A woman, I think. I can't really tell." The soldiers stopped at their cell and the door slid open.

Malinda moved back and Sarah stood up. The soldiers stepped into the room and dropped the person on the floor without a word, turned around and left. The door slid closed behind them. Malinda and Sarah worked together to move their new cellmate to one of the bed slabs. They gently laid her down on her back and gingerly moved her bloody matted hair out of the way. Malinda gasped, "It's Jessica." she said

"Damn, they really did a number on her," Sarah tore the bottom off of her t-shirt, wet it in the sink and began to clean away the blood that covered Jessica's face. The pain caused Jessica to jerk her head back. She defensively moved her hands in front of her and let out an agonizing scream.

Malinda gently grabbed her hands, "It's okay, Jessica. It's me, Malinda."

Jessica seemed to recognize the voice. It could have been a dream. She had no way to know for sure. She relaxed her hands.

Sarah continued to clean away the blood. Her face was badly bruised and had several deep fresh cuts. Each time she dabbed at the wounds Jessica would whimper. This was not something Sarah was used to. She fought back tears and forced herself to keep it together; more for her own sake than that of Malinda or Jessica.

Jessica's lips struggled to move, "Malin..."

"Jessica?" Malinda whispered as she leaned over her.

"Malinmmph..." Jessica labored. Through her pain it was obvious that she wanted to tell them something. She reached up and lightly clasped Malinda's upper arm to pull her closer.

Malinda placed her ear as close to Jessica's mouth as she could. She tried to make out what was being said. She concentrated. Once she thought she understood she sat up.

"Hmm, I think I caught that."

"What?" Sarah asked.

"I think..." Malinda started to say when Jessica grabbed her hand and guided it down the front of her pants in between her legs.

"Oh!?" Blurted Sarah, not sure how to process what was going on.

Malinda wasn't known to be a prude, in fact, she had a reputation for just the opposite, but even she felt a little uncomfortable with what she was about to do given Jessica's current condition. She unzipped Jessica's pants, spread her legs and went in. Her expression of discomfort immediately changed when her hand felt something unexpected. Malinda gently worked the communicator out and handed it to Sarah, "Wash this."

"Did you just pull that...?"

"Yup."

"Oh, alright," Sarah took it to the sink and rinsed it off. "What was that doing up there?"

"I think she was trying to hide it."

"That's pretty awesome," She handed it back to Malinda.

Malinda saw two series of numbers scratched into it, "Let's see who answers."

Sam was in the lift on his way to meet Jack when his communicator alerted him to an incoming call. He answered, "This is Sam."

"Sam?"

Sam thought he recognized the voice on the other end, but the only woman he expected to hear from was Jessica, "Yeah, this is Sam. Is that you Malinda?"

"Yeah. Sam. Bad news. Jessica was just dumped in our cell beaten half to death."

"Those sons-of-bitches!"

"She needs medical attention."

"Okay, I'll send Darrel down."

"Darrel's with you?"

"No, but he's probably in the infirmary."

"Have you seen Jack?"

"Yes, Jack's okay. I'm on my way to him now. There should be a second number on that communicator."

"There is."

"That's Jack. Contact him," Sam disconnected with Malinda and immediately contacted Darrel.

Darrel was in the infirmary looking after a few wounded Chinese soldiers when his communicator started to vibrate. He stepped into his office for some privacy, "This is Darrel."

"Darrel, it's Sam."

"Hey Sam, what's up?"

"I need you to get to the security deck. Bad shit's happening and Jessica needs some medical attention."

"I'm on it Sam."

"Take Marie. This might be a one way trip."

"Why's that?"

"Darrel, they've started floating groups of colonists."

"You can't be serious."

"I am. Jack and I are working the problem. Please try to help Jess. We'll be in touch."

Darrel's trauma training kicked in, "I'll do what I can."

Malinda nearly dropped the communicator after Sam had disconnected. The news that Jack was alive and well sent a wave of relief through her body. If there was ever any doubt how much she loved him, there was no trace of it now. She would never openly admit to it, but she had many dark thoughts of his fate while she sat hopeless and helpless in that cell. The relief of knowing that he was all right gave her a new hope. She steadied herself and, with a sense of urgency, keyed in the second code on the communicator.

Jack had wedged himself into the drone bay. It was a tight fit even for his bony ass. The bay wasn't meant for humans. It was only meant to hold the drones while they recharged. He had removed the access panel to the Alpha Drone and pulled out the small data input pad. Every Alpha had one for "in the field" input.

Jack had become very familiar with drone programming over the years. Many hours had been spent coding repairs with non-standard parts. Those long and tedious days spent hunched over a terminal had garnered him a high level of proficiency on the matter. He sat there, wedged quite uncomfortably between two drones, and methodically worked to update the Alpha Drone's code to execute his plan. Once the Alpha Drone was programmed it would disseminate the code to the others in its group.

The communicator in his pocket began to vibrate. He struggled to get into a position where he could actually reach it. After a few seconds of shifting and contorting he was able to pull it out.

"This is Jack."

Her knees gave out as she heard his voice and she was forced to sit on the bed slab, "Jack?"

"Malinda?" he said with excited disbelief.

"Yes"

THE TRIALS OF JACK KEMPER

"Are you okay?"

"Yes. Sarah is here with me. Jessica's here too and in pretty bad shape. I just spoke to Sam. He's sending Darrel to help." She tried to bring Jack up to speed on the situation.

"Slow down a bit there, babe."

"What happened to Jessica?"

"We don't know. The soldiers just dragged her in here beaten and unconscious."

"DAMN IT!" he yelled. "Listen, the Chinese are floating colonists to make room for their own people."

The horror of Jack's revelation caught her off guard, "Oh, my god!" She turned to look at Sarah.

Sarah slowly walked over and sat down on her bed slab. She was stunned to silence by the news.

Jack's voice was filled with remorse, "I told her to send out a distress call."

"Jack," Malinda tried to be supportive, "she did what she had to do." There was a short silence before Malinda continued, "Jack, what are we going to do?"

"I'm working on something to prevent any further floatings."

"Okay, what about the Chinese?"

"Sam and I are working on a plan."

The door to the drone bay slid open, as if on cue, and Sam was standing there in a small maintenance room, "Sam just got here. Listen babe, keep the communicator close. One of us will be in touch. And take care of Jess," Jack closed the channel and put the communicator in his pocket before Malinda could reply.

"How's it going, Jack."

"Jumbled code on top of jumbled code."

"Your confidence inspires me." Sam could tell something new was weighing on Jack. He instinctively knew exactly what to say, "Darrel is on his way to check on Jess."

"Finally, some good news." Jack replied.

"I asked him to take Marie with him."

"That's good thinking, Sam."

"So, what are your plans for the drones?" Sam asked, focused on the task at hand.

"The bastards can't float people if the hatches are welded shut."

"Straight and to the point. I like it."

Jack put the input pad back inside the drone and replaced the access panel, "Help me out of here, would ya?"

Sam began to help Jack disengage himself. "How the fuck did you manage to wedge yourself in there?"

"Remember that contortionist I used to date back in KC?"

"Oh yeah, Kimmy."

Jack spilled out into the small maintenance room, "I guess I learned a few things," he said as he picked himself up off the floor.

The room was very small. Its purpose was to allow a single person access to the drone bay in case a drone needed to be pulled out and taken for repair. There wasn't really enough room for two grown men. It was awkward.

THE TRIALS OF JACK KEMPER

The door to the drone bay slid shut and the drones could be heard powering up, "Alright, so that should put a stop to that." Jack stated.

"How long do you think it will be before they notice?"

"Well, if what Jess said was accurate, I expect they'll be getting the next group in place pretty soon. The drones will have the waste hatch sealed pretty quickly."

"That's going to trigger a response. We'll need to get moving on a way off of here."

"Any thoughts on that, Sam?"

"We need to trigger the emergency evacuation systems to give everyone a chance."

"So, the nuclear option?"

"Give me a better one."

They both stood there for a few minutes, in those uncomfortably close quarters, trying as hard as they could to come up with a solution that removed the Chinese menace and left the colony in a position to survive. These were the two men that could do it if it were possible. They knew every system, every nut, every bolt, and every line of code.

"I've got nothing, Sam."

"Reactor overload is the only way."

"Alright, so now it comes down to killing the Chinese and getting as many of our people out as possible."

"We'll need distractions."

"You'll need to hit the reactor. I'm likely to blow

myself up."

"Okay. Hey, Ricky is working on the Docking Bay."

"I bet I can walk him through triggering an explosive decompression."

"They still have Carl working sensors. We could have him trigger some alarms."

Jack finished Sam's thought, "And disable the reactor alarm. That's good. Get them chasing their tails a bit."

"Think Darrel can get the ladies?"

"I can give him some help with that."

"Well, I guess that's a plan."

"It is a plan."

"It's not a great plan."

"No, it's not."

"Odds?"

Jack shook his head, "Sam, you've been a great friend."

"Fuck you, Jack."

Jack truly believed this could be the last time he saw his oldest friend. He put his arms around him and gave him a hug.

Sam had the same thought in his head. It made him very uncomfortable. He tried to play it off, "If you leave without me, I'm going to punch you in the face the next time I see you."

Darrel stood at the window of the security desk while he argued, "What do you mean authorization? I'm a doctor. I was told there's a wounded woman who needs medical attention."

A small Chinese man sat behind the desk. He swiped through screens on his terminal, "I'm sorry doctor, but without authorization there's nothing I can do."

Marie paced the corridor impatiently. She walked over to the door that led to the cell blocks and jiggled the handle. It wouldn't open.

"Miss. Please." the man behind the desk said.

Darrel continued to argue, "Listen, get that interrogator fellow. He knows who I am. He knows I'm a Doctor."

"I'm afraid he's predisposed at the moment."

Marie could see through a window on the door that a few soldiers had just rounded the corner of the cellblock. Shackled colonists followed in rows of two, "Darrel, come here."

Darrel walked over to the door and looked. The soldiers had stopped just on the other side of it. The colonists continued to round the corner and line up behind them. He saw a familiar face round the corner, "Marie, it's Malinda."

"What are they doing?" Marie asked.

"It looks like they're moving them."

Darrel knew exactly what was happening. He hadn't told Marie about it yet; primarily because he didn't want to believe it. He couldn't believe it. As a doctor it was hard to accept that humans could be so heartless.

Darrel pulled Marie over to where he felt they had

some privacy, "Marie, there's something I need to tell you."

Marie noticed the serious nature of Darrel's facial expression, "What is it Darrel?"

"Marie, when Sam contacted me earlier he gave me some information." Marie started to respond but he grasped her arm and continued, "What he told me was disturbing. I didn't tell you then because I couldn't actually believe it was happening."

"What's happening, Darrel?"

"I need you to remain calm."

Marie agreed, "Okay."

"Sam told me that they've started floating groups of colonists."

A look of disbelief came over Marie, "Is he sure?"

"I don't think he would have said it if he wasn't." Darrel peered back over his shoulder, "I think that's what they're doing here. I think they're taking this group to be floated."

"We can't let that happen."

"Sam told me that he and Jack were working that problem."

"You should contact them and let them know they're taking Malinda," Marie walked back over to the door and looked through the window. She turned back to Darrel and mouthed, "And Sarah."

CHAPTER 6

Jack was once again crawling through service tunnels. This time he was on his way to the cellblock to help Darrel free the ladies. He tried to explain to Ricky how to go about setting off and explosive decompression as he made his way. Unfortunately, while Ricky was a wonderful Project Manager he wasn't exactly mechanically inclined. "You're in the shuttle though, right?"

"Yes, Jack. Well kind of. There's no real way to be in it."

"What does that mean?"

"It's mangled."

"Do you see anything like I described?"

"Describe it again?

Jack sighed, "It has a yellow and black sticker on it. It's rectangular. About the size of the box that a bottle of Glenfiddich would come in"

"No, I don't see that."

Jack was at a loss. He didn't blame Ricky for his

shortcomings, "Okay," Jack's communicator beeped. He took a look at it and noticed Darrel was trying to contact him, "Keep looking. It's there somewhere. Darrel's trying to contact me. I should answer it."

"Alright Jack. I'll keep looking."

Jack switched channels, "What's up Darrel?"

"I couldn't get to Jessica." Darrel replied.

"Damn it."

"Jack, they're on the move. They're taking the ladies."

"Shit! Shit! Shit!"

"What should we do?"

"Follow them. I'll meet you there."

Jack switched back over to Ricky, "Any luck?"

"Yep, yep found it!" Ricky proudly exclaimed.

"That's good work Ricky. Now for the fun part."

"Oh, I was hoping for a fun part."

Darrel slid the communicator back into his pocket, "Jack wants us to follow them."

Marie looked puzzled, "How are we supposed to that? Don't you think they'll get a little suspicious?"

"I don't think he meant walk right behind them."

"Oh. Okay. How are we going to do it then?"

Darrel had learned a few things from Jack over the last couple of days. One of them was how to access service tunnels. He had to follow the colonists, but he knew the corridor near the waste ejection hatch would be guarded. Darrel pointed to a grate, "Let's wait until they clear out and use that service tunnel."

The security door opened and the soldiers stepped

through. About ten shackled colonists followed in rows of two. Malinda and Sarah brought up the rear followed by another pair of soldiers carrying Jessica.

Malinda locked eyes with Darrel as she passed. He gave her a slight nod. They dared not speak to each other, but that little nod meant the world to her. She knew that Jack knew. And that's all she needed to know.

The soldiers escorted the group down the corridor and into the lift. The lift doors closed and Darrel immediately sprang into action. He reached into his medical kit, as he began to walk toward the grate, and pulled out a pair of forceps. It was the closest instrument he had to a spanner.

Marie followed closely behind and stood in between him and the security desk. She tried to be as nonchalant as possible in her attempt to shield him from their prying eyes. Truth be told, anytime someone tries to act nonchalant they're probably doing just the opposite, but she managed.

Darrel went to work quickly twisting off the bolts that attached the grate to the wall. He pulled the grate off and Marie wasted no time sliding herself into the service tunnel. Darrel got down on his knees and backed in. He took one last look around just to make sure nobody had noticed and snapped the grate back in place. He put the bolts back in and gave them just enough twists to hold it there.

Sam had made his way back to the Operations Center so he could let Carl in on the plan. He immediately noticed that tension levels were significantly higher than the last time he was here. Jessica's actions had everyone stressed; especially their Chinese overseers.

Fortunately it appeared that they still needed the operations crew to run Bravo Colony's systems and Sam saw that Carl continued to operate the sensor console. He walked over to the Lieutenant in charge and said, "Sir, we've been reading a fault with one of the sensor boards we installed yesterday. Permission to take a look at it?"

The Lieutenant looked over toward Carl, "I haven't had any reports of that."

"No Sir, it's not causing any issues at the moment but the power fluctuations we're seeing could possibly short out the entire system if we don't address it."

"I see." He paused and reluctantly agreed, "Thank you for your attentiveness to the matter."

Sam walked over to the sensor console and put his hand on Carl's shoulder, "Carl."

Carl turned and was relieved to see a friendly face, "Sam, good to see you."

"Holding things together?"

"Trying my best."

Sam winked at him, "I need your help under the console."

"Okay, sure no problem." Carl pushed his chair back and stood up.

Sam pulled the access panel off of the console and slid underneath. He was joined by Carl who slid in next to him, "Carl, Jack and I have a plan."

"Oh, thank the gods. Did you hear about the floating's?"

"Yes, Jessica let us know."

"They killed her, Sam. Beat her to death right here in the OC"

"She's alive, Carl."

"Wow! That's great news. That girl can really take a beating."

"She's in bad shape, Carl, but my contacts told me she's alive."

"That's great Sam," he paused to let the good news sink in, "so, about this plan?"

"Jack has reprogrammed the maintenance drones to weld the hatches shut."

A look of relief came over Carl's face, "Thank you, Jack. They're moving another group right now. Do you think they'll get to it in time?"

"They're working on it right now."

"God, Sam. That's really great news. I've been watching people get floated all night. It's been hard to sit here. I'm useless man. Useless."

"No, Carl, you did good. It's because of you that Jessica knew. It's because of you that we know. Sometimes doing the right thing is hard, man."

"I should have done more," he looked away as the grief began to overwhelm him, "All those people."

"Carl," Sam tried to calm him down, "Carl, look at me."

Carl turned back to Sam. He wiped tears away.

"What's the plan, Sam?"

"I'm going to set the reactor to overload."

"What?!?"

"Listen, it will trigger the overrides on the evacuation system."

"So, that's it? We're done?"

"We're done if we stay. At least down there we have a fighting chance."

"Sam, it's hell down there."

"I know."

"Sam, they eat people down there."

"We've all heard the stories, Carl."

"There's no other way?"

"That depends. Do you have some soldiers hidden away somewhere that could take back the colony?"

"No, of course not but..."

"Nor do we. Our only hope is to evacuate," Sam said cutting him off.

Carl lied there silent for a moment. The gravity of the situation had just become so much heavier. He felt he might have been able to live with the guilt of the floating's provided enough alcohol. He wasn't so sure he could survive on the planet that Earth had become. He steeled himself and replied, "I understand."

"It's not about us, Carl."

"No. Of course it's not."

"We need you to do some things."

"Yeah Sam, of course, whatever you need man."

"First we need you to disable the overload alarm on the reactor."

"That's easy enough."

"Great. When you see it get triggered we need you to set off a bunch of false alarms."

"Goose chase?"

"Right Carl, when the shit starts. Get out of here. Get to the Evac Deck. You've done enough."

"Okay Sam. I'll meet you there."

"Carl, I really hope you do."

Jack was in the ventilation duct above the corridor that led to the waste evacuation room. He had always hated the service tunnels and ventilation ducts, but lately, he had really begun to appreciate them.

Jack watched as Malinda and Sarah were loaded into the waste evacuation room. He had faith in his programming. By his math the drones had already sealed the hatch. So, he actually felt better now that there was a door between them and the soldiers. He knew he had time. They were only two in a group of ten. There would be more groups to come and, anyway, his queue would be the evacuation alert. He patiently waited.

Darrel had carefully led Marie through a series of tunnels and shafts and they had finally reached the waste deck. It smelled. It didn't smell like organic waste. Organic waste was recycled on Subdeck "C". It smelled like industrial waste; synthetic; burnt; offensive.

Darrel poked his head up into the ventilation duct. He could see Jack ahead. He looked back at Marie, "He's up here." Darrel helped Marie up into the ventilation duct and they inched their way toward Jack.

Jack heard Darrel's voice and looked behind him. He was relieved to see his friends were safe, but he knew if he could hear them it was likely the soldiers could as well. He put his finger to his mouth to indicate that they should be quiet.

Ricky had completed the modifications to the shuttles power supply as per Jack's instruction. He walked over to an exterior wall and set it on the floor. The unit began to buzz ever louder as he slid the power indicator to its max setting. He didn't know how long it would take, but he figured it was designed to function at its max setting for quite a while. He had done what he was instructed to do. He put his faith in Jack and left for the evacuation deck.

Sam carefully made his way deep into the reactor room. He had to negotiate a labyrinth of hot pipes and cooling pumps. Along the way his mind plodded through the numerous protocols involved in preventing exactly what he was hoping to achieve. The colony's reactor had several built in safeties to stave off a catastrophic failure. He would have to disable each of them manually before he could initiate the reactor overload. And even more importantly there was a specific order in which they would have to be done.

Sam hopped over the last couple of pipes and found himself face to face with the reaction chamber. It always felt a bit odd standing here. Just on the other side of the wall was enough radiation to kill him in a matter of seconds. And the duct tape that held the cover on the control panel did little for his confidence in the chamber's shielding.

Sam pulled at the duct tape and removed the cover from the control panel. This was the only panel that could give him direct access to the reaction chamber. It took several minutes to negotiate the security screens that sought to prevent him access to the safety override menus, "Do you really want to do this?" It asked him, "No, seriously. Do you really really really want to do this?" That last screen must have been Jack's handy work.

Being the Engineering Supervisor had its benefits. One by one his security code disabled the safety protocols. After the last one was disabled, Sam quickly entered the keystrokes to turn off all of the cooling pumps. The room fell silent. No alarms sounded. Carl had done his job. The temperature display on the reactor immediately started to climb. Once the coolant reached its boiling point it wouldn't take long for the reactor to go into overload. Sam couldn't get out of there fast enough.

He dialed up Jack as he hopped on the lift and headed for the evacuation deck, "It's done, Jack."

The waste ejection room was dark. A small maintenance bulb encased in a wire cover provided the only light. There was also an overpowering hydraulic smell to the room. Malinda had helped Sarah get Jessica to the floor. They sat her up to lean against the wall just inside the door. They were finding it quite difficult to keep her conscious.

Sarah sat down next to Jessica to help keep her from falling to one side while Malinda stood guard over the two of them. The room was actually kind of small and she had a feeling it was about to become quite crowded. Sarah continuously tried to encourage Jessica to fight herself awake.

Over the next few minutes the doors opened several times to let more colonists in. It became difficult to breathe and even more difficult to move. The colonists began to chatter. Most of these people were service staff of the colony. They did laundry, swept floors, and worked the Mess hall; busy work to the elite, essential services to everyone else and totally expendable to the Chinese.

A tall, skinny, brown skinned man spoke up, "Everyone. Listen," he pleaded, "we can't just wait here."

A frail looking grandmother figure agreed, "I'm not going without a fight, damn it!"

The conversations continued and rumors swirled. Malinda was encouraged. It seemed like attitudes among the colonists were beginning to shift. She listened for her moment to step into the conversation and said, "I agree." Malinda had a natural leadership quality about her. She was quite a beautiful woman. She was also very well spoken. Her eyes projected a true sense of caring while having the steely resolve of a warrior woman. People got quiet and listened, "We shouldn't just lie down and roll over for these assholes. But, listen to me, while it might appear that it's now or never," she held up her communicator and continued,

THE TRIALS OF JACK KEMPER

"let me assure you that we have people working on our situation and, when it is time, we're going to need you all to fight. As hard as you can."

An old man replied, "Who are these people, honey?"

"The people that built this place. The engineers."

"That's great, but we need soldiers."

Malinda fought back, "We are the soldiers. You are the soldier. We can all fight."

"Sure, I can fight. I won't last long against guns though."

"You're right. You are absolutely right," she paused and looked at each of the other faces staring back at her looking for any sliver of hope, "soldiers die. It's what they do. It's duty that pushes them forward. It's honor. It's not actions they take for their own survival. It's the actions they take for the survival of others."

She knew by the looks in their eyes that she had them, "My friends are out there right now, fighting, risking their own lives to save us. They could very easily get to the evacuation deck and save themselves. But, they won't do that. They would never leave us behind."

The brown skinned man replied, "I'm with you."

The frail old woman replied, "That's right. Let's kick some Chinese ass!"

The door began to slide open and everyone got quiet once again. Ten more colonists were loaded in. Malinda fought to keep Jessica from being trampled.

The door to the ejection room closed once again, but this time the locks engaged with an audible clunk.

The brown skinned man noticed and said, "What now?"

Malinda held up the communicator and spoke, "Jack?"

A whisper responded, "Wait for it."

Ricky stood alone on the evacuation deck. It was an unsettling feeling. Nerves began to creep up on him. The flask called to him. He pulled it out of his pocket, twisted off the top and took a swig. It probably would have helped had he not been forced to spin around at the sound of the lift door sliding open.

He wasn't supposed to be here so he quickly tried to think up an excuse, "Play dumb?" he thought, "Play drunk?" He settled on play drunk. He had more experience with it. Much to Ricky's relief, however, a familiar face appeared.

Sam exited the lift and his eyes lit up when he saw that Ricky was there waiting. He even had a flask in hand for him. He walked up to Ricky and said, "What a gent you are, Ricky. Got the flask ready for me aye?"

Ricky smiled at Sam and handed him the flask, "Always my friend. Always."

Sam took a swig and handed it back to Ricky, "That Jim, he sure knows how to cook up the Red Eye."

"Well he's from my neck of the woods. We're born to it."

"You're from Tennessee, right?"

"Yep," Ricky took another swig and handed it back

THE TRIALS OF JACK KEMPER

to Sam, "so, how long ya think?"

Sam took a swig and grinned, "Hopefully long enough to finish this off."

"I was thinking it would happen by now."

"Oh right. You set that power supply to blow," Sam looked around, "We should find something to hold on to."

"I don't see anything."

Sam took another swig. Ricky corrected his etiquette, "It's not a joint Sam. It's not puff, puff, pass. It's take a swig and pass."

Sam was amused, "Hah! You got me Ricky!" He handed the flask back to Ricky and continued, "Follow me, I have an idea."

Sam walked over to a pod bay door and entered a code on the adjacent control panel. The door to the pod bay opened. Sam pointed inside to the pods seats, "Let's strap ourselves in."

"Brilliant!" Ricky exclaimed just as the evacuation alarm began to sound.

The light flickered as the outer doors of the waste ejection room were activated. Some of the colonists began to scream. It took Malinda off guard that the rest of them actually had that much faith in her. The hydraulic pumps began to whine as they strained to open the doors, but they didn't budge. Jack's plan had worked!

The hydraulic pumps went silent. Malinda spoke, "When the door opens."

They could hear the lock release. The motor to the

door engaged and it began to open. It was three quarters of the way opened when Malinda yelled, "GO!" and charged out the door tackling the first soldier she saw. Colonists stampeded through the door with intent to do the other soldiers great harm - just as the entire colony lurched several feet and sent everyone flying.

The colony continued to shake violently for what seemed like an hour to all those involved, but it was really only a minute. Alarms began to sound, "Way to go Ricky," Jack said as the trio braced themselves in the ventilation shaft. There wasn't enough room for them to fly anywhere.

Jack peered through the grate. The soldiers were down and struggling to get to their feet. Most of the colonists had been thrown back into the ejection room. Malinda was, already, back on top of the soldier she had tackled and continued strangling the life out of him. This was their chance.

Jack shouted, "Let's move!" as he knocked out the ventilation grate and dropped into the corridor. Darrel followed closely behind him. Jack tumbled down to the floor, jumped to his feet and lunged at the nearest soldier. He rammed his shoulder squarely into the man's midsection which lifted him off of his feet. Jack slammed him violently to the floor. His long spindly legs rapidly coiled around the soldier like a snake trying to prevent its prey from squirming away.

Colonists began to regain their footing and quickly reasserted themselves. They charged out of the room attacking the nearest soldiers they could find. Shots rang out and several colonists fell. This did nothing to dissuade the others.

Darrel was determined to do his part. The anger he had been suppressing instantly boiled into a fierce rage. He was a large barrel chested man who was surprisingly fast for his size. He darted towards a soldier and delivered a crushing hit. The impact caused the soldier to squeeze the trigger of his rifle which sent a few errant rounds flying into the ceiling above them. The wind rushed out of the soldier as he was crushed against the wall.

Darrel quickly hooked arms with the soldier, rotated his hips and slammed him to the ground. The gun slid across the floor. Darrel picked up his foot, as the soldier laid beneath him trying to force air back into his lungs, and stomped as hard as he could on the soldier's face. That confrontation was over.

Jack had his opponent pinned to the floor. He released a barrage of violent blows to the soldier's face. His rage drove him to continue long after the man had lost consciousness.

"Jack," Darrel reached his hand out. He caught one of Jack's arms as he brought it back in preparation for another blow, "I think that's enough."

Jack glanced back at Darrel and then looked back at the soldier's bloody face, "Yeah, I think you're right." Darrel clasped Jack's hand and pulled him to his feet.

Malinda had long since finished off the soldier she

was on and already had his gun slung over her shoulder. She flashed a smile at Jack when she found him through crowd and quickly resumed directing the other colonists, "Grab the guns and ammo."

Jack and Darrel helped Marie down into the corridor. She turned to Darrel and said, "There's wounded."

Things started to come back into focus, for Darrel, as the burst of adrenaline began to wane, "Right." He looked around and saw several colonists lying wounded on the floor. A sense of duty took over, "Let's get on it," and he and Marie began to triage the wounded.

Malinda continued to give the orders, "Everyone!" she tried to shout above the chatter of colonists, "Everyone make your way to the evacuation deck." The colonists with guns began to lead the way toward the lift.

Malinda returned to the waste ejection room to find her friends. Sarah and Jessica were now on the opposite side of the room. It was apparent they had been thrown with some force when the station jolted, "Are you two okay?" Malinda asked.

Sarah grimaced, "I hit my head pretty good but I managed to land in between Jess and the floor."

"Can you stand?"

"Yeah, I'm pretty sure."

Malinda helped Sarah to her feet and said, "Grab her arm. Let's get moving."

They both scooped up Jessica and had started out of the room when they saw Jack come through the doorway, "Jack!" Malinda called out as he approached.

Jack rushed up to her and pulled her into his arms. He kissed her like he never thought he'd kiss her again. He whispered, "I missed you." into her ear as they embraced.

Malinda got lost in the moment and had let go of Jessica. This left Sarah struggling to hold her up, "Umm, Jack?" Sarah interrupted them, "How about giving a lady a hand?"

Jack and Malinda regained their composure. He reluctantly released her and stepped in to take Jessica, "Sorry about that." He yelled out the door, "Hey, Darrel!"

Darrel walked in wiping blood off his hands with his shirt. He reported, "We got a couple back on their feet and on their way but the others were DOA."

Jack nodded, "That's too bad. Hey grab her other arm, would ya?"

"Oh, yeah of course," Darrel moved in to relieve Sarah. He tried to examine Jessica, "Wow, they really did a number on her."

Jack interjected, "We don't have time Darrel. The reactor..."

"Right."

The group left the waste ejection room and met Marie in the corridor, "Everyone that could leave has gone to the Evac Deck." she stated.

"And we should be right behind them," Malinda said as she ran ahead to call the lift.

The evacuation deck was once again a chaotic

scene. This time it was a different kind of chaos. The pod bays were humming. Colonists were loading into pods as fast as they could to get off the colony.

There was also a familiar group of colonists with guns that guarded the lifts. A tall brown skinned man barked orders, "Be ready!" And they were ready. If the lift doors opened to reveal soldiers it would be a bad time - for the soldiers. There would be no repeat of their last experience here.

Sam and Ricky weren't going anywhere without the others so they tried valiantly to help organize the departures. It wasn't going so well. Some pods left with as little as four people. Ricky fought with impatient, and some quite rude, people he used to call friends in an effort to prevent this from happening, but he could only be in one place at a time. Inevitably some pods left light.

Random pod bays would have their control systems freeze up. This would force Sam to intervene. He'd jump into the pod, hack the control system and get the system to reboot. The countdown would begin and he'd immediately jump out to fight the next issue. It was a good thing really. It kept his mind off the fate of his friends. He was actually quite surprised that the damned things were working as well as they were.

The lift doors opened to reveal soldiers! Gunfire rang out. The shots went back and forth for about thirty seconds. Colonists on the deck screamed and pushed at the others in front of them. The brown skinned man barked orders over the noise, "Pull them out. Get our wounded on a pod!"

Several colonists jumped into the lift and started pulling out dead soldiers. Others worked to take their guns and distribute their ammo. Still others carried off wounded colonists for priority evacuation.

The lift doors slid open again and the colonists took aim, "Don't shoot!" Malinda yelled. As the group exited the lift she saw the bodies of soldiers and an even larger group of colonists with guns. She gave the brown skinned man an approving look and said, "Well done. Expect gas." She pointed to a couple groups of colonists at the closest pod bays, "Move these colonists back farther."

Jack took note of Malinda's leadership as he and Darrel carried Jessica away from the lift. He knew she had many skills but he had never even imagined this side of her. To say it was unexpected would be a dramatic understatement. She clearly had some training. It would have to be a conversation for later.

Ricky heard the familiar voice and immediately started toward it. He raised his hand up over the crowd and shouted toward her, "Malinda! Malinda! Over here!"

Malinda was too caught up in organizing the defense of the deck to notice. Jack noticed, "Ricky!" he yelled.

"Jack! You made it!"

"We need to get Jessica in a pod so Darrel can get a better look."

Ricky said, "Follow me," and escorted them to the

shortest line.

They set Jessica down and Darrel began to look her over. He started calling out what he found to Marie, "Broken ribs. 3.. No 4. Ruptured spleen. Serious internal bleeding."

Sam jumped out of the pod bay just as the hatch closed. He was relieved to find Jack standing there, "Jack!"

"Sam!" Jack could feel a sense of relief come over him. Everyone was here. Now if he could just get them all into an escape pod.

"Sam, it looks like we're next. Stay close."

The doors to the lift slid open once again. This time gas bellowed out. It forced Malinda and the others to back up. She started feeling a little woozy, "Move back farther! Back it up!"

The pod bay reopened with a fresh empty escape pod and Jack shouted to Malinda, "Malinda, let's go!" She couldn't hear him.

The gas caused Malinda to gag and cough. She recoiled and stumbled even farther away from the lift. Her eyes watered. She struggled to regain her senses. After about sixty seconds her head started to clear.

The pod bay next to theirs was having problems. Sam looked at Jack, "They've been freezing up left and right."

"Forget it." Jack coldly replied.

"Can't do that, Jack," and with that Sam hopped into action.

Malinda took a deep breath and turned back toward the lift to continue their defense. Just as she was about to bark out another order she saw something out of the corner of her eye. She stopped dead in her tracks and fixed her gaze.

A despicable little Asian man was in line to get on one of the escape pods. She shouted, "HARRY FUCKING TANG!" and leveled her rifle.

Harry's heart instantly sank. He knew the voice. He had seen her arrive. He was just hoping to get on a pod before she noticed him. He hoped if he ignored her she might think she was mistaken.

Malinda took a few steps toward him and shouted again. The colonists between them parted, "Turn around you slimy little piece of shit!"

Harry slowly turned, "Malinda, hey about yesterday."

Malinda cut him off, "Whore was it?"

"I might have been a little harsh."

She smiled, "Well, now you're a little dead." and squeezed the trigger. Harry's head exploded quite abruptly. The colonist near him weren't all that happy about the splattering grey matter but Malinda was more than satisfied.

Jack and Ricky watched the entire thing. They were speechless. They thought it was brilliant but they were still speechless. Jack finally snapped out of it, "Malinda! It's time to go!" he shouted.

Malinda heard his voice and saw Darrel and Marie carrying Jessica into a pod. Jack and Ricky were waving their arms for her to come. She looked back towards the lift. She saw that the colonists were still holding their position. It was time to get her friends to safety. She started moving through the crowd toward them.

The lift doors opened once again and another firefight broke out. This one lasted a bit longer. Malinda watched intently but kept walking toward Jack. She saw the brown skinned man go down just as she felt Jack grab her arm and pull her into the pod.

Jack pushed her toward a seat and barked, "Get in a seat, babe."

There were ten seats in each pod. Darrel had just finished strapping Jessica into one of them. He quickly moved to the next seat where Marie was strapping herself in. He helped her finish.

Ricky had already strapped himself in and Malinda sat down next to him, "Glad to see you made it, Ricky." she said.

"I blew up the docking bay!" he said proudly.

"That was you?"

"It was!"

"Well done. I guess I owe you a drink."

"Noted." he replied, "By the way," he continued, "nice shot!"

Malinda shot him a smile as she finished strapping herself in.

Carl walked into the pod, "Room for one more?"

"You're just in time, Carl. Get strapped in." Jack said.

Jack grabbed his communicator and tried to contact Sam. He waited impatiently for a response.

"What Jack?" A terse response came back.

"Are you coming man?"

"This fucking thing shorted out. The program is shot!"

"Ditch it let's go!"

"I can't do that Jack."

"What then?"

"I'm going to have to take them down manually."

"Do you even know how to do that?"

"It's falling Jack. The damn things fall back to Earth. I just need to release the chute at the right time. I think I can manage."

"Well fuck man."

"I know," he paused, "I'll see you soon friend."

"You better."

Jack put down the communicator, hit a button on the command console and began to strap himself in as the pod door closed. A short countdown began. Ten, nine, eight.

CHAPTER 7

The escape pod slowly drifted away from the colony with its eight passengers. Inside the pod, Jack unbuckled his straps and began floating weightless. He enjoyed weightlessness. Once, a few years back, he tried to convince Jim that a weightless night at the bar would be a great idea. He had all kinds of clever engineering plans for delivering the drinks. They all seemed much too complicated for Jim.

Jack floated over toward Malinda, grabbed onto her seat, smiled at her and gave her a peck on the cheek, "Let me check these straps, gorgeous." He tugged on her straps and found one a little loose, "This needs to be tighter," he said as he pulled the strap through the buckle, "re-entry is going to be a little bumpy."

"I hope the duct tape holds." she said with a smile.

He offered her a straight response, "I'm sure it will. It was the silver stuff."

She grew concerned, "Wait, did you actually repair

this pod with duct tape?"

"I've repaired just about everything on the colony with duct tape. So, yeah, I'm pretty sure there's duct tape holding something together on this pod!" he said confidently.

"Great, that's reassuring." Her words were dripping with sarcasm.

Ricky had a great buzz going, "Heavenly Father, we pray to our Patron Saint, Vesta, bless the skills of her humble servant, Jack Kemper, and grant us a safe and blessed re-entry, in Vesta's name. Amen!"

It was offered as a joke but not a single one of them hesitated to follow it with, "Amen!" They weren't even being sarcastic!

The weightless environment had actually helped Jessica by taking pressure off of her broken bones. Darrel unstrapped himself and began attending to her. He lifted her shirt exposing a blackish purple midsection, "Jack, toss me that duct tape."

Jack pulled a roll of pink duct tape out of his belt and floated it across to Darrel, "Incoming."

Marie knew what Darrel was thinking and interjected, "You're not going to tape them are you?"

Darrel caught the roll, "I know. It's not standard practice these days, but it used to be."

"But it could increase the risk of pneumonia, Darrel."

"Marie, we're about to plummet to the Earth. I'm more concerned with immobilizing the damaged ribs." Darrel tore off strips of tape and began taping Jessica's ribs.

"I guess we can always remove it when we land. What about her spleen?"

"Given the time it's been since the injury I'd say it's a minor issue. I think she'll be fine if she remains immobilized." Darrel finished applying the duct tape, "I think that should do." he said, "Damn Jack, you're right. Duct tape can fix anything!"

This prompted Jack to raise his hand in adulation, "Praise Vesta!'

Malinda and Sarah followed, "Praise Vesta!" and the group laughed at the impromptu adoption of their new religion. They needed to laugh. They needed to believe in something. It was an impossible situation; a fact that wasn't lost on any of them.

Ricky was in the seat next to Sarah. He pulled his flask out of his pocket and twisted off the top. His precious alcohol began to float out in spherical blobs. Ricky wasn't a physicist. It took him totally by surprise.

Sarah was watching Ricky and she started to chuckle, "Oh no! They're making a break for it!"

Ricky looked like a giraffe stretching his neck to reach the farthest droplet first. It seemed that he had discovered a new talent. Not a single drop escaped. He turned to Sarah and said, "Close one."

"Well done!" she replied, "Buy one for the lady?"

"Of course, my dear," he floated the flask over to Sarah.

Sarah carefully twisted off the top and promptly replaced it with her mouth before any of the precious liquid could escape. She began to suck on it.

"That brings back memories," Ricky smiled and winked at her.

She pulled her mouth off the flask and twisted the top back on, "Good ones I hope," she said coyly and sent the flask floating back over toward Ricky.

Jack flew in between them and intercepted it, "Sounds like a fun night!" he said as he floated by. The wall of the pod stopped him. His face pushed up against one of the pod's window portals. The sight took his breath away. He steadied himself and flatly stated. "Well, it looks like they couldn't get it stabilized."

Bravo Colony, once the pinnacle of human advancement, was breaking up. It was hard to fathom. Their home for the past fourteen years was gone. Replacing it was an uncertain future on Earth. A place they had been happy to leave. A place that had gotten exponentially worse as the years passed.

Earth suffered from radical weather. Extremes caused by climate change; massive hurricanes, endless droughts, rising seas, dust and sand storms. Entire cities existed in clouds of smog and their inhabitants were forced to wear rebreathers as if they lived under the sea. Chemical storms were uncommon but not rare.

Overpopulation led to waves of disease. Plagues killed billions of people and left millions more deformed. Pollution left people cancer ridden and prone to illness. Those that survived the caustic weather, disease and pollution were greeted with starvation and worse; the extreme violence that only mankind is capable of inflicting on its self.

Most of the old governments of the world had collapsed. Warlords, Pirates and Slavers ruled as much area as their brutality would allow. Violence was a daily reality for those unfortunate enough to live on land. The elite had long ago fled to their manmade islands. Those islands were the last bastions of civilization and as many of those had failed as had succeeded.

Jack thought out loud, "I wonder how long before the reactor," and at that very moment there was a bright flash, it was a blinding flash, "blows!" Jack concluded.

"You better get strapped in, Jack!" said Darrel.

Jack pushed himself back to his seat, still holding onto Ricky's precious flask and began to strap himself in. He had just got his last strap buckled when turbulence rocked the pod causing it to start tumbling.

Sarah grabbed Ricky's hand and screamed, "Oh my god!"

Jack reassured them, "The guidance system should kick in the thrusters to correct!"

"Should?" Malinda shot Jack a hard stare.

The thrusters kicked in correcting the tumble, "See, we're good." Jack said confidently. Then an alarm started to ring from the control panel. He hedged, "I think."

Jack leaned to his side to look at the at the control panel, "It's time! We're coming up on re-entry. Hold on everybody! It's going to get bumpy!" Jack shouted as he held out his hand to Malinda.

THE TRIALS OF JACK KEMPER

Malinda grabbed it. She squeezed, "About that duct tape?"

He reassured her, "It'll hold!"

The pod started to enter the upper atmosphere. It jostled and jolted as it met the first bit of resistance. It banged and moaned; unhappy with the forces that stressed its metal. The group began to feel the slight tug of gravity and the friction of reentry caused the air around it to become superheated. A fiery red glow from outside lit the interior causing the temperature to rise.

"We're on fire!" Sarah screamed, "Oh my God we're on fire!"

Jack tried to calm her down. He yelled over the noise, "It's just the atmospheric friction. The pod is built for this."

Sarah whimpered and dug her fingers into the armrests. She was rightfully terrified.

A sudden violent jolt rocked the pod. It let out a piercing screech that sounded like metal angrily tearing away. Marie joined Sarah in a scream. It took all of Jack's strength not to join them. He squeezed Malinda's hand ever tighter.

The pod began spinning. Faster and faster it spun. Breathing became hard. Faeries danced in their eyes. It no longer felt like a controlled descent. Buzzers and alarms rang out. Jack took a moment to capture one last look at each of his friends just in case this was it. And it was a terrifying display of contorted faces emitting terrified screams while macabrely lit with a fiery glow.

Then it all went dark.

Liberty Island was a product of the greatest minds that walked among humanity. And in being such, its Operational Command Center had technology that didn't exist elsewhere on the planet. It didn't consist of displays and consoles. Holographic projectors filled the room with three dimensional renderings. Controls were issued through gestures, speech and for a few of the higher functioning individuals; thought.

An artificial intelligence, named Kali, was ever present. Kali monitored every known transmission frequency. It even analyzed the noise for any patterns of relevance.

Currently displayed above the heads of the OCC personnel was a rendering of the remnants of Bravo Colony. Hundreds of pods were being tracked as they fell back to Earth. Each location noted by technicians for subsequent recovery missions.

The OCC was always an active and serious place. The mission of Liberty Island was to save civilization. It wasn't a grandiose vision. The mission was one of action. It involved a myriad of hard choices and they worked it every day. Their people suffered no delusion that it would be achieved overnight, after all, the island was one of a very few civilized places that remained.

The OCC's daily operations were led by Vera Eriksen, Command Marshall of Strategic Operations. She was a rather tall woman with the characteristic fair skin and blond hair of her Nordic ancestry. In her distinguished slate gray uniform with delicate black epaulettes she projected the confidence of a strong leader.

"Kali, are you getting a match on any of the bio-sensors?" she asked.

"I'm afraid the honorable leadership of Bravo Colony did not make it." Kali responded.

"That's too bad."

"I am however getting a few matches in the technical fields."

"Okay, let's prioritize recovery. Can I get a list of names?"

A well-defined holographic projection appeared before her. The projection displayed a list of names with portraits. Jack and Sam were the top two on the list. There were a half dozen others listed as well, "This is it?"

"Sorry Ma'am, it's hard to get clear readings with all the background radiation and atmospheric disturbances."

The Command Marshall made a gesture with her fingers causing the portraits to separate and with a flick of her wrists the renderings before her flew across the room assigning themselves to the technicians on duty.

Technician First Class, Chester Alswettle, sat silently and attentively as he reclined in his chair. The dossier of Jack Kemper had landed in his queue. He had broad spectrum communications opened to the effort within seconds. Chester was one of the high functioning techs who interfaced with Kali and the island's systems through a neural interface. The neural interface allowed him to leverage the non-linear thought processes of a human brain while tapping into the processing power of the AI, which, basically meant; he could think outside of the box very, very quickly.

Jack was reclining nude on a beach chair sipping a margarita. Vivid deep blue ocean waves rolled onto the beach. The intoxicating warm salt air and the sound of rolling water put him at ease. Malinda and Sarah were also there. Each one naked and slathering him in warm oil. Sarah massaged his legs while Malinda stood behind him massaging his shoulders, "So this is heaven?" He wondered. He accepted his fate. He wanted to believe.

"Jack!" he heard an angelic voice, "Come on, Jack! Wake up!" it said. But, Jack didn't want to wake up. He wanted to stay in that wonderful heaven, "Wake the fuck up!" it commanded. And Jack woke up.

"You're crushing my hand!" Malinda screamed as Jack came around.

Jack let go and raised his arms in front of his face to protect himself. It was instinct. He was in shock. Darrel was standing in front of him waving a smelling salt under his nose. It took a minute for him to regain his senses.

Darrel reassured him, "We're good, Jack. The pod's intact."

Malinda replied, "The pod may be intact but my fucking hand is killing me!"

Jack wondered aloud, "How?"

Darrel explained, "The thrusters fired to correct the spin. Once we stopped spinning the chute deployed," he

THE TRIALS OF JACK KEMPER

turned to Malinda, "Let me look at it."

Jack looked to Malinda, "Sorry."

"Not your fault." she said.

Darrel wiggled her fingers and checked every bone he could, "You'll be fine. Just a little bruised."

Sarah made everyone aware, "I pissed myself."

"You too?" Darrel had to chuckle. Everyone chuckled. They had all pissed themselves.

"Well, if that's the worst of it I call it a win." Ricky said.

Malinda replied, "Well, you piss yourself on a nightly basis. You must be used to it."

Ricky admitted, "It's not the first time. It won't be the last. There are worse things to happen. Although, this is the first time I've pissed myself in fear. Not as pleasant."

It took Jack quite by surprise when the communicator in his pocket began to vibrate. Communicators had a short range and certainly shouldn't work without the colonies network. He reached into his pocket and pulled it out, "Uh, this is Jack."

The return from the other end was static. He wondered if he might still be dreaming. It didn't seem right. The static cleared for just a second and he just made out, ".iber.. Isl…"

"Hello? You're breaking up."

"Liberty Island…" The static made it almost impossible to make out.

"We're barely getting that, Liberty Island."

"Southern Tasm… As …en route…" At least that's

what Jack thought they said. Not that it made much sense to him.

"Beware... cannib…"

"Say again?"

"Chem… … front."

He turned to Malinda, "Are you understanding any of this?"

She replied, "There's too much static. I did hear 'beware' though."

The communicator went dead. Jack tried to reconnect but he had no idea how to connect out of network, "I think it was Liberty Island." he said.

"That's good right?" Carl asked, "They must have gotten Jessica's transmission."

T.FC. Alswettle thought, "Kali, let the CM know communications were unsuccessful due to atmospheric interference." He reached above him as if plucking an apple from a tree and pulled the Tasmania region down to him. A quick sweeping gesture of his arms expanded the view providing greater detail of the terrain and Liberty Island assets in the area.

The tracking beacon for Corporal Stoudt, Reconnaissance Specialist with the Liberty Island Advance Interdiction Unit was only a few miles away from the projected landing zone for the pod. T.FC. Alswettle made contact with the field asset, "Corporal Stoudt, mission update; priority recovery target."

A female voice responded, "Understood."

Corporal Stoudt was holed up in a field shelter she had erected to take cover from a nasty chemical storm that currently battered the area. She had been assigned to Southern Tasmania to gather intelligence for an upcoming mission against a group of pirates, but it appeared the pirates would have to wait.

Her system received the updated mission information and an alert appeared on her retinal HUD. She began to scroll through the dossier of Jack Kemper. She wondered why anyone would want to rescue a person from Kansas, but as she read through his accomplishments it became quite clear. She shut down the feed and as she worked to fall asleep, she mentally went over the plans to break camp in the morning and head for the downed Bravo Colony escape pod.

The holographic projection returned to CM. Erikson updated with the added information from T.FC. Alswettle. She would have preferred more precise information from their communication attempts, but acting on limited information was a part of the job.

"Kali, what's the status of our recovery teams?" she asked.

"All teams are in route to their designated rescue areas."

"Where is the Elon?"

"The L.I.S. Elon is currently docked at Keflavik Air Base in Iceland, delivering medical supplies."

"Very well. As soon as they've finished there, I want them underway for central Congo. Ensure that they are data linked to our systems for real time situational updates."

CM. Erikson needed to ensure that the high value

personnel were recovered first. Liberty Island was highly capable and well suited to these types of operations, but they had limited resources. Unfortunately, they wouldn't be able to rescue all of the colonists that returned to Earth.

The Elon was not your typical airship. A full 750 feet long and 250 feet wide, it was shaped like a horseshoe crab, curved on top and flat on the bottom with the exception of the carriage protruding beneath it. The top was covered with multiple high efficiency solar panel arrays causing it to look much like the shell of a beetle as the sun reflected off of it. There were four pylons, two fore and two aft, extending downward from the edges. Each of these contained fully articulated ducted fans which were used for slow speed maneuvering. At the rear of the ship were three large ducted turbofan engines used for primary propulsion.

The bridge of the Airship Elon was an orderly place; just the way Captain Dent liked it. His crew was well trained and performed their duties with the artistry of a choreographed ballet. The Captain had spent his career in the navy and he took his command of the Elon as a great honor. As the flagship of the Liberty Island fleet, he knew that every man and woman serving on his ship was the best in their fields; he had hand-picked each one himself.

First Officer De'Goya approached the Captain, "Communique from the OCC." The Captain nodded curtly. F.O. De'Goya continued, "Orders for priority rescue operations in central Congo and Tasmania. Apparently Bravo Colony has broken up. Evacuation has commenced."

"Have the medical supplies been delivered?" he asked.

"Yes, sir. Dr. Vilhjalmsson and the people of Reykjavik are extremely grateful for our efforts."

"Pass along the relevant information to Reaper Squad. I want full mission briefings ready at 0600."

"Aye, aye, Sir," De'Goya snapped to attention and pivoted away from Captain Dent to carry out his orders.

Jack unstrapped himself and walked over to the control panel. He opened the compartment just beneath it. Inside were eight small belt packs and two backpacks, "Great! It's all here."

"What is?" Malinda asked.

"Each pod has survival gear; rations, water, flare gun, a fire starter and such," Jack said as he handed a belt pack and backpack to Darrel, "the backpacks also have a small field shelter in them." He slung the other backpack over his shoulder, attached a belt pack to his tool belt and then handed belt packs to the others one by one. He pulled a roll of duct tape out of his tool belt, "Here." He handed it to Darrel, "help me get their belt packs secured."

The pod was being buffeted by high winds, as it descended, making it hard for Jack and Darrel to remain standing as they moved. Darrel lost his balance and rolled across the floor until the wall stopped him.

Jack was sent flying and his trajectory had him on

course to land on Sarah. He landed short but his momentum carried his face right into her crotch.

"Boy, I've had more action in the last couple of days than I have in months!" She laughed.

Jack lifted his face up and looked her right in the eyes, "You weren't kidding. You really pissed yourself!"

"Oh. Yeah. Sorry about that."

Jack politely and somewhat embarrassingly said, "Nope, nope, not your fault," he pulled out a roll of pink duct tape and reached around her waist. He pointed to her hip, "Hold the belt pack here."

Sarah held the belt pack while Jack ran the duct tape around her waist a few times, "That should hold it."

Darrel had picked himself up off the floor and made his way over to Marie. He had just finished taping her belt pack on when the pod was blown full on sideways. This time he and Jack both ended up wedged against the wall together. He looked Jack in the eyes, "I need a drink."

The pod straightened itself out once again allowing the pair to regain their footing. Jack pulled a flask out of his tool belt and handed it to Darrel, "You get Ricky and I'll get Malinda."

Darrel put the flask in his pocket and walked over to Ricky while he could.

Jack could see lightning flash outside of the pod. He got to Malinda and began to secure her belt pack. His eyes were full of concern.

THE TRIALS OF JACK KEMPER

"Are you okay?" Malinda asked.

"It looks like we're coming down in a nasty storm."

"I noticed that too."

"The rain is green."

"Crap. I didn't notice that." she said.

"That's what they were trying to tell us. It's a chemical storm."

"Well, hopefully we'll be able to stay in the pod until it passes."

Jack knew that nothing had really been going their way for the past forty-eight hours. He wondered why that would change now. He figured it wouldn't, "Yeah, we'll be fine," but he didn't want to worry Malinda.

Darrel handed Ricky the duct tape and while Ricky was securing his belt pack he took the time to twist off the top of the flask and take a few swigs. Ricky handed him the duct tape when he was finished and said, "Trade ya?"

"Woah, that's some good stuff."

Ricky looked kind of puzzled. After all, it was just Jim's sink swill.

An alarm on the console started to sound. Darrel walked over to look and announced, "5,000 feet. Let's get strapped in, Jack."

Just as they got strapped into their seats turbulence started to shake the pod. Thunder rumbled. The pod swayed back and forth. Jack wasn't sure how much more the chute or the pod could take.

The hangar deck of the Elon wasn't quite as ballet like as the command deck. It was more of an orchestrated chaos, per se. To the untrained eye it might appear that no one knew what they were doing, but the support and maintenance teams moved about as if being conducted by the wand of a rhythmic genius.

Sergeant Joey "Oddball" MacIntyre, stood with his team as F.O. De'Goya finished the mission briefing, "Yes, it's very likely. His followers are fanatics. They see him as a messiah figure. Do you have any other questions?" she paused to allow the team members to respond then continued, "Okay, good luck out there men."

The sergeant called the room to attention as the F.O. turned to leave. Oddball was a stocky, brusk, Scotsman who some might say had been in the Mechanized Assault force just a bit too long. His team, the Reapers, consisted of five subordinate members. Corporal Maria "Bean" Fuentes, Latina by birth; lesbian by choice, Corporal Duke "Steel" Richards, a Brit of African descent, Corporal Kent "Junior" Lawson, a good ole boy from Alabama, Petty Officer Carter "Doc" Daniels the squad medic, a vanilla from Manilla and the aforementioned, but rarely present, Corporal Jan "Scout" Stoudt.

"At ease," Sgt. MacIntyre barked, stepping in front of the team.

Junior's ass growled like a tuba; followed by a smell that could best be described as a three day old shit that had refused to exit, "That was close. I almost didn't make it."

"Smells like you didn't." Steel chided, pulling the

collar of his shirt over his nose and mouth.

"I don't think the hrutspungar agreed with me."

Doc doubled over and began to dry heave.

"Jesus Doc, you gonna throw up?" Bean joked, putting some space between herself and the squad medic.

Junior began to laugh, "Apparently, the hrutspungar didn't agree with him either."

"Yeah, that must be it, Junior." Steel stood there unaffected while the others contorted and eventually started laughing with Junior.

Doc tried to straighten himself as the air cleared a bit, "Dude, next time someone bets you to eat goat dick; just say no."

Junior shot back, "It wasn't goat dick. It was sheep testicles."

"It looked like quite a bit of the stem was still attached." Bean added.

Sgt. MacIntyre the ever serious Staff NCO even joined in, but knew they needed to get back to business, "Alright, alright. It's not the first time Junior's shit himself. At ease Marines!"

The use of the more formal command language triggered an almost reflexive response. The members of Reaper squad may be a bit undisciplined at times, but they were still trained Marines. Each of them came to a standing position, feet shoulder width apart, hands clasped just below the small of the back.

"You heard the F.O., we've got a priority rescue. I want everyone to review their assignments and be on the flight deck, ready to go, by 1400."

The alarm changed pitch. Jack looked at the control panel and announced, "1000 feet. Get ready for impact!"

The descent continued and thunder rolled continuously. The pod shook, dipped and went sideways. It was all over the place. Then they heard a loud bang from above them. It was followed by another one. Jack knew exactly what it was happening. His mind raced. He could feel the pod's descent accelerate. The chute was gone. The pod was in freefall!

CHAPTER 8

A violent chemical storm ravaged the Tasmanian landscape with caustic precipitation and hurricane strength winds. The storm was a product of past industrialization, chemically enhanced agriculture and rampant unregulated fossil fuel consumption during the nineteenth and twentieth centuries; a lingering gift from the past that it kept giving to the future.

Very intense wind shear had ripped the parachute off of the pod. In the end, it had fallen several hundred feet through the air. Fortunately, for all of those involved, a would-be hard impact was greatly softened by a somewhat lucky splashdown. Unfortunately, for all of those involved, the pod instantly began to take on water and sink.

Marie gasped for air as she reached the surface with Jessica in hand. The fierce storm whipped up waves that tossed them without a care. The dirty water stung Marie's eyes and caused her to retch when she swallowed it. And it was virtually impossible not to swallow it.

It was also impossible for her to see anything. The escape pod and her friends had vanished. All lost long ago in waves and darkness as the current carried her and Jessica away. It was a continuous struggle for her to breathe. Even when she could keep her head above water the air she breathed had a strong chemical element to it. It wasn't going well at all, but her hands locked on to Jessica like vice grips. She wasn't letting go!

Darrel fought against the waves with all of his might. He wasn't the strongest of swimmers, but he somehow managed to keep himself from sinking. He tried to shout, "Marie!" just as a wave crested over him. The water hit him so hard it forced itself down his throat. It had the same nasty taste as Jim's red eye sink whiskey on day three. All he heard in response to his screams were wind, thunder and rain. He was lost. And he was alone.

Darrel's mind raced with the thought of a single subject. That subject was Marie. Darrel, like most colonists, tried to push personal attachment to the side. An attachment to hopelessness and alcohol was the meme of the times. But, try as they might to appear hopefully hopeless and wash their fears aside with copious amounts of cheap drink, they were after all only human. And it is human nature to want close personal meaning with another.

Darrel had worked with Marie for the past several

years. The pair had been friendly, exchanged glances and even flirted with each over those years, but for some reason they had only recently taken that next step; the hook-up.

Darrel continued his fight to stay on top of the waves and as he did it became increasingly clear to him why that next step had taken so long to happen. He knew that he would quickly become entangled in a minefield of emotions. The hopefully hopeless man would turn hopelessly hopeful and though it's hard to understand; one state of being would be far worse for him than the other. That state being his current state. It may be, as Tennyson would say, better to have loved and lost, but a colonist would argue that it's better to drink, fuck and only slightly care.

Ricky held on to Sarah for dear life. He couldn't swim, in fact, he was terrified of water. It was a fear born through a childhood of poor parenting, or more specifically, a fatherly toss with the words, "Sink or Swim!" He sank.

Sarah did what she could to keep them afloat, but Ricky seemed determined to pull her under. Fatigue had quickly set in. Her lungs felt like they were on fire and her head started to feel light. The water stung her eyes and her vision blurred. She kept fighting. She kept pushing.

This is exactly how Sarah remembered life on Earth although, growing up in Lucas Kansas, she couldn't imagine it being this wet anywhere. She had spent her youth in the last great dust bowl. It was a dust bowl that continued even to this day.

Her eyes burned. And her mind burned with painful memories. These were the events that had made her much stronger than she would ever appear. She fought to breathe, but there was more chemical than oxygen in the air. Her distant past became ever more vivid with each putrid breath. At one moment she was swimming with Ricky on her back. A moment later she was trying to lead her little brother through a blinding dust storm. She wouldn't allow herself to fail again. She was determined to keep Ricky alive.

Jack and Malinda were the last ones out of the escape pod. Carl was the only person they could see when they came up. He was fifty yards off and being swept further away by the current and wind. They tried to swim toward him but the storm conspired against them. The waves slowly, but inevitably, increased the distance.

"Jack, I can't see him," Malinda shouted over the storm.

Jack shouted back to her, "He'll turn up. Conserve your strength." Jack had no idea if Carl would actually turn up or not. Nor, did he really know where any of his other friends were. Hell, he didn't even know if they were alive at this point.

The impact of the landing had caused utter chaos in the pod. Ricky and Jack's strap buckles had jammed and they were effectively stuck in their seats. While Malinda and Sarah had worked to get them free Darrel had to focus on helping Marie get Jessica out. And the pod took on water almost immediately. It had quickly filled the cabin. It was amazing, to Jack, that any of them survived the landing, but against all odds they somehow got out alive.

Jack knew they couldn't be more than a mile from land. The body of water they landed in wasn't the ocean or even a sea. According to the pod's radar it was a small inlet in southern Tasmania. If they could just stay afloat they'd eventually wash up on land. He just hoped the others could make it through the storm and find their way to shore. After everything they had been through he found it hard to believe that they wouldn't somehow find each other.

Darrel had been treading water for about two hours when he first spotted what he thought was a coastline about five hundred yards away. The rain and wind had subsided, but it was still difficult to see much through the haze of lingering greenish brown fog. He mustered what was left of his strength and began to swim toward the shore.

Fatigue had rendered Darrel's limbs all but useless. He tried to stand and walk as the water got shallow but could only stumble forward eventually settling on crawling and then dragging his tired ass onto the rocks at the edge of the water.

Darrel laid there for a few minutes trying to catch his breath. It wasn't coming easy. Thoughts were hard for him to process and his heart; he hadn't felt his heart race this fast since his little med school experiment with amphetamines. He diagnosed himself with hypoxemia, but there wasn't much he could do except hope the air cleared up before it turned into full blown hypoxia; and it wouldn't be long before that happened.

Marie pulled Jessica up onto the shore. There was just a bit of tree line about fifteen yards in. She hoped it was enough to make some sort of shelter. Her muscles screamed at her with every tug, but she was relentless in her efforts.

Marie didn't become a nurse because it was a good career choice. She was one of those people that had a calling and answered it. She had been raised through the constant misery of those around her as she cared for her family members who suffered the ravages of disease. Those diseases largely caused by smog; much like the haze left behind by the chemical storm she was dropped into. It instantly brought back those memories which only served to strengthen her determination. It wasn't until she had Jessica safely in the tree line that she realized how woozy she had become. She collapsed from exhaustion.

Ricky lay on the beach in a state of shock after two hours of absolute terror. Unless he drowned in alcohol he had absolutely no interest in doing so at all. On the bright side, since all he had to do was focus on floating, he didn't find it all that hard to catch his breath. He did what he always did in times like these. He reached into his pocket for his flask.

Sarah was lying on the beach next to him. She was spent. She rested her head on Ricky's chest trying to catch her breath. Her legs were numb and she really wanted to take a nap. She noticed him fishing around his pocket, "I think you have a drinking problem, Daddy."

"Nope, got my flask right here!" He straightly replied. He pulled it out and quickly realized it wasn't in fact his flask, "Oh, this is Jack's flask. Wait, did you just call me daddy?"

"Mommy doesn't like it when you drink." She was only half conscious.

He twisted the top off and took a drink. Nobody could see it but his eyes lit up, "Oh wow!" He exclaimed. The wonderful essence of his home state began to course through his veins igniting some sort of innate reaction that sent a wild energy coursing through him. He shrugged off the remnants of his fear and turned his attention to Sarah.

"Sarah?" He rolled her onto her back. He could see she was only semi lucid.

"Daddy?" she replied.

"Crap," he wasn't equipped for these situations. He tried to hide his concern, "Look, I like where you're going with this, Sarah, but maybe another time? C'mon let's get you up on your feet."

Ricky got to his feet and reached down for one of Sarah's arms. He put it around his shoulder and lifted her up to her feet; something he had done for Jack at the end of many a fun night. With his help she was barely able to stand.

The sun had been up for a couple of hours. Long enough to begin burning off the lingering haze left behind by the storm. Visibility was slowly returning to normal allowing Ricky to see a fair distance down the beach in each direction. He saw a river inlet to the east. There's no way he could drag her through that. What he didn't see was any sign of his friends, so, they turned west and started walking.

Jack and Malinda plodded along the beach, like a couple of zombies, under a dull green sky. The morning sun had finally cleared the haze enough so that, even though they were still a bit groggy, they could begin their search for the others. Jack looked up at the sky and memories of his childhood crept in. This color of sky usually signified tornado weather back home.

"I keep thinking about Kansas City," Jack said.

"Oh, really," Malinda responded, "Missing home now that we're back down here?"

"Actually, I am, but I'm so hungry all I can think about is a nice big plate of burnt ends," Jack's eyes drifted off as his thought became so vivid he could smell them.

Malinda replied, "You know, they quit using meat for those about fifty years ago, right? It's all made out of Soylent now."

"I think the lack of oxygen might be fucking with your head. I don't think they'd use Soylent for Barbeque in KC." he scoffed.

Malinda couldn't help but pluck this nerve, "Really? Well let me ask you this; when is the last time you saw a cow?"

Jack thought for a second. His mind was clearing

but it was still difficult, "Where would I see a cow?"

"Nowhere, I'm pretty sure they went extinct." Malinda smirked. She knew they weren't quite extinct yet.

Jack's memory began to function again, "Wait, no, I saw one at the zoo about twenty years ago."

Now it was Malinda's turn to scoff, "Okay, but one cow at a zoo isn't going to make enough burnt ends for everyone."

"Actually, I think it was part of a herd." Jack stated.

"It still wouldn't be enough, Jack."

"But they breed them, Malinda."

Malinda flatly rejected the notion, "Not enough."

Jack was incredulous, "Soylent? I think I would have heard about that."

Malinda kept at it, "Well, they changed the name after that guy broke into the Soylent factory a few years ago. Remember? They did that big expose?"

Jack seemed surprised to have missed it, "I didn't see that. Are you serious?"

"Yep! It killed the Soylent brand. Turns out they used dead people to make that stuff! Now it's just called 'organic additive'."

Jack started to chuckle, "That's great! How did I not hear about this?"

Malinda seemed a bit shocked, "Great? I don't know about that."

Jack replied, "Yeah it's fantastic. I always felt bad for the cows, especially, after I saw them at the zoo."

"The cows? What about the corpses?" Malinda could barely hold back her laugh.

Again Jacks sarcasm kicked in, "I've seen corpses. They just lie there and rot. Who cares about a rotting corpse?"

Malinda acted incredulous, but it was getting harder and harder for her not to bust out in laughter, "Their relatives!"

Jack winked at Malinda, "What? The worms should eat and we should starve? Get over it!"

Malinda shook her head feigning disbelief, "Cold man."

Jack thought about those Soylent burnt ends, "Nah, warm with a spicy sauce. Delicious!"

Malinda chuckled, "Maybe I'll get to try some one day."

"Maybe..." Jack was interrupted when he saw a figure in the distance jumping up and down waving his hands, "Hey is that Carl?"

Malinda waved her hands and shouted, "Carl!"

Carl saw Malinda wave back to him and picked up his pace. He was elated to see that they had made it to shore, "Hey!" he yelled as he waved his arms over his head and broke into a trot. It was an action that every muscle in his legs protested. He barely noticed the sound of his feet hitting the sand through his labored breathing. That is until he heard the loud pop of a snapping branch beneath him. That sound was followed by the whirring of a rope as it was pulled rapidly through the sand.

Carl was quite surprised by the sudden flurry of action. It caused him to stop running. He watched as the sand was kicked up in a line that drew a path towards the brush at the edge of the beach. It was a curious sight that he puzzled over for a moment, "Why would someone...." His thought was cut short by a sharpened spike of bamboo that was driven through his eye.

A trap snapped closed on Carl, like a clam shell, sandwiching him between the frames of two bamboo trellis laced with spikes. The spikes held him in a standing position like some sort of life sized marionette.

Jessica had finally regained consciousness, but her lucidity seemed to fade in and out, "Where am I?" she asked.

Marie was finishing up a lean-to she had been working on to shelter Jessica, "We're back on Earth." The response caused Jessica to try and move, "Don't move, Jess."

Jessica didn't recognize the voice she heard, "Who are you?" she asked.

"Marie Perez, from the infirmary," Marie replied.

"I can't see."

"Your eyes are swollen shut. They beat you pretty badly, hon."

"Oh, that's too bad, Remember when you found sis and I naked in Tom's room..." She faded out.

Marie had experienced these semi-lucid conversations before, "I don't hon, but that sounds like an interesting story."

Jessica continued to mumble incomprehensibly for

a few more moments then laid there silent. Marie had done her best. She was no survivalist. Her shelter making skills were, at best, rudimentary. The lean-to would, at least, shelter Jessica from the afternoon sun and hopefully she wouldn't be there too long.

Marie started fishing through her belt pack. Between her and Jessica they had already drank most of the water. She pulled out the flare gun and read the instructions on the side of it. She turned to look at Jessica and said, "Hmm Jess, this should let them know where we are."

She stood up, pointed the flare gun in the air and pulled the trigger. A red flare shot up into the sky above them. She didn't know if Jessica was still conscious or even in a state of mind to understand her but there was a small chance that she might so she said, "Jess, I'm going to walk along the beach a bit and see if I can locate any of the others. Hopefully they saw that flare and I can flag them down if they're close."

Jack and Malinda stood on the beach looking at Carl, "I think he's dead, Jack."

"That's a rough way to go." Jack replied

"Seems like an awful big trap for game."

"I can't imagine what kind of game would be that big."

"I haven't seen anything alive around here at all let alone something to eat."

"True, that's kind of odd. You'd think there'd still be some birds at least."

"Maybe they flew off to get away from the chem

storm."

"Seems likely. But, anyway, that isn't a bird trap."

"Seems to me like.."

Jack finished her sentence. "A human trap."

"That's a scary thought."

"Earth is a scary thought."

"True."

Jack started to examine the mechanism. He looked at how it was constructed. He noted how it was concealed and explained to Malinda exactly how it worked. He pointed to Carl's feet, "You see that branch? It was pinned into the sand. When he stepped on it, the rope that was attached came free. That released the springs of the spiked trellis' that were buried under the sand."

"That's all pretty elaborate. Why not a pit trap?"

"Too close to the water."

"Ah. Good point."

"But, we should probably watch out for those as well if we go inland. Someone doesn't want people around." Jack pulled out his flask, twisted off the top and took a drink. It wasn't what he was expecting. He gagged a bit, "Ugh."

"Not sure I've ever seen that reaction from you after taking a drink."

"Shit balls!"

Malinda chuckled, "What?"

"This is Ricky's flask!"

"It has booze in it then?" She held out her hand.

"Yes." Jack handed her the flask.

Malinda took a swig, "Tastes the same as always."

"My flask had the rest of that whiskey you got me."

"Wow, I wonder what that will do to Ricky?"

"What do you mean?"

"Well, he's been living off this garbage for a decade."

"True. I guess it will be a nice treat for him. He probably needs one right about now anyway." Jack pointed to the trap, "So you know what this means, right?"

"Someone is eating people?"

"That's the only conclusion I can come to."

"Well we've all heard the stories. Should we bury him?"

"Seems like the decent thing to do. Doesn't it?"

"It does." Malinda paused for a moment and let a truly horrific thought process play out in her head. She took another swig and said, "Whoever put this trap here must be desperate."

Jack grabbed the flask back and took a swig, "I can't imagine being that desperate." He screwed the top back on and slid the flask back into his pocket.

"Let's leave him. At least someone will get a meal out of it." Malinda said.

"Wow. And you thought I was cold for eating soylent burnt ends!"

"Alright, let's start digging then," she said as she feigned looking around for a good spot.

Jack thought, for a moment, about the physical effort involved in digging a grave. He took a breath and choked on it a bit, "Fair enough. Let's get out of here before whoever set this trap up comes back to check on it."

"Jack, we should at least say some words or something for Carl."

"Words? A bit old fashioned; don't you think?"

"Damn it, Jack, we're leaving him here to be eaten. It is, quite literally, the least we can do."

Jack realized she wasn't going to let this one go. He raised his flask to Carl, "Carl, you were a good man. I wish we could have shared one last drink together. I will always cherish the good times we had." He paused for a moment of contemplation, "Carl, I was quite shocked to learn that Soylent was people." He smirked at Malinda, "I had been eating people, Carl. And now it appears to be a sport. I hope those receiving the gift of your sacrifice appreciate how lean colony life has left your meat."

Malinda stared at Jack as she shook her head, "Well, that was certainly moving."

Darrel saw a flare go up about a half mile south of him and started to walk toward it. He figured it was probably Ricky. It just seemed like something he would do after a couple of swigs from his flask. While it appeared to be a logical decision, Darrel understood the dangers that surrounded them.

Of course, the flare wasn't shot by Ricky. Much to Darrel's surprise and relief he saw Marie walking toward him on the beach. As his excitement took over he began to run toward her.

Darrel heard a loud snap underneath his feet as he ran. He didn't stop running even when he saw the sand begin to fly into the air on his periphery. By the time the trap activated he was already past it. The loud slap of the two trellis' coming together, however, caused him to look behind him as he ran. He promptly tripped over his own two feet and tumbled to the ground.

Darrel spit sand out of his mouth and sat up. He took a long hard stare at the trap he had just sprung, "Shit, that was close." he said.

Marie arrived a few seconds later, "Darrel, are you alright?"

"I'm fine, Marie."

She dropped to her knees and hugged him from behind, "I'm so glad to see you." She teared up, "You can't even imagine."

Darrel got to his knees and turned around to greet her properly with a long, passionate kiss. It didn't even matter to Marie that he still had some sand in his mouth. He pulled back and asked, "Is Jessica with you?"

"Yes. I tried to make a shelter for her over in that grove of trees."

"How's she doing?"

"She's in and out. I think she's going to pull through."

"That's great news. Really great news. Amazing. I can't believe we made it through all that."

"It wasn't easy. I thought I was going to drown a

few times last night."

"Yeah me too. I'm not that good of a swimmer."

"Good enough apparently. I could sure go for a couple drinks and a day of sleep."

"Well, hopefully Ricky will turn up. I honestly thought he was the one that set off the flare."

"Why?"

"His flask is full of some really good whiskey. I have no idea where he got it from."

"No, I meant why did you think it was Ricky."

"Oh, uh, yeah. Just because there might be some dangerous people lurking about." He looked back at the trap, "It kind of worried me that it might draw the wrong kind of attention."

"Oh shit, I didn't even think about that.'

"Well, we better go check on Jessica. I want to check on that spleen."

"It's not far. Follow me." Marie grabbed ahold of Darrel's hand and stood up.

They started heading back toward Jessica. Marie noted, "The air seems to have cleared up quite a bit."

"Yeah, I was worried about hypoxia there for a bit."

"I know. It took me a good hour to get moving after we washed up on shore."

"You're an amazing gal, Marie."

"Awe, aren't you sweet," she turned and gave him a peck on the cheek. "She's right over here," She turned toward the trees and immediately saw a problem. Her moment of happiness was instantly dashed, "Oh, no!"

Darrel was puzzled, "What?"

"She's not there!" Marie ran the last fifty yards to where she had left Jessica. The lean-to had been destroyed and there was a bloody trail. She fell to her knees in disbelief.

Darrel scanned the immediate area, "It looks like someone dragged her off."

"I never should have left!" Marie dropped to her knees and began to cry, "I'm so stupid!"

Darrel tried to comfort her, "Well, that's just not true. What would you have done? At least now we're together and we can go after her."

"I never should have left." She sobbed.

"We don't even know what happened. Maybe the others found her. They might be close."

Marie knew what Darrel was trying to do. She could tell just by the scene that this wasn't Jack's work. Not even Ricky would attempt to move her. She stood up and started following the drag marks.

Darrel instinctively moved to get in front of Marie. If there was someone hostile at the end of the trail, he certainly didn't want Marie to be in between him and whoever it might be.

Ricky and Sarah noticed a flare go up just to the west of them. It had taken about an hour but Sarah's brain was working once again. She did, however, have a terrible headache to match the throbbing muscles of her arms and legs.

Ricky tried to take it slow. Every couple of hundred feet they'd sit down. He'd take a few sips out of his flask. He'd offer it to her and she'd politely decline. She had gone through both of their bottles of water. Ricky didn't mind. He had exactly what he needed.

"Do you think that was Jack?" Sarah asked.

"I don't think so." he replied.

"Why not?"

"Well, the same reason we haven't shot off our flares. We don't know who might be around here. Probably best not to draw attention to ourselves. I'd imagine Jack is doing what we're doing. Walking the beach. He'll turn up. I'm certain of it."

"Well it has to be one of us don't you think?"

"Maybe Darrel or Marie? They might be needing help with Jessica. That's the only thing I can think of that would be urgent enough to warrant doing that."

"That makes sense," she paused for a second, "It seems like you're making more sense than normal today."

"Am I?"

"Yeah and you don't seem as scared as you were."

He held up the flask, "It must be the whiskey."

"No, I've seen you drunk before."

"Well you've seen me drinking Jim's scatter brain sink swill."

"Isn't that what's in the flask?"

Ricky chuckled, "Oh yeah, you were a bit out of it earlier. No, somehow mine and Jack's flasks got switched."

"Well, what's in his?"

Ricky handed her the flask, "Here. Have a taste."

Sarah took a sip and her eyes lit up, "Oh wow! That's the stuff!"

Ricky nodded and joked, "Who's your daddy?"

Sarah gave him a very confused look, "What?"

Ricky busted out in laughter, "That's right, I'm your daddy!"

"Okay weirdo."

He continued to chuckle, "Come on. Let's get moving."

CHAPTER 9

Darrel heard a noise up ahead. He stopped, turned to Marie and put his finger up to his mouth, "Shhh." He could hear what sounded like chopping. He whispered, "Stay here. I'm going to go up ahead a bit."

The terrain had changed from dead and dying trees into barren rocky outcrops. There were no other signs of life anywhere. Darrel could hear the sounds coming from behind a rather large boulder. Smaller rocks were stacked up against it. The structure almost looked man made; as if someone had tried to make a crude wall for shelter.

Darrel moved closer to the rocks and heard what sounded like grunting. It seemed somewhat animalistic, but as he listened closer he noticed it had a structure; like some sort of crude primitive language. He could also smell a fire. He approached the rocks and looked them over. If he went around them, whatever was on the other side was sure to notice him; climbing the smaller rocks to get on top if the boulder seemed like the smartest play to him.

Slowly and methodically he negotiated the smaller rocks until he could lift himself up on top of the boulder. He laid flat and slowly scooted forward the last few feet. And what he saw; well, what he saw would remain with him until the day he died. There wasn't enough alcohol in existence to drink that sight away.

Jessica's torso was roasting on a crude spit over a campfire. Her arms and legs had been removed and reduced to smaller pieces that were hanging, tied by rope, from large crude poles in the ground. A naked greyish man, or beast, or whatever it was, had just finished hanging the last piece from one of her legs.

Darrel froze. He wanted to scream. He wanted to jump down and kill whatever those… things… were. He was a large man, but even being as big as he was, he counted three of them; there was no way he stood a chance. He closed his eyes to avoid seeing that horror any longer and started to inch his way backwards.

Darrel carefully dismounted the boulder and returned to Marie. How was he going to explain this to her? He really had no idea. He felt sick. By the time he had gotten back to Marie he was ready to vomit, but he didn't want to make a sound. He grabbed Marie by the hand and walked swiftly back towards the beach. When they were finally a safe distance away he let it go. He spewed like he hadn't spewed in months.

Marie rubbed his back, "Are you okay? What was it?"

THE TRIALS OF JACK KEMPER

Darrel wiped his mouth and turned toward Marie. He took a couple deep breaths, "You really don't want to know."

"Did you find Jessica?"

"Jessica is gone, Marie."

"What?!?" she said raising her voice.

This alarmed Darrel, "Shhh. Come on, let's keep moving," he grabbed her hand and pulled her behind him.

Marie was in a state of shock. She wanted to know what Darrel had seen but clearly he wanted to put some distance in between them and whatever it was, so, she remained silent while he pulled her along.

Jack and Malinda walked eastward along the beach. They took their time about it. They didn't want to set off another trap. Every few minutes Jack would take out his flask, take a swig and hand it to Malinda. Malinda would take a swig and hand it back.

"I bet it was Ricky." Malinda said.

"Why's that?"

"He's probably drunk off that whiskey."

"That does sound like him. Remember that time he ran through the bar naked with his dick in a bun?"

"Oh yeah, he ran around asking the ladies, 'Would you like a hot dog?' that was fucking funny."

"That guy's a hilarious drunk. We've known him what, 11 years now?" Jack said.

"Yeah, and Darrel for 12."

"Did you know Ricky used to be the Mayor of small town in Tennessee?"

"No, he never mentioned that to me."

"He doesn't like to talk about it much. They impeached him after they found him naked in the town fountain after an all-night bender."

Malinda chuckled, "That's our Ricky."

"Probably wouldn't have been so bad if it wasn't for the dead hooker that was floating beside him," Jack paused for effect and then continued, "he was on a shuttle to Bravo Colony before the proceedings were even finished."

"I guess we were all running from something." Malinda conceded.

"I was running from the plague. When it hit Kansas City I couldn't get on that shuttle fast enough. Luckily, I had a ticket waiting. Sam had been trying to get me up there for a couple years."

"Yeah, plague will do it. Personally, I got tired of killing people."

Jack was shocked, "What!?"

"Things got pretty bleak in Odrick's Corner. The rape gangs, starvers and just the odd asshole here and there that wanted what I had."

"How many did you kill?"

"I don't know. I quit putting notches in my gun when I hit 15."

"15? Holy shit!"

"No, I quit counting at 15. Like I said, it was pretty bleak."

"Is that where you learned to shoot?"

"Nah, my dad taught me when I was a kid."

"Wow, here I thought you were just another civil servant."

"I was Jack. Jesus, you're gullible."

"What?"

"I'm fucking with you. My assignment to Bravo Colony was just dumb luck."

Jack shook his head at Malinda, "I guess I'm too damned tired to catch that."

She nudged him with her shoulder, "Tired; Drunk; Why split hairs?"

Ricky and Sarah stood on the beach examining what appeared to be a sprung trap. Ricky took a swig of whiskey, "Wow, I'm glad we haven't run into one of these."

Sarah replied, "I couldn't even imagine. It looks like it would be quite painful."

"I see the footprints continue on past it so I'm guessing whoever left those didn't get caught in it."

"Not a very good trap then is it?"

"I don't know. My dad used to trap animals back home in the hills of Tennessee. It's not so easy."

"Really? It seems like it would be."

"You'd think, but anytime you're dealing with intelligence it always has a chance to beat you."

"Aren't they called dumb animals for a reason?"

"It's all relative. They still have a brain and instincts."

"I guess that's why we created grocery stores."

Ricky laughed at her funny logic, "I guess so!"

"God, could you imagine a grocery store? All that

food! I wonder what it was like."

"I'm pretty sure I'd be really fat if I had lived back then."

"I read that a lot of people were."

"I can't blame them. If I had access to all that food all I'd do is eat and drink."

"Well you'd have to work too."

"Would I?"

"I would think so."

"What if I got so fat that I couldn't?"

"Then you wouldn't be able to afford to eat and you'd lose the weight."

"Do you think they would have let me starve?"

"Maybe not starve, but at least you'd have to moderate."

"Would I?"

Sarah's stomach started to growl, "I get it! You're hungry! So am I! Let's stop talking about food!"

"Hey, you brought it up," Ricky handed her the flask, "Drink up!"

Darrel had pulled Marie behind him all the way to the beach without another word said. They emerged from the trees and Darrel once again tried to vomit but instead only heaved.

"What do you mean she's gone?" Marie asked.

Darrel spit and continued to stare down at the sand. He didn't want to see her face when he said it. "Cannibals," was his short response.

"Cannibals? Oh my god!"

He turned his head to look at her, "There's nothing

we can do for her, Marie."

Darrel thought he heard someone yelling his name, "Darrel!" He looked up and saw Ricky and Sarah standing near the trap. "Well, finally, some good news," he pointed down the beach, "Look, there's Ricky and Sarah."

Marie wiped away tears as she looked down the beach. A wave of relief came over her. At least Ricky and Sarah were safe, "Let's head over there."

"Alright"

The group met up a short distance from the trap. Ricky immediately hugged Darrel, "It's great to see you! I really wasn't sure we'd see any of you again."

"I'm glad you made it Ricky. Any sign of Jack and Malinda?"

Sarah answered, "You two are the first living things we've seen all day. Thank Vesta you're okay. Is Jessica with you?"

This triggered Marie to begin crying once again. Through her tears she answered, "No, the cannibals got her."

Sarah's response was almost a shout, "Cannibals!?!"

"Yeah, they dragged her into the rocks. There was nothing I could do."

Ricky looked around quite nervously, "They aren't near are they?"

Darrel pointed past the trees, "They're just over that ridge behind that small group of trees."

"So, we should head the other way then?" Sarah

asked.

"That would probably be a good idea." Darrel responded. He looked at Ricky, "Hey buddy, anything left in that flask?"

Ricky smiled and handed it to him, "Maybe a bit."

Darrel twisted off the top and took a swig. He handed it to Marie and she jiggled the last few drops out.

"Oh! No! Man down!" Ricky lamented.

Sarah looked at Ricky and said, "This shit is getting serious!"

The group didn't notice that, as they were grieving, drinking, joking and trying to cope with recent events, a large group of armed men had jumped out from behind the rocks that laid just off the beach and begun to approach them.

Marie was the first to notice and she promptly dropped the flask to the ground, "Uh, guys."

"Hey, that's a nice flask. Just because it's empty…" Darrel's response stopped mid-sentence when he noticed someone come at him out of the corner of his eye. The day had not been going well and he was ready to fight. He turned and began swinging; unaware that he was badly outnumbered. He managed to tag one of the men quite solidly in the face and take him to the ground. The punches flew for about ten seconds before another man kicked Darrel squarely in the head sending him tumbling into the sand.

"Leh's not go doin' som'tin 'ero like, mate," growled a stocky, grizzled, man that now towered over

THE TRIALS OF JACK KEMPER

Darrel. A twisted, mostly toothless, smile revealed the pleasure he felt as he put his foot on Darrel's chest.

The others stood frozen in fear. There was a gun to each of their heads before they even realized what was happening. A muscular, unarmed man stood at the center of the group staring them down. He pointed to a couple of the men on the perimeter and growled, "Joo's go watch for dem canni's," he then turned his attention to Darrel.

The man standing over Darrel reported, "tough'n 'ere, Chappy."

Chappy, the man standing in the center, spat at Darrel. "If'n I let you up, e're not go'a have any trouble out'ya?"

Darrel replied, "That's a promise I can't make."

"Oi, like dis'un boys! Ee's got spirit! Beat'm a bi'more Otis and leh's see 'ow'it 'old's up!"

Otis, the man standing over Darrel, joyfully handed his gun to another man and began to beat Darrel with his fists. The beating lasted only a few minutes, but for Ricky, Marie and Sarah it felt like it lasted much longer. They couldn't watch. It wasn't finished until Darrel was rendered unconscious by the assault.

"Ats 'nuff." Chappy said nonchalantly.

Otis had a big smile on his face as he looked down at a bloodied and unconscious Darrel lying in the sand. He took his rifle back and slung it over his shoulder; satisfied with his handy work.

Chappy looked at the others, "So, an'ee ohn els got spirit?" The question was met with silence, "Ai'ght, get'em toid up. Joo' two 'pic'up dat un," he gestured towards two of his men then to Darrel, "Le'z get mov'n. Oi'wan'be bak a'camp 'fore dark."

The pirates set about the binding of hands. Two of them seemed to take a special interest in Sarah, "Oi', Chappy," one of them called out.

"Wut's it?'

"'Oi joos go'ed. We gon' trumpfuck dis un."

"Sud'jerself, if joos wan'be canni bait," Chappy replied over his shoulder as he and the others headed back into the rocky terrain just off the beach.

CHAPTER 10

Sarah struggled with the two goons as they dragged her to a secluded spot in the rocks that lined the beach, "Dis gun be fun, Max."

"Seriously guys? Can't we work something out?" Sarah pleaded.

Max ignored her, "Aye Sid, bedd'r dan da'canni bitch we 'ad wylbak"

"I bet dis'un aint even got'da warts."

"Warts!?!" Sarah yelled, "Oh my god!"

Max laughed, "Dat's not the last time we'll hear that. Oi, Sid?"

They tossed her to the ground, "Nup joo'll 'ear it plen'ny whil'ya wach'n"

Sarah began to quietly pray, "Oh Great and Holy Vesta. I, being your humble..."

Max began to unbutton his pants, "Oi, ya bast'd, jus fer 'dat I'm gon'na first."

"Fook y'are!"

"Joo ga' prol'm wid'dat lil'un?"

It was a provocation that Sid could not allow to go unchallenged. He immediately lunged at Max's legs and took him to the ground. He reached up and clawed at Max's face trying to get the better of him. Sid was the smaller of the two. He was also the quicker one. Sid pulled his hand away and with it a large clump of Max's beard. Max let out a howl, "So, dat's 'ow i's gon'be eh?"

Max's anger took hold. He grabbed Sid by the hair and wrenched his head back. The scarred knuckles of his left hand were planted squarely into the Sid's cheek. The blow sent Sid rolling into the rocks.

Sid swiftly popped up on his knees as he steadied himself with one arm. He touched a newly opened cut on his cheek then held his fingers out to check for blood. He looked at the bloody digits and spit angrily, "Joos gon'a 'gret dat, Max." he snarled.

Max was already on his feet, arms slightly out in front of him. He was ready and waiting for whatever came next, "Stoy dewn lit'l man." he growled.

Sid's eyes were ablaze with rage as he charged at Max and caught him in the midsection with his shoulder. The impact caused Max to take a couple of steps back but it didn't knock him off balance. Sid's attack had less than the desired effect.

Max raised his arms up above his head, clasped his hands together and brought them down hard on the Sid's back. The blow dropped Sid to his knees, yet his grip around Max's waist remained firm.

With the two men distracted by their ongoing fight,

THE TRIALS OF JACK KEMPER

Sarah saw her chance to escape. She flipped over and started scrambling away towards the rocks and scrub.

Sid continued trying to gain an advantage, but a second heavy blow to his back finally loosened his grip. Max grabbed Sid, spun him around and locked his arm around his neck. He began to squeeze slightly; cutting off the airway. Sid valiantly struggled to pull Max's arm away, but there was no substitute for brute strength. He recognized that he was defeated and stopped struggling. He tapped out.

Max didn't hesitate to release him. A good scrum is no reason to kill a friend, especially when the scrum was over a woman, "See' I go'firs." Max claimed. "Oi'l mak'sur I fook her goo' and bloody for yeh."

Sid didn't respond. He just lay on the ground trying to catch his breath.

Max turned back to where Sarah had been laying only to find that she wasn't there. It didn't take long to spot her scrambling through the scrub beyond the rocks. He started after her, "Sid, ge'up. She's mak'n a ruh'fer it".

Sid got to his feet and hurried after Max.

Unfortunately, Sarah hadn't made it very far into the scrub. The pair quickly caught up to her. There would be no arguing about who went first now as Max grabbed her by the ankles and twisted her onto her back.

Sarah screamed and kicked at her attacker. She fought back with everything she had. Twisting and writhing while trying to delay the inevitable.

Sid moved to help hold her down. He used his knees to pin her arms down while violently ripping off her shirt. He then used it to bind her hands over her head.

Max tore off her sweatpants while maintaining his grip on her legs, "Ey! Sid get'a loo' at dat."

"Dem's sexy," Sid replied as he ogled Sarah's thong.

Max worked his trousers loose and lowered them to his ankles. Just as he began to remove Sarah's thong he caught a glimpse of a small silver canister flying above his head, "Oi Sid, wat's dat?"

The canister burst open releasing a thousand pieces of foil that floated around them. The air around them electrified and charged the foil pieces. The two hapless pirates and Sarah let out agonized grunts as a high voltage charge coursed through their bodies. All three were rendered unconscious after only a few seconds.

Cpl. Stoudt uncloaked and moved in to bind the two men. She pulled two short lengths of wire from a dispensing mechanism on her belt and rolled Max over onto his stomach. She put his hands behind his back and slapped the wire around his wrists. It tightened itself snug. She then proceeded to bind Sid. With this completed she moved to check Sarah. She swiped the panel on her forearm activating her bio scanner. Jan held her arm out and starting at Sarah's head moved it slowly along her body. The information from the scan displayed in her retinal HUD.

THE TRIALS OF JACK KEMPER

Jack's voice called out from behind her, "Who the hell are you and what did you do to our friend?" Jan spun around to find Jack and Malinda glaring at her. Each one was holding a big rock.

Jan answered, "I was hoping that was you, Mr. Kemper."

"You were?" the answer caught Jack off guard, "Wait. How do you know who I am?"

"I have quite a bit of information on you Mr. Kemper."

Sarah began to regain consciousness, "Why does my mouth taste like metal?" she asked as she tried to force herself awake.

"Sorry, that's the after effect of my foil grenade," Jan replied, turning back to Sarah.

Sarah asked, "Who are you?" and then noticed Jack and Malinda standing there. She tried to get to her feet but only made it to her knees, "I'd hug you but my legs aren't quite working yet."

Malinda dropped her rock and moved past Jan to embrace Sarah, "Are you okay?"

"I think so," she replied, but then realized she was once again sporting only a thong. "You have got to be kidding me!"

"Jack, give her your shirt."

"Why, she'd just lose it." he said.

Jack pulled a roll off duct tape out of his tool belt while trying to refocus the conversation, "You have me at a bit of a disadvantage," he said to Jan as he ripped off two small pieces of tape and walked over to Sarah.

"Let's start from the beginning. Who are you?"

"I'm Corporal Stoudt, Lead Recon...," Jan stuttered, distracted by the fluidity with which Jack quickly slapped the tape on Sarah's nipples, "Uh, Lead Recon Specialist for the Liberty Island Quick Response Unit. You can call me Jan."

Jack perked up, "Stoudt? Did you say Stoudt?"

Even Malinda and Sarah were struck by the coincidence. They looked at each other out of the corner of their eyes, "Praise Vesta." they reflexively murmured to each other. To them it was clearly a sign.

"Yes, Jan Stoudt," she extended her hand formally, "Why?"

Jack thought about dropping to one knee and kissing her hand as a sign of reverence but in the back of his head he reasoned it must be entirely coincidental. And he might appear to be crazy. Instead he chose to shake her hand, "Are you familiar with duct tape?"

Jan seemed a bit bewildered by the question, "Of course," she turned toward Sarah, "Nice pasties by the way."

Sarah pointed at Jack, "Space Engineer."

Jack shook his head, chuckled a bit and continued, "It was invented by Mrs. Vesta Stoudt in 1943."

Jan's curiosity was somewhat piqued but it didn't seem like the appropriate time for such a trivial conversation, "Well, that's quite interesting but..."

Malinda cut her off, "Jan, duct tape is a large reason why we're even alive today."

Sarah added, "It's covered my tits twice!"

Malinda said, "Oh, and mine once as well!"

"She was the trend setter. Really, I'm just following her fashion choices."

Jack continued, "What we're trying to say, is, that we have a certain sacred reverence for duct tape. It basically held Bravo Colony together for the last 5 years, Praise Vesta."

Jan wasn't quite sure how to interpret all of this. She wondered if the chemical content of the air was having an impact on their mental capacity.

Sarah looked at Jan and added, "You know, up until now I thought Jack was being funny. It was a nice way to alleviate stress in the moment and we all played along, but even I have to admit that this is far too much to just be coincidental."

"Are you actually related to Vesta?" Jack had to ask.

Jan replied, "Well, actually Vesta is a family name. My great grandmother was named Vesta and I do believe she was named after her great, great grandmother. Hmm, that is kind of weird. Isn't it?"

Jack, Malinda and Sarah all stared at each other in a state of utter shock, "She answered my prayers!" Sarah said.

Their conversation was cut short as the pirates began to regain consciousness, "Da'h fuk?" grunted Sid, laying face first on the ground, "Joos shite in me mouf?"

Max unsuccessfully tried to roll over, turning his head to one side instead, "I aint 'ad nuffin dis awful in me mouf sin dat canni girl." he said spitting sand out as he spoke.

It didn't take long for the two pirates to realize they weren't alone. They both craned and wriggled their bodies to where they could see the others, "Oi, ee' din'a mean any'ting by it," Max pleaded, trying to act remorseful.

Sarah looked to Malinda, "Help me up." She stumbled to her feet, with Malinda's help and moved towards Max. She stood above him; her light mood replaced by rage, "Didn't mean anything by it?"

She grabbed the back of Max's head and thrust her knee into his face. The blow split his nose and forced him back to the ground. Sarah then moved towards Sid, who tried in vain to squirm away, "Where's that fucking rock you had, Malinda?"

"Oi, Oi, c'mon dunt broain me."

"I was just going to smash your dick off but now that you mention it I might just brain you after."

"Aight, un secen touht mehbe broain me foist."

Jan spoke up, "Wait, maybe they can be of use to us."

"Yea, yea, ee can'elp ya git ur'frens bak"

Sarah, Malinda, and Jack all looked at each other. The mention of their friends pulled them out of the immediate situation. Jan looked at the three of them and beckoned them closer to her. She had an idea.

"I know where your friends are being taken." She started in a hushed tone.

"Where is that?" Jack asked

THE TRIALS OF JACK KEMPER

"To a camp on the other side of the bay. In this terrain, it will take several hours to get there."

"So, what do we do with these guys?"

"Kill them." Sarah responded.

"They could be of use to us. All of you have seen the traps on the beach?" The others nodded and she continued, "They were put there by the cannibals that roam through this area. These two might be useful in keeping them off of us until we get clear of them."

"You're suggesting we leave them as bait?" Malinda asked.

"That is exactly what I am suggesting."

"I don't have a problem with that." Sarah added.

Jack was already starting to like Jan. He put his hand on Sarah's shoulder and said, "Sounds good to me." These animals had tried to rape her, their cohorts had his friends, and it seemed reasonable to him that a cannibal with a full belly might be less likely to get hungry in the near future.

Jack walked over to Max and Sid. He kneeled down next to them, "You say you can help us get our friends back?"

"Sur, sur. Ee cun'elp." Max replied.

"Well, we'd appreciate it if you put up a good fight when the cannibals show up to eat you. You know, buy us some time."

"Wat?" Sid tried to choke back his fear.

Max begged, "Oi now mate, lehs be roisanble 'ere."

"Oh, I think it's quite reasonable."

Jan had another thought, "We should take their

clothes." she said.

Sarah was in the mood to make them as miserable as possible, "Ooo yeah. Let's do that." she replied.

"Wat? Why ya gun do dat?" Sid asked.

"Something for Sarah to wear and I bet Jack would make quite the handsome pirate."

Jack interjected, "Hey, I don't want to wear those smelly rags all day. No thank you."

Malinda agreed with Jan, "It could help us blend in."

"Can't I just go with the pasties?" Sarah asked.

"I agree. It's a good look for her." Jack smiled at Sarah.

"It would make for good camo. If someone off in the distance sees us they'll just think we're part of their group."

"Dats a 'orrible idea, mate." Sid argued.

"Yea, terrible. 'Ave ya smelt us?" Max agreed.

The sun was high in the sky. Its chemically filtered light washed out the color of the landscape. A slight breeze delivered the hint of a familiar stench in the area. So slight was this smell that only a heightened, preternatural, awareness could sense it.

The lead hunter stopped momentarily. His eyes closed slightly as he focused. There were many scents, but he was only searching for the one. And he found it; the distinct scent of fear. It was the scent of a meal. He slowly glanced to his left and right making eye contact with the other hunters. The signal was a subtle one; a mere twitch. In just an instant their spears rose to the ready and they silently moved off in different directions.

These were the tainted ones. Born as a lineage of the afflicted, their disease addled bodies rendered them into, what many considered, a sub-human species with minds that were barely capable of functioning beyond a primal level, but those primal instincts were almost all they required.

Howling and screaming rose above the terrain around them. The hunt was on. Each of the hunters knew their roles. Their movements were more instinct than intent. They covered the ground between them and their prey in virtual silence while their eyes darted back and forth scanning the brush for signs of movement.

Jack and Sarah had donned the pirate's ragged clothing. Their noses quickly went blind to the accompanying scent. Their eyes on the other hand watered like a faucet stuck in the on position.

Jack looked toward Max, "You weren't kidding about the smell."

"Oi, is not loik 'ee 'ave bafs in camp."

Sid added, "Yeh gotta go to da port fer dat."

Malinda walked over carrying the pirate's guns and handed one of them to Jack. She recoiled immediately, "Oh my. That is a powerful stench."

Jack agreed, "I hope it washes off."

"Da'Piss 'ill git it off" Sid said.

"Piss? You bathe in piss?" Sarah asked.

"Nuh, not piss. Da'Piss."

Sarah shook her head and look toward Malinda, "I'm missing something."

"Da'Piss! Da'Piss!" Sid reiterated.

Max clarified, "Foimented tit piss. From's da goats."

Jan translated, "I think they're trying to say that fermented goats milk will wash the stench away. It's their homebrew."

Jack said, "That sounds awful. I mean I'd drink it, but it sounds awful."

"Joos get'us'ta it, mate." Max said.

Malinda replied, "Can't be any worse than Jim's sink whiskey."

An alarm started to sound. It was coming from Jan's arm mounted data pad. She raised her arm out in front of her and swiped the control panel sending the data to her retinal HUD. She could see a group of six figures superimposed over the terrain, "We have multiple bogies coming our way. Looks like a hunting pack. Let's get moving!"

"Oi, yer not go'n leev us fer da canni's." Max pleaded.

"C'mon mate. 'Ee's nah baht'guys!"

Sarah walked over to Max and kicked him square in the teeth. She turned to Sid and tried to do the same but he turned his head. This left her feeling a bit short changed so she took better aim and kicked him again. This time her foot landed squarely on his nuts before he could react. She held it there as he squirmed.

"You know, had you just asked," she paused for a

second wrinkling her nose at their smell, "and taken a bath. I probably would have thought it fun."

He let out a grunt which ended in a high pitch, "Oi! Oi!"

Malinda walked over to pull Sarah away and get them moving, "Really Sarah, pirate fantasies?"

"I read a book once," she said nonchalantly as she removed her foot from Sid's testicles. Sid fell to his side and whimpered.

"Oh yeah?"

"Captive of My Desires. It was an oldy but damn. Ever since then..."

Ricky trudged along. His mind drifted back to Sarah. He felt helpless and hopeless, "Marie," he mumbled, "do you think Sarah is still alive?"

"Of course she is." Marie replied. She was trying hard not to think about what happened to her friend.

"I can't help but think it may be better if she were dead."

"What?!" Marie yelled.

"At least it would be over for her."

Marie understood the logic and on some level she even agreed with him. There was no telling what lie in store for them.

"Oi, Chappy." called out one of the pirates carrying Darrel.

"Whas'it?"

"Dis'uns wak'n up."

"Goot. G'head n'put'm down." Chappy said.

The pirates dropped Darrel to the ground. He laid

there for a moment still not fully conscious. Slowly he brought himself up to his hands and knees, the movement made more difficult by the bindings around his wrists. He looked up at his captors; one eye partially swollen shut. Chappy, Otis and the others stood there looking at him as they passed around a water skin.

"A'ight, hook'm up wit'dem oth'rs." Chappy ordered.

One of the pirates grabbed Darrel's bindings and jerked him over to where Marie and Ricky stood. As he was tied to the rope linking Marie and Ricky together, they got their first look at his bruised and bloody face. Marie instinctively reached for him but was abruptly stopped by the pull of the rope as the pirates started walking again.

They walked in silence for some time. It was obvious that Darrel was slowly becoming aware of the situation. He looked at Marie then back towards Ricky.

"Where's Sarah?" he asked.

"She's..." Ricky started.

"She was kept at the beach." Marie finished.

Darrel struggled with what he heard, "What?"

"Two pirates kept her," she stopped short of saying what she felt their intentions were.

This was more than Darrel could take. Beating or not, he had to act. He glanced at the pirate closest to him. He noticed that the guy wasn't really paying all that much attention to him. Darrel seized on this opportunity and tripped him.

Darrel's action was wholly unexpected by the pirate who tumbled to the ground clumsily. Darrel was fast to jump on top of him. His sudden flurry of movement jerked on the rope that tied him to Ricky and Marie.

Now, if someone were to total up the mass of a Ricky and a Marie and then compare their total mass with the mass of one large black man from Mooseknuckle, Manitoba, they would come to the same conclusion that nature itself had come to at that very moment. The force that his mass exerted on the rope would jolt them right off of their feet. And it did just that. It jerked them to the ground in a tangle of limbs and rope.

Darrel wasted no time wrapping his arms around the pirate's neck. It was almost a surprise to him when he snapped it. It took less effort than he thought it should. He reached for the dead man's weapon, but before he could work it free he felt the barrel of a rifle pressed against his temple. Darrel froze.

An angry Chappy stood over Darrel, "Joos mor' trubl'dan u'wirth. Joos payin fer..." Chappy's anger was interrupted by wild screams that rose up from all directions. The sounds immediately drew his attention away from Darrel. Such were the nature of these screams that they caused the hair on the back of his neck to stand up and triggered his more primal survival instinct.

Chappy carefully scanned the area for any signs of unnatural movement. A threat caught his eye. It was a mere blur. His reflexes took over just in the nick of time and he dove to the left. A spear flew past him just to his right piercing the head of a pirate that was standing just behind him, "CANNIS!" he yelled.

A large group of cannibal hunters rushed at the pirates from all directions. Chappy rapidly got back to his feet and deftly swung his rifle around to meet the oncoming attack. He did some quick math and came to the logical conclusion that there were far too many of them for his group to hold their ground.

Chappy screamed the order, "'R'treat! R'treat!" as he sprayed a volley of shots towards the aggressors.

Otis shouted at his three prisoners, "Oi ain't woitin on ya's! Git'up or Git'et!"

Ricky and Marie hurriedly untangled themselves. As they got to their feet they could see just how big the group of hunters was. They stood for a brief second in a state of shock; Petrified by the alien horde of greyish human-like animals rushing toward them.

Darrel grabbed onto Marie's arm and pulled, "Let's go! Run!"

The pirates were leaving them behind. They didn't have much use for prisoners anyway. If the trio managed to distract the hunters and provide enough time to get away, that would be quite sufficient. But, Darrel and the others realized their only hope of surviving was to run towards the guys with the guns. And run they did.

The hunters didn't follow. They weren't looking for a fight. It was a meal they were after. And the two fallen pirates would suffice. As quickly as it started, it

THE TRIALS OF JACK KEMPER

was over. The cannibals grabbed the corpses and melted back into the scrub and rocks just as quickly as they had appeared.

Sid and Max sat alone, hogtied and naked on the beach near the sprung trap. It was late afternoon and a sweltering heat had set in. They wiggled and shifted and did everything they could to try and free themselves.

"Oi, Sid, scooch yer back up ag'in moine." Max said.

Sid used every muscle he could to make his way through the sand until they were back to back, "O'right now wat?" Sid asked.

"Woik da tie!" Max ordered.

"Wat da fook am I 'sposed to woik it wit?"

"Anyting. Is dere a wiik'spot?"

"I dun fil'un."

"No luock?"

"Nah no luck."

"Not luck. LUOCK! LUOCK!" Max reiterated.

"Yeh, no luock eifer."

"Sid, oi tank dis'izit."

"I dun wan'doi Maxxie."

"Fuk'n 'ell. Cun'be anee' woise den dis shite."

"Maxxie, Oi got'a cum'clen mate."

"Cum'clen?"

"Yeh, joo memba'ow joo'd wake up afta a bender'n joor arse 'ould be bleedn?"

"Yeh, da fookin 'emroids. Oi wunna miss'em."

"Yeh, mate. Dat's on me."

"What ya soyin, Sid?"
"Oi dun'yer arse lik'a canni bitch."
"Yeh wat?"
"Oi fook'd yer arse loik a canni bitch's twat."
"Oi dun even nuh wat'ta say ta dat."
"Oi luv ya, Maxxie."
"Go'un fook yer'self, Sid. Ya puf'ter!"
"C'mon Max. Oi dun wanna g'out li'dat."
"Wat ya wan'me ta say? Joos been stick'n it ta' me all dis'time."
"Oi, dat eh'hev."
Max yelled, "Oi, canni's! Weez ova'ere!"
"Oi Max wat da fook?"
"I'ma moike'm eat joo foist, Sid."
"Oi wuz jes kiddin joo fuck!"
"Yeh, sur!"

Sid couldn't contain his laughter any longer, "Dat wut ya'get for call'n me'lil. Ood wan go no'ere dat'airy stink'ole a'yers n'ways?"

"'Ow ya know iss'airy den?"

Sid began to respond but stopped. He could just make out the muted calls of a cannibal hunting party nearby.

"Joos 'ere dat?"

"'Cors I'did." Max looked around trying to come up with an escape plan, "C'mon, Sid, lez git t'da water."

"Ow ees gun'da dat?"

Max laid out as flat as he could and began to roll himself down the beach. Sid recognized immediately what Max was trying to do and followed suit. They had only covered a few feet when Max's progress was stopped by a gnarled and abnormally large greyish foot. He craned his neck to look up. His gaze was met by a hulking, gray skinned beast glowering down at him. It was obvious to Max that this was the alpha hunter. He shouted, "Shite, we's dun fer, Sid!"

The beast was covered in the tell-tale sores of the afflicted. Many of the sores were surrounded by decorative tribal scars. There were other scars as well; remnants of a thousand hunts and his numerous victories over would-be challengers. Across his chest hung a bandolier made of tanned human hide adorned with the bones and teeth of his prey.

The alpha hunter was soon joined by the rest of his hunting party. They jostled for a prime position as they drooled in anticipation of the meal to come. He stood guard over the two pirates and growled. He could sense the excitement in his hunters and waved a level hand to settle them. He signaled for two of them to grab Sid. As they obeyed and moved in to grab a hold of Sid, he knelt down in front of Max. The hunger in his eyes revealed his desire.

Max knew what was coming. In one last defiant act he spat in the beast's face and shouted, "Fook off, ya'cunt! Oi ain gun squ'rm fer'ya!"

The alpha stared, almost hypnotically, into Max's eyes. With a deft, almost imperceptible movement, the razor sharp edge of a stone knife effortlessly opened Max's throat; severing his carotid artery. Blood sprayed from his neck.

Max couldn't help but wonder, "Wer'd dat knife com'frum?"

Sid watched helplessly as Max's blood drained down the slope of the beach towards the water, "Maxxss." he sobbed.

The hunters knew their roles. They set to work dismembering the now lifeless body of Max. The arms and legs were severed and packed. Then the head was removed and packed. The torso was opened up and the vital organs carefully removed. All were packed away except one.

The heart was left sitting in the chest cavity. This was the alpha's prize; devouring the spirit of his prey. He turned his icy stare to Sid and, almost taunting him, scooped the heart out of Max's chest and bit into it.

Jan led the group through scrub and rocks. She kept a brisk pace in an attempt to put some distance in between their group and the hunting pack. And she figured that they were only about an hour behind the pirates that had the others, so, she hoped to catch them before they made camp.

Sarah looked up at the late afternoon sun. It's brilliance dulled by the greenish brown sky above, "I can't believe what we did to this planet." she said.

"Pretty sad isn't it." Malinda replied.

"Makes me wonder what they were thinking. They had to see it happening."

"I'm sure they did."

"Well why didn't they stop it?"

"I think they talked themselves into believing it wasn't happening for so long that, by the time it got to the point that it was obvious, it was too late."

"I guess they weren't as smart back then as we are today."

"They were, but sometimes it takes more than just knowledge to get people to act."

The two continued looking at the sky as they walked. Their silent pondering was interrupted by the sound of Jan's alarm.

Jan stopped immediately, silenced the alarm and analyzed the information on her retinal HUD. She turned and looked toward the northeast horizon. A slight incline ran for about one hundred yards before dropping off. It was virtually barren with only small scrub and dead trees dotting its landscape. The small rise cloaked whatever was coming behind it, "I'm reading some bogies heading this way."

"How many are there?" Jack asked.

"I can't get a clear reading. They're on the other side of that hill."

"Canni's or Pirates?"

"They're moving too fast to be pirates."

Jack chambered a round, "Well, we have about 100 yards to work with here. I doubt they'll get closer than 50."

"We should spread out for a wider field of fire. Try to triangulate a bit," she turned to Malinda, "We only have a few minutes before they crest that hill," She pointed to the southeast, "go 25 yards and take up a prone position."

"You got it," Malinda replied and quickly moved southeast.

She turned to Jack and pointed northwest, "Do the same over there."

"Right."

"What do I do?" Sarah asked.

Jan replied, "Just stand behind me."

"So what? I'm bait?"

Jan felt a bit guilty after what Sarah had already been through but she knew nothing would get close, "Well, sort of. They won't get very close."

Sarah moved a few feet behind Jan, "So what's wrong with these people?"

"They're the surviving descendants of victims of Ural Synth Syndrome."

"I've never heard of that."

"It wasn't widespread. It was first noticed in a small mining village in the Ural Mountains in 2127. A synthetic organism they used to accelerate the breakdown of spent nuclear fuel suffered a radical mutation which allowed it to infect humans. It caused severe genetic damage to the victims and their offspring."

"So how did they get here?"

"The U.N. put them here to isolate the spread of the infection."

"And now they're cannibals?"

"They're so deformed I'd hesitate to even classify them as human. So they're probably not cannibals in the purest sense of the word. They don't eat their own,"

Jan looked down at the panel on her arm, "we should see them any second," and raised her gun toward the horizon.

A man's head popped up above the horizon. He was a man who was clearly familiar to Sarah, Jack and Malinda.

"Don't shoot!" Sarah yelled.

It was Jim! He was running at full speed and the sight almost brought Jack to tears. In his hands were four full bottles of what appeared to be whiskey.

Jack yelled, "Get down Jim!"

Jim heard the familiar voice. He had been running so long. It must have been his fatigued mind playing tricks on him. He turned his head toward Jack but kept running straight ahead. A few seconds later they saw why he was running so fast. A large group of cannibals were chasing him.

Malinda, Sarah and Jack all yelled, "Get down Jim!"

Jim was tired. He felt that, if this was a delusion, it was a very elaborate delusion, but, mostly he was just tired of running. He slid down to the ground and, without a second's hesitation, the bullets began to fly.

It took only a minute to lay waste to the pack of cannibals that had been chasing Jim. Laying there in a fetal position, he clutched his precious liquor close to his chest. He didn't dare move. He could barely catch his breath. He heard another familiar voice.

"Jim, you okay?" Malinda asked.

"More importantly, is that whiskey in those bottles

and is it okay?" Jack asked.

Jim opened his eyes. It was no delusion. Malinda and Jack were standing over him, "It's really you?"

"It is." Jack replied.

"Oh thank the gods!" Jim teared up, "I thought I was done for."

Sarah came running up to greet Jim while Jan checked the corpses to make sure they were down for good.

"Jim! I can't believe it!" Sarah dove on top of him; embracing him like someone she thought she would never see again.

Jack pulled his flask out, "Well, you're plenty alive, so, about that whiskey?"

Malinda had picked up Ricky's flask off the beach. She held it out, "Fill'er up for the lady too."

"Sure. Sure. You saved my life," Jim said as Sarah helped him to sit up.

"Hey, that's my flask!" Jack said.

"Yeah, I found it lying in the sand by that trap."

"That's not good."

"Well it's better than it being lost."

"Well, yeah, but that means Ricky has nothing."

"Shit, I guess the clock is ticking then."

Jan arrived, overhearing the last bit of their conversation and asked, "What clock is that?"

"Ricky's sobriety clock."

"What?"

"Our friend Ricky is an alcoholic."

"And you aren't?"

"Well... uh..." Jack choked, "yeah maybe."

Malinda came to his defense, "Look, we cope with things the best as we can. Don't you dare fucking judge us."

"I didn't mean any..."

Malinda cut her off, "You have no idea what we've gone through over the last few years."

"You're right. It's impossible for me to know. I'm sorry if I sounded judgmental."

"I'm sure you didn't mean anything by it." Jack said.

Malinda wasn't so sure. She glared at Jan, "Yeah, I'm sure."

Jim took the flask from Malinda. He took pride in his pour even in such a fatigued state. Carefully, he gave one of the bottles a twist; breaking the seal. He opened the flask and slowly poured until the flask was full. Not a drop was spilled. Jim was a true professional.

"Really, I've heard stories about the culture of Bravo Colony," Jan tried to explain, "I understand things were pretty hopeless up there. It's just different here."

"Different sure, but I haven't seen anything demonstrating that it's better." Malinda retorted.

"Well, not here that's for sure, but the people of Liberty Island are still trying. We haven't given up. That's why I'm here. I'm not here to judge you, but you should be aware that on the Island there are expectations. And more importantly - hope."

Malinda lifted the flask to her mouth and took a swig before handing it to Jack, "Do you remember what it was like to have hope?"

Jack took a swig and laughed, "Hell, I hoped every day that the duct tape would hold that reactor together!"

"Not exactly what I meant," Malinda turned to Jan, "Wait, why are you here?"

"Initially I was here to gather intel on the pirates. We're about to begin an operation to take them out."

Jack recalled Jan's earlier statement, "You said you knew me and had information about me, but we got sidetracked. Care to fill me in?"

"You're Jack Kemper. Mechanical Engineer. You helped design Bravo Colony with Sam Dillinger at General Dynamics."

"Okay, so you do know who I am."

"Your skills are quite valuable to Liberty Island. When they read your bio signature in the pod I was re-tasked to your recovery. Your file was transferred to me so that I could identify you."

"What if I don't want to go to Liberty Island?"

"It's your choice, although, I'm not sure why you wouldn't."

"I was just curious. I've heard a lot about your operation. I wouldn't be opposed to seeing it. And honestly if it looks good, well, it's not like I have better offers at the moment."

Jan smiled at Jack, "There is no better offer."

Malinda grabbed the flask and took another swig,

"So, what about Sarah, Jim and myself?"

"Look, whatever happens when we get back to the island; that's all up to the powers that be. I'm just following orders. I was asked to retrieve Jack, but I'm not going to leave you all behind. Clearly you have some military training that might be useful."

Malinda quickly moved past the last part of her comment, "And Ricky, Marie and Darrel?"

"That's where we're heading. They've been taken to a small camp just west of here.

"What's the distance to the camp?" Malinda asked.

Jan pointed to the ridge that rose up above the horizon to the west, "It's about a mile from that ridge. If we don't waste any time we should be able to get into position up there before dawn. Once the sun comes up and we get a good look in on the camp; we can work on a plan to rescue them."

Jan's alarm began to sound again, "Be quiet." she ordered. She scanned the horizon to the west, "We have a three bogeys heading this way."

"More of these canni's?" Sarah asked.

"Pirates."

Sarah coldly replied, "Give me a gun."

As Jan turned back to look at Sarah she noticed movement coming from the east as well, "Shit." she said quietly.

Malinda asked, "What is it?"

"Canni's from the East and pirates from the West. The gunfire must have drawn their attention."

"Not exactly what I'd like to be caught in the middle of." Jack replied.

"We need to move west."

"I thought you said there were pirates?" Sarah asked.

"I can get us by them. We need to put them in between us and the canni's."

"You suppose they're just gonna let us pass on by?" Jack snorted.

"You suppose my people sent me out here ill equipped for this situation?"

"Fair point."

"You all just go on without me. I can't run anymore." Jim said with a heavy dose of resignation in his voice.

Jack replied, "I totally understand, Jim."

This response caught the others off guard. Malinda was just about to chastise Jack's heartless tone when he continued, "You just hand over those bottles so I can get them to... uh... safety."

Jim looked down at his stock. An inner strength welled within him helping him rise to his feet, "Sorry Jack, I can't trust you with that responsibility. It's my duty to see that these get poured properly. Do you even know how long to let a 30 year old scotch breathe before you pour it?"

"It can breathe as it enters my mouth."

"Exactly. I can't allow that. This might be the last bottle of Glenfiddich on the damn planet."

"Okay then. Stay close. You drop and those bottles are mine."

THE TRIALS OF JACK KEMPER

Malinda smiled at Jack in appreciation of his motivational techniques. She turned to Jan and asked, "So, how are we going to do this?"

"I'll use my cloaking field. Everyone get close to me and stay within 5 feet. If you get out of range they'll see you."

Malinda was impressed, "You have a cloaking field?"

"Standard issue for recon."

"How long can you keep it up?"

"Probably one tenth of what I can manage." Jack remarked with a mischievous smile.

Sarah laughed, "You're awful."

Jan played along, "Jesus Jack, seriously? I'd like to see that. I can keep it up for about an hour."

Malinda replied, "Hmm. Sorry hon, but I think that's about 40 minutes longer than you."

Jim busted out in laughter, "Ouch!"

Jan tried to bring things back into focus, "Okay, okay, you drunkards, quiet down!"

Sarah looked toward Malinda and said, "I'm really starting to like her."

The others moved in around Jan. She raised her arm and swiped the control console. A shimmer expanded outwards from a unit on her back. Like a bubble it enveloped them; rendering them unseen from the outside.

"We'll move slowly west. Stay quiet. When the pirates get near we'll stop. Hopefully they'll pass us by."

The sun was beginning to set, but the heat and humidity were resilient even if they were no longer oppressive. A cadre of pirates was sent to retrace their path along the trail heading east; the gunfire, although not all that alarming, did merit further investigation.

These pirates were used to walking. They weren't the smartest nor were they the toughest, in fact they had very little skill at anything, and that's exactly what gets a man assigned to inland patrol, or as the port commander called it - buffer duty. The idea was to give the afflicted just enough to eat and keep them from making their way to the port.

Jack would later say that he could have been drinking buddies with these pirates if the situation was different. They had very similar interests after all. Drinking and fucking. And neither party was all that discerning about the quality of their vice.

"Oi Jones, if'n Max'n Sid's out'ere wit dat red'ed oi tink oim gon 'ave a go at'r."

"Yeh, 'dat soun's goot, Finny," came Jones' reply from behind him.

"En' if she'ded, 'opeflee she still'fresh."

Jones chuckled at Finny, "Wut d'ya 'tink they's shoot'n at?"

"Prolly, sum'cannis."

"Canni's dun use'ly com'down 'dis fah."

"'Dey cood'a bin'trakn 'dem all'dis way."

"Mehbe."

The cooling temperature allowed a green haze to condense over the area. It had an odd shimmering quality as the last rays of the setting sun filtered through it. They played with a man's vision and made it hard to focus as they danced from particle to particle. The world could be a truly beautiful apocalyptic nightmare at times.

Finny shielded his eyes and squinted towards the eastern ridge. He didn't see any sign of Sid, Max or Sarah. He squinted even harder as if to give himself super vision. It worked! He saw fast movement coming down the western slope. Unfortunately, even though he couldn't quite make out who it was, he knew immediately it wasn't Sid or Max. The only thing that moved that fast were the afflicted. He assumed the worst case scenario; a hunting party.

"Oi, cannis cum'n dun'da ridge," he alerted the others, "Take'cov'r, ee'll mow'm dun'fore 'dey git close."

Jones spotted a creek bed ahead of them. He pointed and hollered to the others, "Oi, up'dere."

The three pirates scrambled forward into the creek bed where they instantly realized that this was a terrible idea. While the afternoon heat had dried the surface of the creek bed, it had only dried the surface. The recent storm had been soaked up by the creek like a thirsty sponge leaving the underlying bed a thick viscous mud.

It took all of their effort to pull their feet out of the mud once they had stepped in and why they didn't just turn around and wait for the afflicted on their side of the creek was anyone's guess. As noted earlier they weren't the brightest creatures and, truth be told, some men at the port openly wondered who was more intelligent; the inland patrol or the afflicted. They continued to slog along, however, and struggled to reach the other side where they took up firing positions along the bank.

Finny peaked over the edge of the berm and saw that the afflicted were close, in fact, they were too close. They were practically on top of him. He yelled, "Awe fook! Fir'ya coonts!" and opened fire. The pirate's nervous shots rang harmlessly off the ground around the afflicted while the onrushing creatures weaved erratically to avoid being hit.

Jones finally managed to drop one. It crashed to the ground and slid to a stop just a few feet in front of him. He quickly took aim at another and tensed his finger on the trigger, but before he could fire off the next shot he was surprisingly tackled by another hunter. They flew backwards into the muddy creek bed, but Jones' reaction was swift. A vicious blow to the creature's head with the butt of his rifle knocked it senseless for a second and it slumped into the mud. Jones struggled to pull himself out of the mud and to his feet. He at least wanted to get to his knees.

Not a single one of Finny's shots had landed on target, but he was ready for the creature that lunged at him. He used his rifle while pivoting to deflect the attack. The creature's momentum carried it over the berm, and over Finny, where it landed solidly in the mud of the creek bed.

It somehow managed to remain upright and quickly

pulled a stone knife from a sheath hung around its torso. It let out a growl and pounded its chest. A necklace of bones and teeth rattled. Surely this was an attempt to intimidate Finny.

Finny swung his rifle wildly missing the creature. It ducked the attack and lunged at Finny with a counter attack. The force of the blow knocked him back against the berm and the knife, true to its nature, was driven deep into his side.

Jones had always been a fan of mud wrestling. Before being reassigned to inland patrol he had even won a few Friday night contests against some of the stronger women in port. At least on those nights his reward was free drinks. All he'd get for winning this fight was the right to carry on the struggle of daily life. In the back of his head he almost wanted to resign.

The pair writhed in the mud of the creek bed. A thick slime coated each of them. It was hard, nearly impossible, to get a grip. But, in these conditions and with his Friday night experiences, he knew his strength could be used to his advantage. He locked his legs around the waist of the creature and head butted it as hard as he could. The stunning blow was all that it took to give Jones the opening he needed. He grabbed his attacker by the head and drove his thumbs through its eyes.

Jones was exhausted, but none the less, managed to get himself into a standing position and began to look around. All he saw were the dead bodies of friend and foe. He then heard the suction of muddy footsteps behind him. He turned to see the largest and meanest creature he had ever seen with a knife plunging down in an arch towards him. Jones ducked his head and raised his arms to defend himself from the blow. There was a report off in the distance. The blow never landed.

He lowered his arms and wiped the mud from his eyes. The creature's body laid at his feet with a bullet hole in one side of its head and the other side completely missing. He turned to see where the shot came from. He was hoping to see Finny. Instead he was greeted by five people who appeared to magically materialize from thin air. One of them pointed a rifle in his direction. The sound of a second shot would have rung in his ears if he could have heard it.

CHAPTER 11

It had been a long walk back to the camp. And it was also a total buzz killer. Ricky was stone cold sober. He marveled at how the unbearable afternoon heat of the previous day was so profusely countered by the pre-dawn chill that caused his bones to ache. It made him long for the consistent environmental temperance of the colony; and a buzz.

The pirates used a small, hand rowed, skiff to ferry the group across a canal to a small dock. A couple of larger motorized skiffs were also tied to the dock. There was a well-worn dirt path that led from the dock toward the main camp which was surrounded by a ten foot fence topped off with razor wire.

The group approached the camp's entrance gate with Chappy in the lead. He yelled, "Oi ya dirty fooks gid'up 'n open da'gate!"

There were several shacks along the perimeter surrounding a few larger well-made buildings in the center. A rather large drunken pirate stumbled out of the shack nearest the gate, "O'right. O'right, dun git'yer pan'ees in a bunch lil'goil."

Chappy growled at the man, "Lil'goil? Lil'goil is'it?"

"Das roight," the pirate stooped down to Chappy's level and flexed, "Joos got'a prol'm wit dat?"

Chappy began to laugh, "Shite Ernie. Ow's joo get so big eat'n goat?"

"Tis da'ball jooses, Chaps."

"'Ow's dat?"

"Dey 'as da'vitmens in'em."

Chappy's face recoiled in disgust, "Ugh, I not'eatn no goat'nuts, mate."

"Goot! Mor'fer me den," Ernie said as he unlocked the gate and pushed it open.

Chappy turned toward the group and pointed toward Darrel, "O'right toike da tough'n to da meat lock'r, Otis," he then gestured toward Marie and Ricky, "lock dos'utters up. An' if'n anyun spoils'er 'for I wake up, dey get'n dealt wif by'me!"

Jan and the group took up a position on the west side of a large ridge that overlooked the pirate's camp. The ridge was only about one mile away from the camp and the elevation offered them the perfect perch to scope out a plan. They settled in for a long watch just as the first rays of the sun began to crest over the top of the ridge.

Jan said, "Welcome to my world. I moved inland a few days ago and started watching this place. Their larger base is a port about three miles west at the mouth of the bay."

"How many have you seen stationed here?" Jack asked.

"At most they'll have thirty guys here. And we already took out some of them," Jan pointed to the huts on the periphery of the camp, "See those huts?"

"Yeah," Jack replied.

"That's where the men sleep. I believe the two larger buildings at the center of the camp are a mess hall and probably the brig. The fence around the camp should be easy enough to penetrate. It already has a few holes. And there's some livestock that mills about."

"Do I see boats?" Jack asked.

"I haven't seen them move since I've been here. I don't think any of them are in working order."

Jack produced a spanner and a roll of duct tape from his tool belt, "Give me five minutes and we'll have a ride."

"That's great. The problem is the path out. They have fortified positions along the channel between here and the outer bay. At the port they have three old Navy destroyers and a number of heavy gun emplacements."

"Wow. That's impressive."

Jan gestured to the south and continued, "That canal only has two outposts but it is impassable."

"Why is that?"

"The pirates have sunk steel pylons into the bed of the canal in several spots. It prevents any boats from entering or, in this case, leaving in that direction."

"Neither route would be an easy trek for us in one of those little skiffs."

"Is there another option?" Malinda asked.

"I suggest we wait for my team to come get us. They'll have to fight their way in but they always come through."

"So, we wait?"

"Yes."

The Marine Mechanized Assault Chassis (MMAC) was developed through years of private military research at General Dynamics in the former United States. The MMAC is an exoskeleton covered in reactive armor that carries a full complement of the most advanced weaponry. In its bipedal mode it measures just over 18 feet in height with a width of 7 feet and, as if that wasn't enough to strike fear into any ground combat opponent, it also has the capability to convert into air combat mode where it's slightly shorter and broader. It is capable of sustained air and ground based combat in a myriad of environments. Essentially, it's a tank that can maneuver like a dragonfly.

Sgt. "Oddball" MacIntyre eased off the throttle and levelled out after breaking through the cloud cover into the sunlit, midday sky. From this view, his MMAC appeared to be skipping along the tops of the clouds. It was a peculiarly menacing sight.

He was joined by Cpl. "Steel" Richards who moved into position on his port side. Petty Officer "Doc" Daniels piloted the support craft into the formation. Corporal's "Bean" Fuentes and "Junior" Lawson brought up the rear.

"That guy is going to need some therapy after what he just went through." Bean said.

"No kidding. He was trussed up like a hog for roasting," Junior replied, "an apple in his mouth and a piece of celery sticking out of his ass. That's just not right."

"There are some things you just can't un-see."

Steel's voice crackled in their headsets, "Sounds like every other night for you, Junior."

"Wait, wait, wait, I'm not into vegetables. I would have drawn the line at the celery."

"Seriously, at the celery?"

"Hey, there's something about being trussed up like that and surrendering to someone else completely."

"What the fuck, Junior," Steel cut in, "You are one fucked up individual."

"No kidding." Bean agreed.

Doc finally spoke up, "Sgt. MacIntyre?"

"Go ahead Doc," Sgt. MacIntyre had been shaking his head as he listened to the conversation between the Marines under his command.

"As the medic of this unit, I officially recommend that Cpl. Lawson receive a psych eval to determine the depths of his 'perversions'."

"Agreed, and noted. There'll be no perverts in my unit."

"Wait…what?" Junior's surprise and apprehension

was evident.

"I'm sorry son, but if there's one thing I can't stand it is perverts."

"Sarge, seriously? I was only fucking with Bean and Steel"

"Corporal's Fuentes and Richards, do you think Lawson was joking?"

"He sounded believable to me," Bean reported, her efforts to sound serious while smiling failed miserably.

"I concur with Bean's assessment." Steel added.

"You fuckers!" Junior lashed out at his peers.

"That'll be enough Corporal," The stern warning from Sgt. MacIntyre putting an end to the conversation for now.

Off in the distance, the L.I.S. Elon was barely visible to the naked eye. Its shape and naturally reflective surfaces made it blend in with the surrounding clouds. One would need to know where and what to look for in order to find it in the blue, white and gray patchwork of the sky before them.

Sgt. MacIntyre keyed the communications channel open, "Guardian, this is Reaper 1, requesting clearance for landing."

"Verifying I.F.F sequence." The response came from the Elon's flight controller. After a short pause the controller continued, "Sequence confirmed, approach heading two-five, landing bay three."

"Aye, aye, heading two-five, bay three," Sgt. MacIntyre updated his navigation system with the information then switched back to the squad channel, "If everyone is done going over Junior's perversions, we've received clearance to land. Navigation information is transmitting now."

"Aye, aye," returned the unified response of the Reaper squad Marines.

Captain Dent was enjoying lunch and conversation at the Captain's table in the Mess Hall. His meals were carefully scheduled with a rotation of those that served under him. All ranks were included. The captain felt that sharing a meal was the best way to get a feel for what was happening among the ranks.

The captain encouraged his people to speak freely while at his table. He would insist, "There's no rank at my table," at the start of every meal. Of course, he would regret it on the rare occasion. And usually those occasions included Junior and Bean.

"Captain Dent, sir," a voice came through his communications implant.

The captain excused himself from the conversation with his lunch guests. He stood up, "Please excuse me." and took a few steps away from the table.

He spoke, "Go ahead."

"Response Team One has returned."

"Thank you, Ensign. Have Lieutenant Commander Dubois meet me on the bridge in 10"

"Aye, aye sir"

He returned to the table and his guests, "I'm sorry but I must cut my lunch short, please enjoy the rest of the meal. I look forward to continuing our discussion another time," he put his cap on, cordially tipped it and then turned to leave.

Reaper Squadron reached the controlled airspace around the Elon within moments while they methodically moved into a formation that would allow Doc's support craft, the Archangel, to take the lead position.

The Archangel was almost always the first to dock. The rare exception to that rule would be a damaged MMAC that required immediate landing. Doc usually carried a rescue or someone in need of medical assistance. He gracefully took the lead and slowed the craft to docking speed as he positioned it directly in line with the opening to the hangar bay.

Doc was not only a skilled medic, but also an exceptional pilot. Under the control of his experienced hands the Archangel gently maneuvered into position as he reduced thrust. The Elon's deck chief helped Doc find its final landing position and the craft gently settled onto its skids.

"Archangel is secure." Doc reported

"Copy that," Sgt. MacIntyre called out the clearance, "Steel, Junior. You're good to go."

"Aye, Aye, Sarge." the two MMAC pilots replied.

Bean watched Steel and Junior begin their docking maneuver, "Sarge, why is it that we're always last?"

Steel interjected, "Because we don't want to be stuck out there in a holding pattern while you crash into the dock."

"Yeah, you know that's gonna happen." Junior added.

Sgt. MacIntyre spoke up, "It's because Steel and

Junior can't seem to dodge the flack worth a shit, Bean, best to get them in before they fall out of the sky."

Bean burst into laughter, "Ouch! Noted Sarge."

The activity in landing bay three was always frenzied after docking. As the crews worked through their post flight checks, Oddball jumped down onto the flight deck where he was met by an very eager Junior, "Sarge, let me take over that post flight for you. I noticed one of your thrust actuators had a tremor in it. Wouldn't want that to fail in a firefight."

The crusty Scotsman knew exactly what this was about and decided to play along, "Thanks for taking the initiative Junior. A tremor in one of the thrust actuators eh?" He rubbed his stubbly chin in mock contemplation, "Now that you mention it, I did notice a slight lag in the flight controls during our return flight."

"Let me get someone to take a look at it."

"Sounds good," Sgt. MacIntyre decided to take it a bit farther, "oh and Corporal, it looks like there's an awful lot of carbon residue on some of those joints. Think you can take a look at that while you're having the thrust actuator checked?"

Junior continued to fall all over himself, "Definitely, I'll get it all cleaned up."

Sgt. MacIntyre began to walk across the deck towards the flight room. He barked back towards Junior and the others, "Debrief in 30."

"Aye, aye. Sarge." They replied.

Doc double timed it across the deck to catch up with the sergeant, "Sarge, you're not going to actually submit Junior for a psych eval, are you? I wasn't being serious when I recommended it."

Sgt. MacIntyre turned to face Doc wearing a big smirk on his face. It was all he could do not to laugh, "Of course not, Doc, it's all just patter, but I might as well get some work out of him before he figures it out."

"Well played, Sarge." he replied.

Oddball put his hand on Doc's shoulder, "Besides, if I turned in Junior for being a dafty, I'd have to turn in the whole lot of you," and gave him a shake and continued on his way.

Lieutenant Commander Dubois was already on the Elon's bridge in discussion with First Officer De'Goya when Captain Dent arrived. F.O. De'goya barked, "Captain on deck!" and everyone snapped to attention.

Captain Dent moved quickly to his command console at the center of the bridge. As he sat he replied, "At ease."

F.O. De'Goya and Lt. Cdr. Dubois approached the captain and took positions to each side. Lt. Cdr. Dubois spoke first, "Sir."

"Sorry about the early wake up Lieutenant Commander."

"No apologies necessary, Sir." Lt. Cdr. Dubois gestured with his hand and a holographic chart appeared in front of the captain, "Here is the navigational and weather information for our route to Tasmania."

The captain stared hard at the chart and studied the information as Lt. Cdr. Dubois briefed him, "The chemical front that pushed through 24 hours ago has weakened and moved south of our plotted course. Satellites and terrestrial sensors don't indicate any additional disturbances for the next couple of days. We should make Tasmania in 10 hours, putting us within deployment range by 06:00 zulu, 17:00 local time."

The captain glanced at his watch, "That's good time," he turned to the First Officer, "Any updates on the Reapers recovery mission?"

F.O. De'Goya answered, "We just received the report, sir. The primary target was recovered successfully. There were no other survivors."

The captain pursed his lips, "Bloody savages."

Otis stood in the center of a primitive wooden hut. It had one small window that allowed just enough light in. It had a dirt floor and a blood stained table that sat along one wall. Several indelicate looking tools took up space on the table. Otis snarled, "Welcomes 'oo Otis's play'ouse."

Darrel was bound at his wrists, with his hands above his head, by a rope that was attached to a log in the roof. His face was already swollen from yesterday's beatings to a point that only one eye could open. He snarled at Otis, "Don't choke on the third person there fella," and spat.

Otis looked around, "Wher's dey at?"

"In your fucking head you moron."

"Oi's we gun 'ave a goo'time ain't we?"

"Why don't you just tell me what you want?"

"A'ight, leh's starcha wit an easy one. oo's yeh

wit?"

"Bravo Colony." Darrel replied.

"En' erre's dat den?"

"It was in orbit. I doubt much of it is left."

"En' da spoice?"

"Right."

Otis didn't like that answer. He punched Darrel in the stomach, "Oo's gun pay fer yeh den?"

"Nobody."

Otis didn't like that answer either. Darrel once again became his punching bag. The hut was filled with deafening screams as pain set in on top of pain.

Jack had been sitting on the ridge for several hours. The hours were filled by blood curdling screams emanating from the camp. There was no doubt in Jack's mind that it was Darrel screaming. He couldn't even imagine what was being done to make him cry out like that. It was becoming ever harder for Jack to contain his rage. It wasn't something he felt often so he had little experience in trying to control it.

Malinda tried to steady Jack by putting her arm around him. In truth, she was just as furious as he was. Her mind raced with visions of violence; acts that she could only hope to perpetrate soon.

Sarah couldn't stand it any longer. She had cried all the tears she had to cry. She spoke up, "We have to do something."

Malinda agreed. She turned to Jan and said, "She's right, we can't just sit here and let them torture our friends."

THE TRIALS OF JACK KEMPER

Jack added, "We have 8 mags. That's 240 bullets, about 20 bullets for each one of them by my math."

"And he's an engineer. He can do math." Sarah said.

Jan was feeling powerless. There's no way she was going to be able to talk them down. And they had the guns. It's not like she didn't understand. If those were members of her team she'd feel the same exact way, "My team is still about 3 hours out. They haven't even engaged the harbor yet."

Jack replied, "Some things just can't wait, Jan."

"Okay, look. It's going to take us about two hours to get inside. We need to head south so that we can cross the river unseen. If we can just wait a couple of hours that would put us there right around dusk."

"Jan, we need to go now." Malinda said.

"I know. I know you do. But we need to coordinate the fight with my team. If we go in before they engage the port forces then the port will send reinforcements. We'll have no chance. You'll have no chance. The friends you want to save will have no chance. It's failed before it even began."

The group looked back and forth at each other for a valid response. None of them could come up with one. She made perfect sense. Jack looked toward Malinda, "There's no point in getting them out if we all die in the process." He resigned himself to waiting. He turned to Jan, "I'll give your team three hours. I'm not waiting 'til dusk."

"Thank you, Jack."

"We're moving now." Jack gave the order, "We'll be ready the minute they engage."

Ricky had been placed in a crude holding cell in one of the other primitive huts in the camp. He was sitting on the dirt floor struggling to keep it together. The shakes were in full control of his muscles. He hadn't gone twelve hours without a drink in nearly twenty years. Hell, he hadn't gone longer than five hours without a drink.

Marie was in the cell next to him. She knew exactly what Ricky was going through. He was treading in dangerous waters. He could have a seizure at any moment, "You okay, Ricky?"

"I'll be fine."

Their guard sat at a crudely made table where he incessantly spun a knife to kill time. He was short man that stood barely five feet tall, however, he had quite a bit of muscle built on top of his small frame. He was cleaner than most of the other pirates as well. And, apparently, he liked to keep his cells quiet, "Oi, joo shut yer faces o'er dere."

Marie replied, "He's having withdrawals."

"Witdrawerls?"

"He's an alcoholic," she looked at Ricky, "Sorry, Ricky."

"O, e'ryone's a drinka 'ere'."

The guard stood up and walked over to Ricky's cell, "Ey?" he kicked the bars, "Dat tru'? Joo nee'a drink?"

"I...I really do." Ricky stuttered.

"O, o'roight. Leh's 'ave a chat."

The guard opened Ricky's cell door and helped him up and over to the table. It was a strangely compassionate move that caught Marie off guard, "Thank you." she said.

The guard walked over to a cabinet and pulled out two glasses and a jug. He placed a glass in front of Ricky and sat down on the other side of the table. He popped the cork out of the jug and poured himself a drink.

"Where's ya from?" the guard asked.

"Bravo Colony."

He chugged his drink, "En' whers dat den?"

"Space."

"Oi, yer a spoiceman? Oi, i ne'er drank wit a spoiceman b'fur," he said as poured a bit in Ricky's glass.

Ricky immediately gulped it down, "Oh, fuck that's terrible!"

The guard had a laugh, "yeh, is da'piss," as he poured himself another one.

"Piss?"

"Aye, tit piss."

"You mean milk?"

He chugged his drink again, "Was'dat?"

"Never mind," he said as the alcohol hit his bloodstream. It was a sweet relief, "Might I get another?"

"If'n ya tells me oo's gun pay fer yehs."

"Pay? Like a ransom?"

"uh recov'ry fee."

Ricky looked at Marie unsure how to answer their captor. As their eyes met, he winked at Marie and turned back to the guard, "Oh Yeah, of course good sir. They'd be happy to pay!" Ricky tapped his glass on the table expecting a pour.

The guard filled Ricky's glass, "So's oo's dey n 'ow do's we conta't 'em?" he asked.

Ricky raised his glass, "Cheers mate," and took a drink, "oh my, that goes down a bit easier the second time around." He smiled, "I'm sure if you were to contact the Tennessee Regional Authority they'd be more than happy to pay whatever egregious amount you were to demand. Tell them you rescued the Mayor of Iron City," and he promptly polished off the second glass of liquor.

Jan had extended her cloak once again as the group moved through dying trees and scrub towards the pirate camp. She stopped as her nearfield radar began to light up her HUD. They were just out of visual range of the camp, "The camp is just up ahead."

The screams had, thankfully, stopped a few hours back. Jack wanted desperately to get on with it and help his dear friends. He looked intensely at Jan, "Where's your team?" he asked.

"I'll check," she poked at the panel on her left arm, "Guardian, this is Recon 1, status check please."

First Officer De'Goya approached the Captain, "Excuse me sir, Recon 1 has contacted us and is requesting our status."

The Captain stared intently through the large windows of the command deck, "Thank you, Commander," he continued, "Lieutenant Commander Dubois!" He spoke without breaking his focus.

Lt. Cdr. Dubois responded while concentrating on the navigation console, "Sir?"

"What is our position and ETA for the port?"

Lieutenant Dubois picked up a small translucent screen from the desk in front of him. With a few swipes and pokes he retrieved the most current information, "Sir, we are currently 10 nautical miles from the port. At our current speed and heading we should arrive in 15 minutes."

"Commander De'Goya, report to Recon 1 that the engagement will commence in 15 minutes."

F.O. De'Goya replied, "Aye, aye, Sir," then turned quickly on her heel and returned to her position at the communications terminal.

Captain Dent continued, "Tactical! What's the intel on the port defenses?"

"Sir," replied Tactical Officer Mueller, "based on the information gathered by Corporal Stoudt the port is primarily defended by one Australian Navy Hobart class destroyer, one Russian Buyan class missile ship, and an American Littoral class frigate. They are supported by several dozen small craft, mostly former fishing vessels, whose main armaments are made up of line of sight weaponry. We are currently tracking all targets and continue to scan for additional threats."

"Thank you Lieutenant. Sound battle stations!" Captain Dent commanded, "Ready the infrared smoke and high explosive missile batteries. Target their ship and shore based armaments!"

"Aye, aye, Sir," T.O. Mueller replied. She punched a sequence of buttons on the terminal in front of her. The lights on the bridge changed to red. The Elon's intercom system began to broadcast a sequence of tones that indicated battle stations to the crew and all non-essential personnel left the bridge and reported to their assigned posts, "Sir, IR and HE batteries charged and ready. All targets locked." she reported.

"Good, set the Reapers loose!" the Captain ordered.

The flight room was a large comfortable area that the pilots used to gear up and go over mission details. Two walls of the room, opposite each other, were lined with large locker stalls where the pilots stowed their combat gear between each mission. Each pilot had their own locker, the placement of which was designated by their position in the flight formation.

Along one wall of the room was a large three dimensional holographic image which had the latest flight plans, tactical analysis, objectives and environmental data on display. Sergeant MacIntyre stood within the hologram, "Okay Reapers, let's go over your assignments." Oddball bellowed with a thick Scottish accent, "Bean, you're with me." He began to point to objectives that were labeled in the image, "Our objective is to mop up the destroyer after the HE batteries do their job."

"Aye aye, Sarge" Bean responded.

THE TRIALS OF JACK KEMPER

"Steel, Junior."

"Sarge?" they spoke in unison.

"You finish off the frigates and clear out any smaller craft. I don't want anything sneaking up my ass from those glorified fish trawlers they're sporting."

"Aye, aye, nothing up the ass, Sarge." Junior responded.

Steel looked at Junior, "You sure, Junior? I got some celery..."

"Alright, you two. Enough. Let's focus! Doc, you'll follow in the Archangel. You're tasked with providing additional covering fire and rescue support for Corporal Stoudt and her civilians."

Sgt. MacIntyre looked at the team in front of him, "Any questions?"

"Negative Sarge." they replied together.

"Good, let's move," he turned and headed out of the flight room onto the hangar deck.

The remaining members of Reaper Squad stood and followed him as they finished shrugging on their assault harnesses. They wasted no time jumping into their cockpits to get strapped in. The flight crews buzzed as pre-flight checks went off like clockwork with each step carefully coordinated by their crew chiefs.

"Reaper squad, check in," the voice of Sgt. MacIntyre crackled over their headsets.

"Reaper 1, I have you five by five." Bean reported.

"Reaper 2, Feel the Steel." Steel growled.

Junior replied, "Reaper 3, comms are lickin' chickin',"

his southern drawl accentuating the last two words.

There was a brief moment of silence in the headset. Sgt. MacIntyre repeated the request, "Reaper Support, comms check?"

Doc's' voice eventually sounded, "This is Reaper Support, finishing pre-flight. Comms are good."

Sgt. MacIntyre changed his comms channel, "Guardian. This is Reaper Squad. We are ready to deploy."

Jan, once again, brought the nearfield radar up on her HUD. The outlines of pirates appeared superimposed on the horizon, "Alright, my team is about to engage the port."

Jack could feel his pulse quicken, "So we can move?" he asked.

Jan had been wracking her brain for a way to keep Jack out of harm's way. She didn't want to risk the recovery of an asset fighting a bunch of pirates for what her superiors would consider "non-essentials", "Yeah we can move, but I've been thinking. It might be good if we could get one of those skiffs. You know - just in case."

"Probably not a bad idea," Jack looked at Jim, "What do you think, Jim? Can you handle that?"

Jan interrupted, "I was thinking you could do that Jack."

"Me? I'm going to get my friends."

"I get that, but it doesn't do any good to get them if we run into reinforcements and can't get away."

Malinda said, "She has a point."

"If they send more, we'll shoot them." Jack protested.

Malinda shook her head in disagreement, "We only have 8 mags, Jack, and 2 of those will be with Jim and Sarah."

"So, who's going in?"

Jan pointed to Malinda, "Malinda and I can handle the rescue."

"What about me?" Sarah asked.

"We need you and Jim to watch the perimeter. If they send reinforcements they'll be coming up this canal from their camp in the South."

"So let me get this shit straight. You and Malinda get to go in shooting up these assholes and I get to stand here watching water with Jim?"

Jim chimed in, "Sounds like a good plan to me. You know they'll be shooting back, right?"

"So I just stand here?" Sarah puzzled out loud.

Jan replied, "Well, really you should hide."

"Hide?"

Jack put his hand on Sarah's shoulder, "Hey, look Sarah, we're not doing this for ourselves. We just want to get our friends and ourselves out safe. If you don't have to risk your life then you shouldn't feel like you need to."

Sarah felt dejected, "I know but..."

"Don't worry, Sarah. I'll shoot a couple for you," Malinda couldn't help but smile as she cycled the chamber on her rifle.

"Jack, give Malinda your ammo," Jan reasoned

that if Jack didn't have anything to shoot at the pirates then it would be less likely the pirates would have a reason to shoot back at him.

"Right," He took the clip out of his rifle and began to hand it to her, but then a thought occurred to him, "Wait, what will I have?" he said.

Jan replied, "Duct tape and a spanner. You have one job."

"Well shit, I hope nobody starts shooting at me."

"If they do, yell and we'll be on it." she said.

"Right, that makes me feel warm and fuzzy."

Jan took a canister out of her leg pouch and held it out towards Jack, "See the button on top? If anyone starts to mess with you, press the button, count to 3 and toss it over their head."

Jack took the canister, "And what will that do?"

"Oh, it will be a shocking experience I assure you. Make sure you're not too close."

In between bouts of unconsciousness, Darrel had worked on loosening the ropes that bound him. At least he thought he was. He couldn't be sure. His fingers had gone numb hours ago and blood had dried his eyes shut.

Otis paced in front of Darrel, "'Ell if nobo'ys gun poay, wha reason oo I 'ave ta feed ya?"

It was hard, if not nearly impossible, for Darrel to speak. His lips were busted open and swollen to twice their size, "I'm a doctor. I'm sure you idiots get sick or better yet, wounded."

"Aye, we's do 'ave wounded."

THE TRIALS OF JACK KEMPER

"I could probably help those men," even though he had been cut on, pissed on and beaten for hours on end; He meant it.

"Nd why 'ould we trust joo?"

"I'm not interested in dying."

"'Ell dat's a point. Okay, I'll's run'it by Chappy."

Darrel was honestly shocked that Otis was capable of such reasoning. It didn't matter. He would still kill him on the first opportunity that presented itself.

Jan and Malinda had made their way through the scrub to the southeastern corner of the camp. They watched as the others slowly and stealthily moved up the bank of the canal toward the southwest of the camp. A patrolling pirate walked north along the inside of the fence. They waited for their opportunity.

The pirate turned and disappeared behind a building. This prompted Jan into action. She said to Malinda, "Wait here. I'll cut the fence." and activated her cloak. She moved to the fence and pulled a "knife like" device from a sheath on her right leg. It took her only a few seconds to slice a four foot high triangle in the fence. The metal fence melted like butter as the blade passed through it.

Malinda immediately ran up and ducked through the hole, taking up a defensive stance just on the other side. Jan followed.

Jack and the others stopped when they got to the last thicket of scrub between the canal and the camp. They could see a dock about eighty yards ahead. There was a small shack near it. Jack pointed to it, "I assume that's a maintenance shed." he said.

There was a small hut near their current position with an attached pen of sickly looking goats. Sarah said, "Looks like that's where they keep their livestock. Think it has chickens inside?"

Jim raised his nose into the air and smelled something familiar, "Doesn't smell like chicken to me." he said.

Sarah joked, "I hope it is. I could go for some chicken," and her stomach audibly rumbled on cue.

Jack reached over, rubbed her belly and spoke directly to it, "Tell me about it," he continued, "I think this is the best spot for you guys. You'll have cover. You'll have a clear line of sight to the dock and be able to watch the canal from here."

Sarah sighed, "Alright Jack," she had resigned herself to being a bystander.

For some reason Jim's eyes were fixated on the shed, "Good luck, Jack." he said.

Jack gave a nod and moved off toward the canal. He figured the easiest way to get to the docks unnoticed was to float there.

Ricky had a nice buzz going. As it turned out; fermented goats milk was quite potent. His guard had been pouring the drinks quite liberally, happy with the prospect of a big payday, and Ricky's brain was finally firing on all cylinders now that it was properly fueled once again.

"I'll tell you what. I bet you'll be able to update your whole camp with the money you get." Ricky said.

"Oi, dat be groit. Moybe 'e'll bouy sum loidies fer fun."

"That's a great idea! There's nothing better than a hard working woman. If you know what I mean?" Ricky winked.

"Aye, aye! I 'aven't 'ad a las in..." he strained to think, "'ell, too long!"

Ricky motioned toward Marie, "Maybe we should get that pretty thing over there out? She looks like a lot of fun to me."

"Oi, now yer tinkin. A litt'l innertainment be noice."

Marie was shocked, "Ricky! What the fuck?"

"'M glad oi dint 'ave ta kill yeh."

The guard stood up. It took more effort than he expected. He wobbled a bit and steadied himself by leaning on the table. He tried to shake his head clear. He took a step and staggered. It was with great focus and effort that he eventually made it to Marie's cell where he propped himself up against the cell door, "Now joo's list'n. Joo look fun. Ploy noice n der wown be no beatin. O'roight?"

Marie backed up to the rear of her cell, "Oh there's going to be a beatin' all right."

"Oi, foisty!" he let out a drunken laugh, "Oi loike foisty!" He reached into one of his pockets looking for the key and seemed a bit bewildered when he didn't find it. He patted on his shirt even though it had no pockets and then figured out they might be in his other pants pocket. They were. He was very pleased with himself. He held them up and smiled at Marie. It took a few tries for him to get the keys into the keyhole, but eventually he managed to do so and started to unlock the cell.

While the guard was searching for the keys, Ricky continued to sit at the table as if nothing was happening, calmly picked up the jug from off of the table and filled both glasses, after which, he stood up and began walking toward the cell. He smiled at Marie and then smashed the thick ceramic jug over the guard's head. The blow, along with a high level of intoxication, rendered the guard unconscious and he collapsed in a heap.

Ricky grabbed the guard's feet and pulled him out of the way while apologizing, "Sorry about that Marie. I needed him to turn his back to me," Ricky felt he may have taken it a bit too far, especially since Marie had no way of knowing what he had planned.

Marie angrily pushed the cell door open, "I picked up on that, Ricky. No worries. I know you're not like that." She walked straight over to the table, picked up the glass and took a few rather large gulps, "Oh my god! You weren't kidding! Wow, that's something."

Ricky said with a little chuckle, "Give it a few seconds to kick in. The next drink won't be so bad." He picked up his glass and took a drink.

Jim and Sarah were hiding behind a small solitary shrub that clung to life on the bank of the canal. The goats were strangely attracted to them and Sarah wasn't happy they were drawing attention, "Shoo!"

she said quietly.

"I don't think that works on goats." Jim replied.

"We should shoot them."

Jim was caught off guard by what seemed to be an overreaction, "The goats?"

"Yes, they're drawing attention to us."

"Don't you think gunshots would do that?"

"You're right. Maybe a big rock?"

Jim's eyes widened. He couldn't believe what he was hearing, "Wait, you want to bash each of these in the head?"

"They're going to get us killed."

Of the four bottles Jim was holding he carefully placed three of them in the shrub and covered them the best he could. The one bottle he continued to hold was the opened one. He twisted off the cap and took a big swig. He held it out for Sarah, "You need a drink." He knew his clientele.

"Oh, thanks!" Sarah's mind quickly ignored the goats and focused on the drink.

Jim was far more shrewd than most people would give him credit for. Decades of bartending experience had given him a keen insight into the minds of men - and ladies. Years of brewing his own stock had also given him keen insight into distilleries. He could smell one a mile away; even over goats.

"Damn, that's good!" Sarah said as she screwed the top back on the bottle.

"Okay, now that you're thinking straight - listen."

"Sure."

"Do you smell that sweetness in the air?"
"I smell goat shit."
"Yeah, of course, but underneath all that?"
"Nope, just goat shit."
"Okay," Jim pointed to the roof of the nearby hut, "see that chimney?"
"Yes."
"I'm betting there's a still in there."
"A still?"
"For making spirits."
Sarah's eyes lit up, "Oh, you mean there's booze in there?"
"Probably so."
Sarah quickly forgot about her duties to watch the perimeter, after all, there was a possibility that booze was at stake! "Let's go see!"

Darrel's continued struggles with his bindings had rubbed his wrists raw and bloody and while he could feel the ropes loosen, the resulting blood provided the small bit of lubrication he needed to free himself completely.

Otis hadn't taken notice of Darrel's efforts. He was focused on the conversation he was having with another cohort. After a few minutes, the other man nodded at Otis and walked out the door. Otis turned to face Darrel just as Darrel's hands came free. Otis did notice this and snarled loudly as he charged at Darrel.

Otis drove his shoulder through Darrel's midsection. The force of the blow lifted Darrel off his feet and slammed him hard to the ground. Darrel had finally proven too difficult. Otis set his mind to putting a permanent end to him; doctor or not.

Darrel recognized immediately that the pirate wasn't trying to subdue him again. This was now a life or death situation. Exhausted and weak from his ordeal so far, he marshalled all of his remaining strength to gain a hold on Otis. He desperately fished for anything that would allow him to get some leverage. He grasped at Otis's shoulder, but the pirate shrugged him off. At a minimum he wanted to keep him close. Darrel resorted to wrapping his legs around Otis's mid-section.

Otis contorted from one side to another trying to raise his torso up but couldn't separate himself from Darrel. He seethed with rage and began to flail, landing short, ineffectual blows, with his fists. It was out of sheer frustration that he finally settled on head butting Darrel.

The blow stunned Darrel, but he forced himself to focus through the stars and darkness that danced in his vision. He knew he couldn't wage this struggle much longer, his stamina was already fading, so he opened his mouth wide and bit into Otis' face. He wrenched his head back and tore away the pirate's flesh. A sudden rush of blood filled his mouth with a sickening iron taste. Otis howled and reeled as a large chunk of his cheek remained in Darrel's teeth.

This was Darrel's chance! He spit out the bloody flesh and twisted his legs to the side using Otis's momentum against him as he carefully wrestled his way on top and gained control. He raised himself up and began raining punches down on him. Otis quickly lost consciousness. Darrel took his head into his hands and savagely dug his thumbs into the eyes. He experienced a twisted pleasure as the pirate's body convulsed beneath him before going limp.

The sudden adrenaline rush was overwhelming, but ultimately short lived. It was all too much for Darrel's weakened physical state. He retched uncontrollably as the darkness finally closed in causing him to collapse unconsciousness atop the dead pirate.

Jack held onto one of the dock's piers as he floated through the water. He looked into the camp and didn't see anyone around. He maneuvered himself over to a skiff and tried to quietly hoist himself out of the water. Unfortunately, he landed on a paddle which promptly banged against a fuel can, "Shit." he muttered to himself.

A head poked out of the small shack and promptly spotted Jack in the skiff, "Oi, wut joo doin' o'er dere?" the pirate shouted as he stepped out of the shack and started to move toward Jack.

Jack quickly searched his belt for the canister that Jan had given him. It was the first time he ever felt that maybe his belt had a few too many pockets. He finally found it on the fourth try. He pressed the button, counted to three and tossed it toward the shack.

The canister flew through the air and as it reached the vicinity of the shack it quietly discharged thousands of tiny foil pieces. This confused the pirate who stopped dead in his tracks. For a brief second he thought, "wuz dis?" and then the electrical charge hit him.

The pirate should have been flailing on the ground as the voltage burned through him, but instead, the entire shack exploded. He had no chance. Pieces of him went flying, along with the shack and its contents, in all directions.

An exasperated Jack ran his hand through his scraggy hair, kicked at the skiff and said, "Well, fuck me." He then realized he was a bit exposed so he ducked down and started to move toward the skiff's engine.

Jim opened the door to the hut and was greeted with a most beautiful sight, "Eureka!" He exclaimed.

A large metal vat sat atop a fire pit. The smell that emanated from within was quite vile. The fire boiled a mix of fermented goats milk and wild grains. Metal tubing spiraled out the top of the vat carrying its precious distilled vapors into a holding tank where they condensed into "da'piss"

Sarah walked in behind him, "That's a still?"

"Yes it is," Jim smiled and pointed over to a stack of small casks in the corner, "but the real prize is over there."

"Is that the booze?"

"Yep."

Sarah walked over to the casks and picked one up, "Let's have a taste."

Jim looked around and saw a mallet lying on a table near the casks. He walked over and picked it up, "Bring that cask over here."

Sarah carried the cask over and set it on the table, "How do we open it?"

"That's what the mallet is for," Jim whacked the top of the cask with the mallet and the plug went flying. He then pulled a collapsible travel cup out of his back pocket and, with one quick jerk, expanded it.

"Oh, that's nifty." Sarah said.

Jim smiled, "Sarah, I'm a professional. I'm always prepared to pour a drink." He lifted the cask, gave it a tilt and carefully filled the cup. As usual, it was a perfect pour. He put the cask down on the table and handed the cup to Sarah, "Give that a try."

Sarah took big gulp. Her lips frowned. Her eyes got wide. She turned to the side and spit, "Oh my god! That's awful!"

It was at the moment that an explosion shook the ground, the hut and everything inside it. Debris could be heard hitting the hut they were in, "What the fuck was that?" Sarah yelled.

Jim replied, "If I had to guess. It's Jack blowing shit up!"

"Well, I guess it's on now. We should get back to the canal and keep watch."

"Right, let's grab a couple casks on our way out."

Sarah shook her head, "Why?"

"You never know. It might mix well."

"I doubt it. But, okay."

The pirate camp was, more or less, laid out in a

wheel and spoke design. There were a couple of large buildings at the center and a little more than a dozen smaller buildings and huts that circled them in two rows.

Malinda started to move in toward the inner circle. Her objective was the two central buildings. That's where she believed her friends were being held. She was surprised that she was able to move so freely without being noticed. With the exception of the one pirate she assumed was on patrol, she hadn't seen anyone else. The pirates didn't appear to be expecting a confrontation.

Jan began to move along the outer circle. She wanted to be as close to Jack as she could. She was going to take the shortest path to the docks while providing support to Malinda. They were only about ten feet apart when the sound of an explosion rumbled through the camp and the east side of the camp was bathed in a bright orange glow.

"What the hell was that?" Malinda asked.

Jan replied, "I hate to say it, but that came from the dock."

"Five minutes in and he's already blowing shit up?"

Jan was bewildered, "With what? All he had was a spanner and duct tape?"

"Space Engineer!" Malinda retorted.

Pirates started stumbling out of huts. It appeared that most of them were either drunk or half asleep. Malinda didn't waste a second. It was payback time. She shouldered her weapon and started firing to the left quickly felling two of them. Malinda would later refer to this moment as the great pirate turkey shoot of 2155.

Jan dropped to one knee, shouldered her weapon and began firing at every available target. She was truly brilliant with a gun. Shot after shot hit true. She shouted to Malinda, "I'm going to move toward the dock. I have a feeling Jack will be in need of some help," while continuing to fire.

Malinda's confidence grew as pirate after pirate fell to the ground, "Okay, I'll round up the others and meet you there."

Sarah and Jim returned to their position by the canal, now three casks richer, however, Sarah would argue that it wasn't in anyway worth the effort. The force of the explosion had sent pieces of burning shack and its contents flying everywhere. A gas can landed near the canal just in front of the solitary bush they were using for cover.

Sarah noticed some pirates pointing toward the dock and heard gunshots coming from the west. She turned toward Jim, "They're going to find Jack! We should create a diversion." She thought for a few seconds. She looked at the goats. She looked at the gas can. She looked back to the goats. And she came to the only conclusion she could have. She darted out from the bush and picked up the gas can. It was heavy with fuel. She ran over to the goat pen, opened the gas can and started showering the goats in it.

Sarah calmly climbed out of the pen, walked over

and picked up a nearby burning timber. She walked back to the pen and said, "Sorry goats," and lit one on fire. It immediately bucked and bumped into a couple of other goats which then also caught fire. They too bucked and caused a chain reaction. Within seconds every goat was on fire, kicking and bucking, letting out the most chilling goat screams!

Sarah moved around to the pen gate and opened it. Several burning goats shot out. A couple goats, however, ran into the attached hut containing the still and casks. Sarah ran back to her spot near the canal and watched the carnage unfold.

The hut was now fully engulfed in flame. Jim said, "Uh, we might want to get down." and lied down on the ground grabbing ahold of Sarah and pulling her toward the ground with him.

Mere seconds had passed before the hut housing the distillery exploded sending burning shrapnel in all directions. The force had also nearly destroyed another nearby hut. The remnants of that hut were also engulfed by fire. The haunting squawks of burning chickens would be hard for Sarah and Jim to ever forget. Flaming chickens came bolting out of the burning hut. Some ran out and collapsed straight off, but oddly, most of them followed the goats!

"Hey Jim, he was right. They had chickens!" Sarah noticed the next hut going up in flames. A few seconds later another hut went up, "Diversion created!" she laughed.

"You sure are an interesting spirit, Sarah." Jim

said.

A naked pirate lay unconscious in Ricky's former cell. Ricky had thought about killing him but it just wasn't the type of thing he'd do. Instead he just took his clothes. He had this farfetched notion that if he dressed like a pirate he might be able to walk right out of the camp with Marie.

"It's never going to work, Ricky." Marie said.

"Sure it is. I make a very convincing pirate don't ya think?"

"No not at all."

"Well that's not a good attitude."

"Ricky, his clothes are wearing you. You haven't done a hard day's work in... well... ever!"

"It's going to work, Marie," Ricky insisted just as an explosion shook the ground beneath him.

"What the hell was that?" Marie asked.

"I'm guessing, Jack?"

Marie replied, "Of course, who else would it be?"

The explosion was followed shortly by the sounds of gunfire. Ricky opened the door and poked his head out to see what was going on. He saw the pirates running around frantically. He'd hear a gunshot and a pirate would fall. One by one all the pirates he saw fell to the ground with a bullet hole in them. He pulled his head back in and closed the door, "Okay, it looks like the pirates are being taken care of."

"By who?" Marie asked.

He replied, "My money is on Malinda. Let's go find Darrel! Stay close."

THE TRIALS OF JACK KEMPER

Ricky opened the door and stepped out. He was greeted by a stampede of burning goats; one of which ran squarely into the side of the hut they were in, lighting it on fire. He grabbed Marie's hand, "Come on, we need to move!" and pulled her along behind him.

It was a chaotic scene of burning huts, goats and chickens. They dodged left as a flaming goat ran by. He pulled Marie with him as he took a step forward and hopped over a Flaming chicken!

Marie didn't know what to make of things. Why were these flaming livestock trying so hard to kill her? This had to be Jack's doing! She pointed to the building that was just in front of them, "Let's get in there!" she said.

Malinda was on a rampage as she cleared the center of the camp. She saw three pirates taking up positions nearby. They hadn't noticed her. They were looking towards the docks. She aimed, she pulled her trigger and one pirate fell. She aimed, she pulled her trigger and another pirate fell. She aimed, she noticed a flaming goat run by, and she thought to herself, "What the fuck was that?" and pulled the trigger. The last pirate fell just as two more flaming goats ran by. She turned around to see several flaming chickens in pursuit and ducked around the corner to avoid them.

Jack tried to crank the skiff's engine, but just as they had suspected it was dead. He pulled out his spanner and had the cover off in seconds. He checked the starter. It looked good. He followed the fuel line. It was all intact. He tried to crank it one more time. Because, you know, it might work this time!

Jack turned his nose up in the air and sniffed. He thought he could smell the slight hint of gas, it was hard to make out over all the other burning smells that permeated the air, but it gave him an idea on where to start. He followed the cables to the spark plug. Well, he followed the cables to where the spark plug should be!

Jack looked up and around for anything that could help. He looked over to the other skiff. It had a motor. It was full of bullet holes, but just maybe its spark plugs were intact. He took a few quick steps and jumped over to it.

His brilliant leap into the other skiff was foiled by an empty bucket. Probably used by the pirates for bailing out water. He fell flat on his face; crashing quite loudly into a toolbox. The bucket went flying off his foot as he lay on his back and kicked it off into the air. He stood up and took a quick look around. Shadows and blurs moved through the fire and smoke that was engulfing the camp.

Jack made his way to the engine and put his spanner to work. He quickly removed the cover and saw, much to his surprise, that the sparkplugs were intact. He couldn't help shouting, "Yes!" as he quickly removed the spark plugs.

The noise and his shouting drew some much unwanted attention. A voice came from the dock, "Oi joo, wat yeh doin on me skiff mate?" Jack looked up and saw a large muscle laden man pointing a pistol at him, "Joo, blow up me shack?"

THE TRIALS OF JACK KEMPER

Jack slipped the plugs in his belt and put his hands up, "Uh, yeah mate sorry about that. It wasn't my intention."

"Yeh? Den joo lit moy goats?" he asked.

"Goats? Uh, no that, that wasn't me. That sounds kind of cruel actually. Maybe your guys did that?"

"Chappy's guys woon't do dat. 'Ow 'bouts yeh geh out da skiff, mate," he motioned with his pistol, "C'mon"

Jack took a step forward just as the side Chappy's head exploded to the left. He looked over to the right and saw Jan about twenty yards away, "I told you I'd have you covered." she said.

Jack replied, "Good timing."

"Did you really have to blow shit up and light the livestock on fire?"

"Hey, I tossed that canister you gave me. That's all I did. I thought it would stun the guy. I didn't know it would explode."

"It shouldn't have exploded."

"Well it did or something it hit did."

Jan turned to look at the smoldering remains of the shack, "Fuel shed?" she asked.

"Shit, yeah that makes sense."

"I got you covered. Get the boat running."

Jack hopped back onto the skiff and got to work.

Ricky and Marie burst through the door expecting a fight, but what they found was a large blood soaked man on top of a larger blood soaked man. Neither was recognizable. The man on the bottom was clearly dead.

And they weren't too sure about the man on top.

Marie walked over and began to wipe the blood off of his face, "Darrel?" Marie asked.

Darrel's eyes didn't open, but a soft reply came, "Praise Vesta."

Ricky moved towards Darrel, "Come on, Marie. Let's help him up."

"Sure. Sure." she stammered. She was quite shocked by Darrel's appearance. His face was terribly swollen and he was covered in so much blood that if he didn't have clothes on it might appear that the top layer of his flesh had been removed.

They each put one of his arms around their shoulders and began to lift. It was a struggle to get him to his feet. He had no strength left in his legs to help them. He screamed in agony as they moved him. Marie wanted to stop and see what was causing him so much pain, but she knew they didn't have time. They needed to get to safety first.

Ricky could sense her hesitation. He reinforced her with the direness of their situation, "We need to get out of here, Marie." he said.

Jim could barely make out the sound of a boat motor over the gunshots, explosions and the squealing and squawking of burning livestock. He looked southward down the canal trying to get a look at its source, "Is that coming our way?"

"It does sound like it's getting louder."

"Ah crap, I was really hoping we were done for the day."

"You're not much of a fighter are you Jim."

"Hey, I can clean up a bar fight just fine but I've never been overly fond of guns; or violence for that matter."

"Don't worry, Jim. I'll protect you."

Jim sarcastically replied, "Thanks. I feel safer already," as he picked up his gun and cycled a round into the chamber, "let's get on the other side of this bush."

The two moved around the bush and ducked down behind it. Whatever was coming was moving at a fast rate. "Let it get close and aim for the engine." Jim said. "Set your rifle to semi auto. We don't have many shots at this."

Sarah was shocked that Jim had such a cogent plan for the situation, "Hmm, here I was thinking you'd shoot yourself in the foot or something."

Jim looked toward Sarah, "I said I wasn't overly fond of guns. That doesn't mean I don't know how to use them."

She smiled at him, "So, how do I do that?"

"Do what?"

"Set it to semi-auto?"

"Oh," Jim chuckled, "I figured you had experience what with all the goat killing and such."

"Yesterday was the first time I ever picked up a gun. I can point. I can shoot."

"Alright," Jim pointed to a switch on the side of his rifle, "slide the switch forward."

Sarah slid the switch into position, "So now I only get one shot per squeeze?"

"A burst of 3."

"Will I still get the glowy ones that show me where they're going?"

"Yes."

She raised her gun and aimed down the canal, "Cool," and cocked her head to the side with a wink at Jim, "I'm so horny right now."

"That's normal."

"Is it?"

"As long as it's not because you lit the goats on fire. Sure."

"Maybe a little," she let out a perverted laugh.

"God help us."

A large skiff, carrying a half dozen armed men rounded the bend of the canal and came into focus. Sarah squeezed the trigger and fired at the boat.

Jim yelled, "I said wait until they're close!"

"Is that not close?"

It was when the bullets started flying at him that Jim realized close was a relative measurement, "My bad, my bad. Should have been more specific!" he yelled.

The pair began squeezing off round after round at the skiff. The pirate at the bow was hit and fell off into the water. The pirate behind him slid up into the previously occupied position and began to fire. The skiff swerved; zig-zagging its way up the canal.

Bullets whizzed over the heads of Jim and Sarah. Some bullets landed short; kicking up dirt in front of the pair. Sarah didn't even flinch. She held steady and fired burst after burst focusing squarely on the motor.

Jim instinctively tried to duck his head every time he heard a bullet whiz by. He wasn't accomplishing much. A round hit directly in front of him sending dirt flying into his face, "This is it," He thought to himself as the skiff came closer and closer. He had just about resigned himself to his fate when a round blasted one of his prized bottles!

Jim sprang to his feet and yelled, "You sons of bitches!" He slid the switch to full auto and instinctively moved toward the edge of the canal while spraying the skiff with bullets. One pirate fell. Then another fell. Then the pilot of the skiff fell. And finally the shot they had been looking for. It must have hit the fuel tank. The skiff exploded sending the last two remaining pirates flying into the canal.

Sarah came running out from behind the bush. She jumped up and down in excitement, "Oh my god that was amazing! You're amazing Jim!"

A somber Jim replied, "Well, they shouldn't have done that."

"Done what?"

Jim walked over and saw two shot up bottles, "What a waste that is. Those might be the last two bottle of Jack Daniels on the planet." He kicked the broken glass to the side, bent down and pulled his one remaining bottle out of the bush, "At least Glen survived."

"Glen?"

Jim cradled the bottle like it was his most precious baby, "Fiddich."

"Right, look on the bright side," Sarah said as she walked behind the bush and returned with a half empty bottle of whiskey, "we still have this one too Jim." She twisted off the top and took a swig. Her eyes lit up, "Whew, that's sooooo good!"

Usually a satisfied drinker was all it took to make Jim's day a good one. On this occasion her satisfaction was only a minor bit of solace, however, his disappointment was quickly forced to the back of his mind by the sound of multiple boat motors coming from the south. He looked over toward the dock and saw Jack working on the skiff, "Doesn't look like he's ready yet," as he walked over and set his bottle down behind the three casks.

Sarah pulled the magazine out of her rifle and looked inside, "I don't have many bullets left."

Jim pulled out his magazine. He sighed, "Make'm count."

Malinda waited for the last of the flaming livestock to run by before she resumed her mission. Just about every structure had been lit on fire except for the one she thought Darrel would be in and it was only a matter of time before it went up. She quickly moved towards it.

The door to the building opened just as she approached. She raised her weapon and took aim; prepared to deal with whoever appeared. Much to her amazement it was her three friends that emerged.

Ricky spotted her immediately, "Don't shoot, Malinda!" he shouted, "It's us! It's us! We have Darrel!"

Malinda lowered her rifle, "Praise Vesta!" she replied, "We need to move toward the docks. Follow me!"

Jack frantically twisted the spark plugs into place. He looked up for just a second and saw that the entire camp was engulfed in flames. His thoughts strayed to his friends and their wellbeing, "Malinda," he thought to himself. What would he ever do without her? What would he do without any of them for that matter? He popped the cables onto the spark plugs, "By Vesta's grace!" he turned the engine over once again. Ignition!

He shouted, "Jim! Sarah!" and waved them over.

Jan turned to look toward the skiff when she heard the engine start, "Well done, Space Engineer!" she shouted. She turned back to see Malinda leading Ricky, Marie and Darrel out of the flames. She shouted, "Jack!" and pointed.

Jack teared up. Emotions swelled in him that he thought had died off years ago. He quickly ran through the checklist in his head. Steering - check! Throttle - check! Fuel level - check!

Malinda, Darrel, Marie, Jim, Sarah, three casks of "da'piss" and one and a half bottles of liquor all arrived on the dock at the same time. Normally that would be indicative that there was one hell of a night ahead, however, Darrel was in no mood to party.

Jack jumped up on the dock. He and Jan took hold of Darrel and began to help him into the skiff while Malinda stood guard.

Sarah embraced Ricky and gave him a kiss, "I was so worried." she said.

"I'm fine. It's all fine," Ricky slurred as they followed Darrel into the skiff.

A flaming goat came running between huts towards the dock, "Hey Jack, burnt ends incoming!" Malinda smirked at Jack over her shoulder.

Jack replied, "What, no fries with that?"

Malinda turned, squeezed off a single round and dropped it before it could reach the dock, "Yeah, it just wouldn't be the same without the fries." she muttered. She turned around, untied the skiff from the dock and hopped in, "Let's go!"

CHAPTER 12

The L.I.S. Elon hovered several hundred feet above the ocean, in relative safety, just ten miles off the coast of Tasmania. It would be from this vantage point that Captain Dent and his well-trained crew would mount their latest operation.

The bridge of the Elon was in combat mode. Overhead lighting was dimmed. The forward wall went translucent. It resembled a window but it was so much more. Powerful cameras on the ship's hull focused on their target, the port, and highlighted tactical objectives.

"Reapers are ready, Captain." Tactical Officer Mueller reported.

"Good," Captain Dent replied with a short pause before he continued, "Let's lay down some cover. Send in the smoke rounds."

T.O. Mueller poked at her screen, "Smoke deployed, Captain."

"Launch the observation drones."

"Drones launched, Captain."

"Fire the IR and HE at their designated targets and let the Reapers loose."

"Aye, aye, sir," without hesitation her hands flew over the keys of the terminal, initiating the missile salvos. She then poked at her communications panel, "Reapers, you're a go. I repeat. You're a go."

The crew of the flight deck stood ready in their launch positions. They were prepared for any number of possible emergencies that could happen during the launch sequence. Flight Chief Terry "Nob" Lewellyn stood by listening for the launch command. As the command was received the signal was given.

Sergeant MacIntyre replied, "Roger that Guardian," and switched back to the squad channel. "Reapers, we're a go for launch. On me!" On his command, his elite squadron of MMAC pilots jammed their controls full forward. Their mechs lurched ahead towards the open hangar bay door. One by one they stepped out of the hanger and dropped away. After a few seconds of freefall, to clear the Elon, the pilots initiated their flight engines, formed up and headed towards the port.

The bridge was mostly empty aboard The Whore's Menace. The pirate destroyer's night watch was nothing more than a skeleton crew. It was a routine start to the evening until a crackling came over the radio.

The gruff old man currently on watch picked up the headset. He keyed the transmit button on the chord, "Oi, wha's dat?" His expression changed. The headset dropped back to the console as rushed to the Captain's quarters.

The old man rapped on the captain's door, "Cap'n!"

"Oi?" growled a half asleep voice from the other side of the door.

"Cap'n, repor' from da'camp. They's unda 'tack or somethin'?"

The door opened and a balding, crusty, old mariner hobbled into the doorway, "Wha's tha' ag'in?" he said.

"Jus' now, on da'radio. Da'camp is unda'tack."

The Captain stood in the doorway and scratched his privates for a good two minutes as he tried to shake off the fog of sleep, "Fook'it, Charlie. Sen'some skiffs thru'da chan'l, 'ave dem go'n check'tout."

Charlie nodded, "O'right cap'n," and turned to head back to the bridge. It didn't sit right with the old timer when his routine got interrupted. That's why he liked his job on the Whore's Menace. Nothing ever happened. The boat was a visual warning to lesser rivals more than a boat of action. He had only managed a few steps down the corridor when the first explosion ripped through the ship. The force of the blast threw him fifteen feet forward and squarely into the bulkhead. His ears rang and blood poured from his head.

Charlie rolled over trying to squint through the smoke and dust that filled the corridor. Flickering lights provided just enough illumination for him to see that his captain was no longer standing there. In his place was nothing more than a smoldering hole created by the blast.

Jack slammed the throttle into reverse and the skiff lurched backwards. Everyone grabbed onto the hull for support. Spinning the wheel hard to the left, he swung the bow around and thrust the throttle forward. The engine howled. The skiff got up to speed quickly and leveled out as it headed into the open water of the bay. It might not look like much, but it was obvious that the pirates prized speed when it came to their boats.

"That went about as well as could be expected," Jack said over the roaring engine.

"It's still a long way to the port." Jan replied.

Malinda made her way to the back of the skiff. She gave Jack a peck on the cheek and sat down next to him. She pulled out a new mag of ammo and cycled a round into the chamber.

Marie used the time to try and clean Darrel up. She had torn off a piece of her shirt and wetted it in the seawater. She wiped away blood until it was saturated then rinsed it out and repeated the process.

Sarah held out the almost empty whiskey bottle, "Hey, Marie!" she shouted.

Ricky took the bottle from Sarah and handed it to Marie. Marie handed it to Darrel who promptly emptied it.

It was a slow day at "the point" and Ollie, the pirate on duty, was ready to get back to camp and get some shut eye. They called this outpost "the point" because it sat at the entrance of the main port channel on a little arm of land that jutted out into the inlet. It was the perfect spot for keeping an eye on the comings and goings between the port and inner camp.

Ollie sipped on a cup of "da'piss" while enjoying the effervescent rays of a chemically enhanced sunset. He leaned back in his chair with his feet up on a small stone wall while his eyes lazily scanned over the water. Off in the distance he noticed one of the camps skiffs heading his way.

Ollie stood up and said, "'bout toime. Dey gotit run'n." He walked around to the rear of the outpost where a generator was housed. He flipped the switch on it, primed the carburetor and fired it up with a couple strong pulls of the cord.

Ollie walked back around to the front and went up some steps to the top of the outpost where they had a signal lamp. He powered it up and flashed the blinds a few times. No return signal was presented. He signaled again; nothing.

Ollie wrinkled his brow and grimaced. This wasn't the way he wanted to end his shift. He reached for the set of binoculars that were kept next to the signal lamp. He peered through them at the oncoming boat, "Blot'y 'ell, dats naw roight!" he said in disgust.

The powerful skiff sped through the waters of the inlet toward the channel. Jack was having so much fun piloting the skiff that he almost forgot how exhausted he was. And his exhaustion was causing him to miss certain key details in his surroundings.

Malinda shouted at Jack, "Did you see that?"

He scanned the water ahead of them, "See what?" he asked.

"The light, up on the ridge, 1 o'clock"

"No."

"It looked like a signal lamp."

"That's an outpost," Jan added, "They have several along the channel."

"At least it's getting dark out. It will be tough for them to see us," Ricky interjected from the bow. Just then a red flare burst overhead. Ricky shrugged and sank a little lower into the bow.

Jack guided the skiff into the channel at full speed. Up ahead he could see that land encroached upon the water ever closer, narrowing the channel to a discomforting width. Another flare burst overhead. It illuminated most of their surroundings. Jack did his best to keep the skiff on the fringes of the lit area, but it was no use.

A chain of bullet splashes raced across the water towards the skiff followed by the staccato report of gunfire, "Stay down and hold on!" Jack yelled as he turned the wheel sharply to the side. The bullets appeared to just miss the skiff as it pitched hard into the turn. He continued to steer the boat erratically in an effort to dodge the gunfire.

Jim shouted, "Man down! Man down!" A cask of "da'piss" had been riddled with bullet holes. He frantically tried to stick his fingers in it to plug the holes. It didn't make it.

THE TRIALS OF JACK KEMPER

Thick smoke drifted up and across the bay. Only the very top of the Whore's Menace poked through. The Reapers watched as the first volley of high explosive missiles impacted their target. The ship heaved and a fiery orange glow began to make the smoke luminesce, "Bean, lock target. Attack pattern Sigma-42."

"Roger that, Oddball. Sigma-42. Locked"

Oddball darted to the left, "Fox 2, Fox 2"

Bean darted to the right, "Fox 2, Fox 2"

A volley of rockets whistled toward the Whore's Menace followed by the report of the concussion rounds hitting their target. The two mechs dove down just above the water. They hid in the smoke as they skimmed along the surface making their approach.

"Guns hot, Bean"

"Roger that! Guns hot, Oddball!"

They lit into the ship with their railguns. The rounds penetrated the aging armor burrowing deep into the decks below.

Steel came over the communications channel, "Alright Junior, let's start with that Russian bitch."

"Roger that, Steel. Chaos-Delta-13?"

"What is it with you and Chaos-Delta-13?"

"It has 'Chaos' in it."

"Sounds tactically sound to me! Roger that, Chaos-Delta-13! Lock that bitch up!"

"Target locked. Let's melt some metal my brotha!"

The mechs swept down from the sky strafing the missile ship with incendiary rounds before the ship's crew even knew they were there. Anyone unfortunate enough to be on deck at the time was torn to shreds as the rounds tore through their bodies before exploding into the ship's armor.

The group's progress through the channel was met with stiff resistance. Bullets raked the hull sending splinters from the console flying. Jack instinctively dropped to the floor of the skiff, but hopped back up almost immediately and veered hard right. Automatic weapon fire continued to splash around them.

The channel began to narrow even more and small rocky islands cluttered the waterway ahead. Suddenly a rush of wind and heat screamed just overhead followed by a large explosion in the water a few yards in front of the skiff.

Marie shielded Darrel from the debris cast up by the explosion, "What the fuck was that!?" she yelled.

Malinda and Jan's eyes snapped to each other's in shock. Their gaze turned to follow the trail of smoke. It led toward the north shore of the channel where it met with two skiffs heading their way.

"They have RPG's!" Jan shouted.

Jack steered for the far side of one of the small rocky islands. The continuous lines of automatic gunfire raked through the water around them.

"Incoming!" Malinda yelled.

Jack deftly turned the skiff hard around the edge of the island. A jet of fire propelled the RPG as it sailed by, so close the occupants of the skiff felt its heat. It exploded into the rocky shore sending rocks and shrapnel into the air.

"How much farther?" Jack asked.

Jan poked at the panel on her right arm, "We'll be through this part of the channel in another 500 yards." she shouted.

Jack peered over his shoulder at the two skiffs chasing them and did a quick mental calculation, "They'll catch us before we get there," he shouted, "Malinda, think you can do something slow down our friends back there?"

Malinda shouted back to him, "I can try!" She turned around and brought herself into position on one knee, shouldered her weapon and began to fire. Almost simultaneously, a spray of bullets riddled the hull next to her and striking the engine.

The skiff sputtered to a dead stop. Jack frantically tried to restart the engine, but it refused to start. Even worse, fuel sprayed out each time he tried, "Ricky! Take the controls!"

Malinda continued to fire on the pirate skiffs forcing them to take evasive action. She wasn't doing any damage, but she was managing to slow their pursuit.

Jan poked at the panel on her right arm, "Guardian, this is Recon 1. Fire Mission. Danger close. Target lit!" She poked at the panel on her left arm activating a laser and pointed her hand at one of the approaching skiffs.

Jack made his way to the stern of the skiff and tore off the engine cover. He looked over the engine for damage. Amazingly, except for severing the engines fuel line, the bullets did little damage. Jack pulled a roll of duct tape from his belt, "Vesta, don't fail me now," he prayed as he wrapped the fuel line, "Crank it, Ricky!"

All eight of them held their collective breath as the engine turned over. It sputtered a couple of times, but it still refused to start. Jack noticed an additional fuel leak further down the hose, "Hold up!" He tore the last of the duct tape from the roll and, once again, applied it to the fuel line, "Again, Ricky! Again," he blurted out. The tension of the situation could be heard in his voice.

Ricky turned the key again. He pushed the choke in an attempt to coax the engine to start. It spit out a last few sputters before it roared back to life. He immediately pushed the throttle down and the boat lurched forward.

The sudden acceleration caused Jan to lose her balance and fall toward the stern. She tried to maintain her laser sight on the target skiff, but it was pointing about fifteen yards in front of it when the missile finally arrived. It exploded into a great fireball spewing water and debris into the air.

The explosion caught the pursuing skiffs by surprise. They swerved to avoid it. One skiff veered hard to the left and collided with the other. The impact of the collision sent pirates in both boats flying into the water.

The pirate piloting one of the skiffs managed to hang on. He tried, but failed, to regain control of his craft and it slammed head on into one of the small rocky islands that dotted this part of the channel. The force of the collision sent him flying over the bow where he landed face first on the rocks.

The channel finally began to widen. Jan looked at her radar, "We're coming up on the port!" she yelled.

The others could see nothing but smoke and flashes of light in the distance. The flashes were followed by the report of loud explosions. Malinda smiled at Jan, "Sounds like your team is giving them hell!"

"I told you they're badass." she replied.

Jack pointed starboard, "Ricky, watch out!" he shouted.

A pirate skiff rapidly approached with some crazy guy standing straight up on its bow shooting wildly. How he even managed to keep his balance was a mystery. His shots tore through the hull.

Jim yelped and dove to the deck as the bullets whizzed by. The grip he had on his last bottle of Glenfiddich didn't fail him. He cradled it to his body as if it were more precious than his life; a true professional.

Sarah instinctively leapt on top of him to protect him. She would later claim that her motive was to protect the liquor. It was the beginning of a long lasting bond between the two of them.

Malinda and Jan returned fire, but the pirates refused to turn away. In fact, there was not even an attempt at evasion. Jan finally managed to land a round to the pirate on the bow and he fell into the sea, but the pilot of the skiff had only one agenda. They could see the other pirates bracing for impact, "BRACE!" Jan screamed.

Ricky tried to out maneuver the other skiff, but its pilot managed to match him move for move. The pirate skiff slammed into them at full speed. The jolt sent Malinda and Jan flying forward. Ricky held the wheel so tight it bent forward as he steadied himself. Marie held on to Darrel for dear life. Jim felt Sarah jiggle and liked it.

The severity of the impact sent Jack flying through the air. He landed on the bow of the pirate skiff. His momentum was such that it allowed him to flawlessly perform a combat roll, spring up to his feet, take two strides and land a flying kick to the chest of one pirate that sent the man flying off the skiff and into the water.

A rather large and angry pirate picked Jack up off the deck, "Joo's t'ink ya'Broos Lee o'sometin'?" He spat through clenched teeth.

Jack struggled to get free but there was no breaking the man's grip. He let loose a flurry of futile blows. Jack just wasn't big enough to have any effect on the man.

In the intervening moments, the pilot had managed to get back to his feet. He saw Jack in the grasp of his buddy and drew his pistol.

Ricky saw this new threat to his friend and reacted quickly; jamming the throttle forward and jerking the wheel hard to starboard. The skiff plowed into the enemy craft just as the pilot pulled the trigger.

The pirate's shot whizzed past Jack's head, but found its mark in the neck of his buddy. He watched as his cohort collapsed over the side of the boat and toppled into the water nearly pulling Jack with him. This wasn't over yet! He furiously clambered past the helm and raised the revolver directly into Jack's face.

Jack stared down the barrel of a gun that had him dead to rights. It triggered an existential moment. Time seemed to slow. Even the loud crack of a gun going off didn't make him flinch. He assumed his mind was playing tricks on him as he saw the pirate's face explode; each piece of flesh and drop of blood appearing in vivid detail. The pirate's body slumped away, eventually landing in the water behind the skiff. Jack just stood there. Lost in what he thought was his final moment.

"Jack!" the scream came again, "Jack!"

Out of the corner of his eye he saw smoke wafting from a gun barrel. It was the barrel of Malinda's gun. He heard her scream yet again, "Jack!" and it finally brought him back to his senses. He was amazed that he was still alive, "Did you see that move?!" Jack asked as he steadied himself.

"That was impressive!" Sarah said.

Malinda rolled her eyes, "Yeah, yeah. Well done. Might have been a little lucky though!" she said.

Jack was incredulous, "Lucky?! Lucky?! A combat roll into a flying kick?! Lucky?!"

"Okay, okay. It was amazing. It was as if Vesta herself was working through you!"

"It was. Wasn't it?" Jack pondered it for a moment, "Hmm, Praise Vesta?"

Sarah and Ricky replied in unison, "Praise Vesta!"

Jan couldn't help but laugh, "Alright, you two and Jim can ride with Vesta's anointed. Malinda and I will nurse this skiff along."

Sarah, Ricky quickly joined Jack in the newly acquired second skiff. They expected Jim to be right behind them but he was lost in grief.

"They're gone!" he said as he held up the last two small casks of "da'piss". They were riddled with bullet holes.

Sarah yelled back to him, "They died heroes, Jim! Don't let their sacrifice be in vain!"

Jim wiped a tear from his eye and jumped over to the other skiff. He took his position next to Sarah on the bow.

Jack moved behind the console and rolled the throttle forward and the two skiffs sped away towards the opening to the port proper.

It didn't take long for the Whore's Menace to go down. She listed to port and began a death roll. Black smoke bellowed from her; mixing with the grey cover smoke deployed by the Elon. The air was so thick there was no way to see if there were any survivors.

The missile frigate launched what missiles it could. The munitions spiraled away in random directions only to fall harmlessly into the sea as infrared rounds from the Elon spoofed false targets for their guidance systems.

Anti-aircraft guns blasted flack into the sky but with the heavy smoke barrage the rounds burst harmlessly away from the Reaper squad pilots.

Bean chided her cohorts, "You need some help over there, Steel?"

"Hey, when I want a fajita; I know who to call. Alright, Bean!"

Junior came over the radio, "Nob says her fajitas' a little on the cheesy side, Steel."

"Nasty!"

Bean replied, "Sarge, permission to lock onto Junior?"

"Denied. Focus on the mission. Target that yankee frigate."

Junior howled into the radio, "Woohoo! The south will rise again! I got this one!"

"I'm sure this isn't the first time you've heard this, Junior. You're just too slow!" Sgt. MacIntyre said.

"Target locked, Oddball." Bean cut in, "Slow in the head, too fast in bed, Junior"

Sgt. MacIntyre and Bean strafed down opposite sides of the frigate. The rocket launchers on their mechs unleashed a barrage of concussion rockets just above the ship's water line. As each round impacted the thick armor plating of the hull; it buckled and split.

"Oh yeah, that bitch is going down!" Bean shouted.

Junior replied, "Hey Steel, I bet that's not the first time Bean has used that line!"

"Nor the first time you've heard it." Bean retorted.

Steel's laughter carried through the radio, "Alright, alright. Enough joking around. Let's finish it off."

"I'm on your 3 o'clock, Steel." Junior replied as the

two mech pilots swept in behind the frigate and leveled out just feet off the water on their attack run.

"Fox 2! Fox 2!" Steel called out.

"Fox 2! Fox 2!" echoed Junior.

The combined missile salvo blew a massive hole in the frigate's stern. Water began to rush in. The mechs soared by, smoke clearing in their wake to reveal pirates jumping into the water as they abandoned the sinking ship.

"Woohoo! That did it, Junior." Steel shouted.

"Look at those rats swim!"

The skiffs plowed headlong into the thick acrid smoke that enveloped the port. Loud explosions rattled over the water accompanied by the screams of wounded and drowning men. Automatic weapons fire came from all around. Stray rounds whizzed past the skiffs as pirates blindly fired at perceived threats.

Jack quickly lost sight of the other skiff due to the thick smoke. He could hear thumps beneath him as his skiff bounced over the bodies of dead pirates floating in the water, but he was effectively driving blind, "I can't see shit!" he shouted to Ricky.

Ricky replied, "This is crazy!"

Sarah pointed dead ahead and shouted, "Ship!"

Jack turned the skiff as hard port as it would go. Ricky grabbed onto the console while Sarah held on tight to Jim. The skiff veered hard to the side coming within inches of an old trawler.

The pirates on the trawler saw Jack's skiff and lined up along the rail to get a shot. It was the first clean sight they had of an enemy. They unleashed a hail of bullets at the skiff as it swerved evasively. The barrage proved effective with several shots finding their way into the engine block. It was cheers all around as they watched the engine tear itself apart.

Jack's skiff was dead, "Into the water!" he barked. The group wasted no time diving into the water. And Jack wasn't far behind.

Jan had also turned port, but with the benefit of radar was able to keep a safe distance from the trawler. Jan turned to Malinda, "Take the wheel. I'm going to light this shit up!"

Jan poked at the panel on her right arm activating her radio, "Guardian, Fire Mission. Laser sighted." Without waiting for a response she poked the panel on her left arm and pointed it at the trawler.

"Fire Mission confirmed." Guardian Fire Control responded.

Thirty seconds later the trawler was wracked by explosions as missiles rained down on it. It was quickly engulfed in flames. Secondary explosions rang through its hull as its fuel store ignited. When it was over, all that remained was flaming bits of debris scattered across the water.

Jan scanned the surface of the water for any sign of the other skiff. She strained to see through the lingering smoke and flaming debris, her retinal HUD struggled to make any positive identification. She saw something floating up ahead, "Oh my god! Is that Jack's skiff?" She shouted.

The bow of a skiff bobbed amidst the burning debris about fifty meters ahead.

Malinda pulled back on the throttle. She peered intently towards the sunken skiff. Malinda willed her eyes to find Jack. She would not lose him now; not after coming this far.

A familiar voice called out, "Malinda!" it was Ricky.

Malinda turned the skiff toward the voice and only then saw Ricky, Sarah and Jim floating in the water. She slowly pulled up to them. Jan reached over the side of the skiff and began helping them climb on board.

"Where's Jack?" Malinda asked hopefully.

"He told us to jump but that's the last…"

Ricky was interrupted by a hand coming over the port bow. Jack's head then popped over.

"Jack!" Malinda shouted. She ran over and grabbed onto him. She helped him up and onto the skiff pulling him on top of her. She grabbed him by the hair on the back of his head and planted a kiss squarely on his lips and before they were even done kissing bullets strafed the air above them.

Jan spun around, "More skiffs incoming!" She moved to the console and pushed the throttle forward as far as it would go.

She steered with her left hand while holding her right hand up so she could see the radar. She veered to the left and then to the right. Bullets and rockets whizzed all around. Somehow she managed to avoid them, "We're almost through!" she shouted.

THE TRIALS OF JACK KEMPER

The smoke turned thinner. Then it began to clear altogether. They were finally through to the other side. The group let out a collective sigh of relief. Then they noticed three pirate skiffs escape the smoke in pursuit of them.

"Malinda, take the wheel!" Jan shouted.

Malinda traded places with Jan. She evasively veered left and right. Unfortunately, the pirates were able to go in a straight line and they were gaining on them quickly.

Jan poked at the panel on her right arm, "Reapers, Reapers, this is Recon 1. 3 skiffs pursuing. Closing fast."

The familiar voice of Doc came through her earpiece, "Hey Scout, good to see you're safe!"

"Not quite safe yet, Doc!"

"Now I don't know if I'd go saying that. If you'd kindly look up."

Jan looked up and saw the Archangel as it nosed up to slow its descent, coming to a stop in the air above them, "You're beautiful Doc!"

The Archangel launched a barrage of missiles at the oncoming attackers. The explosions scattered parts of the three skiffs and their passengers in all directions.

"All clear, Scout!"

"Thank you, Doc."

Jan could see the Elon slowly descending towards the water a few miles out. "Do you see that?!" She yelled.

Jack got his first look at the airship, "Damn, that's impressive!"

"It's the Elon, flagship of Liberty Island!" Jan announced proudly.

"She sure is beautiful." Malinda said.

Marie peeled herself off of Darrel for the first time since their escape from the camp. She sat up and then helped Darrel sit up. They gazed silently as their salvation settled down into the water.

Jim looked down at Glen and said, "We made it buddy."

Sarah stared straight ahead. A tear rolling down her cheek, "That's more spectacular than a stampede of flaming animals."

The entire group slowly turned their looks toward Sarah.

"What? He needed a distraction!"

CHAPTER 13

Upon their arrival Petty Officer "Doc" Daniels, escorted Jack and the others off of the Archangel and into the quarantine area of the L.I.S. Elon. He assured them that quarantine was a prudent policy that covered all rescues and that it was as much for their safety as it was for the crew's.

The risk of exposure to unknown pathogens was not one that Liberty Island personnel, in general, were willing to undertake. So, for the time being, the group would be handled by those professionally trained to limit that risk.

They came to a rather sturdy looking hatch and Doc quickly punched in a code on the adjacent panel. A red light began to flash above the hatch and an alarm began to sound. The hatch slid open and Doc turned to the group to explain the process, "This is the disinfection chamber. Please disrobe, place your clothes in the incinerator chute and then step inside. This process will remove any lingering pathogens on your body. After the process is completed, the hatch on the other side will open and you'll need to exit into the quarantine area for further examination." The group was exhausted, safe and just happy to be alive and together at this point in time. They didn't question the process.

Jack was thrilled to finally shed the disgusting smelling pirate rags he had worn for the last day, although the smell didn't exactly go away. "Man, I think this smell is going to stick with me." he said.

Malinda had gone nose blind from it, "What smell?"

"Really?"

"Guess I got used to it."

"How in the hell is that even possible?" he asked.

Doc was helping Darrel disrobe and interjected, "Actually, the disinfectant should take care of that."

"Praise Vesta!" Jack replied.

The others responded in unison, "Praise Vesta!"

Doc was a little puzzled and just had to ask, "Who's Vesta?"

"Our Most Blessed Patron Saint of Duct Tape." Sarah replied.

"Ah, I see." Doc poked the panel adjacent to the hatch and said, "Quarantine, please be advised. You might want to run mental diagnostics on the incoming rescues."

A woman's voice with a heavy German accent returned over the intercom, "Roger that."

"I assure you we're no crazier than the next guy." Jack said.

THE TRIALS OF JACK KEMPER

Malinda replied, "Unless the next guy is Ricky." She looked to her left, "Oh it is Ricky."

"Hey now, I'm not crazy. I'm a highly functional drunk." he said proudly.

Doc continued to help Darrel disrobe, "Ah well, there's nothing wrong with that!"

Marie replied, "Yeah, the weird thing is he gets smarter as the quality of liquor gets better."

Malinda chuckled, "That's funny. It's like Jack. The better the liquor is. The sexier he is."

Jack winked at Malinda, "Whatever it takes gorgeous."

Jack moved into the disinfection chamber and as the others finished disrobing they followed him. Ricky waited and followed them with Darrel. After they were all in, the hatch slid closed behind them and there was an awkward moment of silence as they waited for whatever was coming next.

Jim said, "This is weird."

Jack replied, "Only because we're sober, Jim."

"Well, when they give me my bottle of Glenfiddich back, I'll rectify that."

Ricky started to reply, "You're a good man…" but was cut off by the sound of another alarm and the red light once again began to flash. This time, instead of a hatch opening, valves in the ceiling, floor and walls began to spew out disinfectant accompanied by a loud hiss. The force was such that the mist was able to work its way into every possible crack and crevice. It lasted less than a minute then subsided.

The hatch to the quarantine area slid open. There were no alarms this time. The group slowly turned around and began to go through the doorway. They had no idea what to expect in the next room. None of them really cared. They were exhausted and standing there naked; at the mercy of whatever came next.

Jack was the first one to enter the quarantine area. He was greeted by Dr. Gladys Brownschidle, a short, pale woman with wire rimmed glasses. A white lab coat wore her more than she did it. She stood there with a tablet staring at Jack in all his naked glory.

She looked at the tablet and then looked at Jack, "Jack Kemper?"

Jack stared past her. His eyes widened in disbelief, "Sam?"

"According to the file you're Jack Kemper." she said.

Sam heard the familiar voice and sat up in his bunk. He looked over and couldn't believe his eyes, "Jack?!" He hopped to his feet just in time to have a naked Jack Kemper put him in a bear hug.

"Sam! I never thought I'd see you again!"

"Hey, you know the rules. You're only allowed to have that thing out if there's a woman in between us. We've gone over this!"

"Damn it, man. Get over it!"

Sam gave in to the embrace, "Damn glad to see you, Jack."

Malinda strolled over, "Now there's a couple slices of white bread that could make me into a meat sandwich any day." She was followed closely by the others who willfully ignored Dr. Brownschidle.

Sam couldn't believe his eyes, "Malinda, I can't believe you kept this guy alive!"

"It wasn't easy!"

He then saw Ricky helping Darrel over, "Darrel? Holy hell what did they do you?"

Darrel replied, "I beat them some. They beat me some. We'll call it a draw."

Everyone had a laugh. They couldn't help it. Here was a man who had spent the last 36 hours being beaten and tortured by pirates, a man that never quit fighting. He simply refused to give up.

Sam looked around and the laughter came to an end. He turned to Jack, "Jessica?"

Marie instantly began to cry, "I'm sorry, Sam."

Sarah put her arm around Marie to comfort her, "It wasn't your fault, Marie."

Darrel replied, "The damn cannibals got her, Sam."

"Cannibals? What?"

Jack answered, "They got Carl too, Sam."

Jim poked his head up so Sam could see him, "And they almost got me!"

Sam was lost in thought as he slowly came to the realization that two of his friends had been eaten. His jaw hung open. Tears welled up in his eyes. Nobody else said a word. They had to let it sink in. He wiped his eyes and looked at Jim, "Jim, I need a drink man."

Jack was reluctant to wake from his first decent night's sleep in days. It was, in fact, the best sleep he had experienced in years. He groggily sat up on his bunk, stretched, yawned and ran his fingers through his hair. He shook his head, craned his neck from side to side, looked around and realized that all the other bunks were already empty. Even Darrel was gone.

The room was rather spacious even with eight bunk beds in it. In between each bunk was a series of shelves for clothing and personal items. Jack saw that there were coveralls, socks and underwear neatly folded on the shelf next to his bunk. A pair of black work boots sat beneath the shelves. He stood up to get dressed and muttered, "Just ain't gonna look right without a tool belt." which made him wonder what they had done with his.

It didn't take long for Jack to get dressed and he could hear his friend's laughter coming from the adjacent room as he finished tying up his boots. He could swear he smelled food as well. That certainly put a little pep in his step as he hopped to his feet.

Jack walked into the room to find all of his friends, except for Darrel and Marie, sitting at a table eating. Everyone looked happy and well rested. He was truly amazed at how resilient these people were. He was even more impressed with the spread of food laid out on the table.

Ricky was the first to notice Jack standing there looking at them, "Finally woke up, eh buddy!"

"Yeah, I really didn't want to."

Malinda stood up, walked over and gave him a kiss, "Come get some lunch." she said.

"Lunch? How long was I out?"

Sarah said, "It's a late lunch."

Malinda replied, "We let you sleep as long as you needed. There was no reason to wake you."

Ricky added, "Yep, nothing has tried to kill us today. Well, yet anyway."

Jack walked over to the table with Malinda and they sat down, "You have to try the breaded fish." she said.

"Real fish?"

Sam had a mouthful, "Sure tastes like it to me!"

"That's incredible hand me a plate!," he said as he looked around, "Where's the booze?"

The room suddenly got quiet and Jim somberly replied, "We only have water."

Jack instantly turned and looked at Ricky. Ricky smiled and said, "I'm fine."

Jack raised an eyebrow wondering how that was even possible, "Are you sure?"

"Yeah, Doc Brownschidle gave me a pill."

Jack patted Ricky on the back, "Well okay then. Pass me the fish!" He piled his plate high with food. It had only been a thing of fantasy for the better part of his life. He thought he had it pretty good on Bravo Colony with Harry's recycled protein dishes. This was something he could barely have imagined, "Are those vegetables?" he asked.

Malinda replied, "yep."

"Oh pass me some of those carrots."

Sarah slid a plate of sliced carrots over to Jack,

"You should try the celery too!" she replied.

Sam winced and his face had a slight nervous tick when she mentioned the celery, "I've repeatedly asked them to stop sending the celery."

"Why's that?" Jack asked.

He coldly replied, "I don't want to talk about it."

Jim's mind was always at work. He interjected, "You know, I bet if they brought me some raw potatoes to go with those tomatoes over there, I could whip us up a batch of Bloody Mary's to go with that celery."

Ricky said, "Oh yeah?"

"Sure, wouldn't take more than 72 hours given the right equipment."

Ricky eagerly asked, "Can we request potatoes?"

"Probably wouldn't hurt to ask." Jack reasoned.

Marie held Darrel's hand as he rested on the doctor's examination table. Dr. Brownschidle carefully looked him over, "They sure did a number on you, Darrel."

"I gave as much as I received, Doctor."

"I'm only concerned with what was received. You have 3 broken ribs, 5 broken fingers and I count 17 lacerations, several of which will require stitching. You're also severely concussed."

"I guess that's why the room won't stop spinning."

"I'm afraid your time on the good ship Elon will be spent in recovery." she replied, "I'm going to give you an injection of genetic stimulators to enhance the repair process."

Marie was impressed, "I've heard about those.

THE TRIALS OF JACK KEMPER

They were developed while we were on the colony."

"Yes indeed. The world might have stopped moving forward but Liberty Island has not."

"So, I'm going to live then?" Darrel asked.

The doctor put the injector up to Darrel's arm and pressed a button. It hissed as it delivered the stimulator, "Yes, Darrel. Barring the onset of infection or a serious pathogen springing up, you should make a complete recovery."

"That's great, Dr. Brownschidle. Thank you so much." Marie replied.

"I've looked over your files. It's not often we rescue such an accomplished surgeon and skilled nurse. I'm sure you'll get the full on recruitment spiel when you arrive at the island and I'm even more sure you'll accept it. Let me be the first to say that we'll be very happy to have you two on our team."

The office of Dr. Brownschidle was actually quite warm. Not in temperature but in aesthetic design. Malinda could see right away that it was meant to put a person at ease. It had all the usual accoutrements; multiple diplomas, photo's with distinguished looking people and it even had a fair share of old fashioned books on a bookshelf. The books caught Malinda's attention and kept it, "You actually have books?"

"Yes, I find it relaxing to flip the pages. And the smell, for some reason, I love the smell."

"Yeah, I get that. My dad used to have a few books. I must have read them a thousand times when I was a kid."

"Well, if you'd like to borrow one to read while you're here in quarantine you're perfectly welcome to do so."

"That would be fantastic."

"I'm afraid most of them are pretty boring, medical texts and such, but there are a few fictions as well as a few historical texts."

"Any pirate fantasy novels? Sarah would love those?"

"Sorry, no. There is one about cowboys though." the doctor scrolled through pages on her tablet, "So, Malinda Hoffman is it?"

"Yes, ma'am."

"And it says here you're from Odrick's Corner, Virginia?"

"That's correct."

"Your father worked for the US Government?"

"He worked for the company."

"CIA?"

"Yes."

"I guess we know how you learned to survive then."

Malinda fidgeted in her seat, "He taught me well."

The doctor sat at her desk waiting for Jim. He was late. It was hard to imagine he had something better to do. After all there wasn't much to do in quarantine. She quickly grew tired of waiting. She stood up and walked out the door.

Dr. Brownschidle walked down the hall to the leisure room. Malinda was sitting there reading a book.

THE TRIALS OF JACK KEMPER

Jack was sprawled out fast asleep with his head in her lap. Sarah was staring out the window lost in a world she never thought she'd see again. But, Jim wasn't there.

The doctor decided she would check the bunk area to see if maybe he was just catching up on some much needed sleep. As she was walking down the hall toward the bunks she heard a loud clang come from her lab. She immediately went to investigate.

She found Jim and Sam in the middle of a heated discussion, "Jim, damn it, listen to me. I'm an engineer. This tube is garbage it will just clog. We need to find one that's made out of an alloy."

"Sam, we're not building one to last for a lifetime. We just need it to work for a couple days."

"You're right. Of course, I'm over analyzing it."

"Well, when we're done you won't have that problem."

The doctor was not impressed, "Ahem."

Jim and Sam slowly turned to face her. Jim said "Oh uh, hi Doctor."

"What are you doing in here?"

"Would you believe it if I said chemistry?"

"Very funny. You're not allowed in my lab, sir. You need to stay in the common areas."

Sam replied, "Oh okay, sorry Doctor. Didn't know this was off limits."

"Jim, I believe we had an appointment?"

"Oh is it that time already? Sorry, you know how it is. Get started on something and lose track of things."

"Can I please see you in my office?"

"Sure thing, Doctor."

The mess hall was serving lunch and today Captain Dent was sharing his table with Reaper Squadron. Sgt. MacIntyre sat across the table from the captain. Cpl.'s Lawson and Richards flanked him. Cpl. Fuentes sat to the left of the captain and PO. Daniels sat to his right. This seating arrangement had been the standard ever since the unfortunate day that the captain was sandwiched between Lawson and Richards.

Lawson always enjoyed lunch with Cpt. Dent. He had plenty of stories to share. There was a standing bet between him and Richards. Lawson won the bet if the captain lost his appetite before the end of his story. And Richards won if the captain was still eating at the end of it.

Cpl. Lawson usually wasted no time starting on a story after they settled down to eat, "Captain, did you hear about our recent rescue in Africa?"

Cpt. Dent nodded, "I don't believe I've had the chance to read that report just yet."

Cpl. Fuentes nudged Sgt. MacInctyre with her elbow, "Here we go."

Cpl. Lawson began, "So we're flying in, lighting the place up naturally, and we're doing our best to protect the high value asset we were sent to recover. It's not like these tribesman were going to put up much of a fight. They're chucking their spears at us. Not the brightest people."

Cpt. Dent continued to eat, "Spears against a fully

armed MMAC. It's a wonder you came back at all, Junior."

Sgt. MacIntyre had to chime in, "When he landed he had 2 spears stuck in his armor."

Cpt. Dent sternly replied, "Let's get him a refresh on evasive maneuvering techniques, Sergeant."

Lawson was caught off guard, "Well if that's an order Captain, but I think I do all right."

The captain couldn't hide his big grin as he took a drink, "Continue with your story, Junior."

"So as we're coming in on our approach we notice the asset isn't moving. We couldn't really make out exactly why that was from that distance. We thought maybe he was already off the grid, but I land and start moving toward him. Pygmy folk were dropping left and right. And I notice the asset is still active. Problem is; he's tied up like a damn hog and hanging from a spit!"

Cpt. Dent looked at Sgt. MacIntyre, "They were going to eat the fellow?"

Before the sergeant could respond Cpl. Lawson did, "They were! He had a damn apple in his mouth to boot."

"Well at least he had a last meal then." The captain joked.

Even Cpl. Lawson had to pause to chuckle at that one, "Here's the strange part."

"Go on."

"He had a damn celery chute stickin' right out of his asshole!"

"Oh my," the captain looked a little startled but then he grinned, "Tell me the truth, Junior. Did you eat that?"

The table erupted in laughter. Cpl. Fuentes almost fell onto the floor. Cpl. Lawson was at a loss for words. What do you do when the captain says something like that?

"Uh, no sir."

Cpt. Dent looked at Cpl. Steele, "Did he?"

Cpl. Steele replied, "I didn't see no celery, sir."

This time Cpl. Fuentes actually did fall on the floor. She had never seen the captain one up Junior before. Sgt. MacIntyre tried to help her back into her chair.

"Sergeant, let's get this man into a psych eval ASAP.!"

"We already have one scheduled, sir. I'll see if I can get it expedited."

Cpl. Lawson fidgeted, "Well come on now. You know I didn't eat it, sarge!"

Sam sat in the chair across from Dr. Brownschidle. Tears were welling up in his eyes as he pointed to the rear end of a stuffed doll, "And worse yet they keep sending up bowls of it at every meal. They even send it for breakfast!"

Dr. Brownschidle nodded, "I see. Yes, I understand how that could be quite traumatizing."

"And I used to love celery!"

"Well, I'll see what I can do to have them stop sending it."

"I'd really appreciate it, doc."

"But, you're feeling okay besides that issue?"

"I could use a drink."

"I could give you a pill for that?"

"I'd prefer a drink."

"I'm afraid I can't let Jim build a still in quarantine."

"Well, I understand he had a bottle with him. Maybe you could pull some strings to get that pushed through?"

"I don't generally condone that sort of thing here, but you've all been through so much and it does seem to be a central part of your relationships. I'll see what I can do."

"We'd really appreciate that, doctor."

Malinda stood under the shower head letting the warm, fresh, water run over her body. It was the first real shower she'd had since she was a child, "Praise Vesta! This is amazing!" She squealed.

Marie stood next to her under another shower head, "Can you believe this? Water!"

"Where do they get it all?" Sarah asked, "I almost feel guilty!"

Malinda replied, "It does seem wasteful, but Jack says they have some sort of system on the ship that pulls the water right out of the air."

Sarah asked, "Why didn't we have that system on Bravo Colony?"

Marie turned and gave Sarah a stare, "Seriously?"

Sarah didn't quite grasp that it was a dumb question, "Yeah."

"Sarah, honey, there's no air in space."

"Oh shit, yeah. Duh."

Malinda said, "I could stand here all day if they'd let me."

"It's a shame we only get five minutes." Marie replied.

"Five minutes of heaven."

The water cut off and there was a collective, "Awe."

Dr. Brownschidle sat at her desk scrolling through pages on her tablet. Jack noticed an abacus on top of her bookshelf, "What possible need would you have for an abacus?"

"It was my father's." she replied.

"It looks old."

"It's an antique. Seventeenth Century Venetian."

Jack replied, "I prefer a calculator."

Dr. Brownschidle set her tablet on the desk, "It says here that you were a prodigy?"

"I know numbers. Know how to make them work. Know how to apply them."

"That's a valuable skill to have."

"My father was a farmer. That's what you're really getting at, right?"

The doctor smiled at Jack, "What did he farm?"

Jack chuckled, "Well, mostly dirt, occasionally food."

Jim was standing at the door staring through the window into the lab of Dr. Brownschidle. She kept the door locked ever since he and Sam were caught rummaging through her equipment. He thought about picking the lock, but he didn't want to cause anymore strife. He just stood there dreaming of the possibilities.

Dr. Brownschidle stood silently behind him. She watched him for a good two minutes. When she realized he wasn't going to try to break in, she spoke, "Jim."

Jim was so startled he jumped. He turned around, "Oh hey, doctor. I wasn't going to go in. You made it clear to me.."

She cut him off, "Jim," Jim was caught so off guard that he didn't even notice his bottle in her hand, "I managed to get this pushed through for you.," she said as she held it out for him.

"Is that?"

"It's your scotch, yes."

Jim grabbed the bottle and then promptly grabbed the doctor. He squeezed her tight, pulled his head back and planted a big kiss square on her lips, "I love you doctor. I truly do! You've made yourself a friend today!"

Dr. Brownschidle blushed, "Enjoy it with your friends, Jim."

"That includes you! Come on let's go have a glass with everyone."

"I'm afraid I can't, Jim. I'm on duty."

Jim nodded, "I get it. It's a damn shame, but I get it."

Ricky had a nice buzz going as he stared across the desk. By the time of his appointment with Dr. Brownschidle, the group had polished off most of the Glenfiddich. Ricky had more than his fair share, "You're from Germany, correct?"

"I am, yes. Bavaria."

"Oh, that's good beer country."

"It was. A century ago. But, you know, drought and failed crops don't leave people much to brew with."

"I bet Jim could have done something about that."

"I'm afraid that unless he could somehow ferment dirt there would be little he could have done."

"Wouldn't put it past him."

Dr. Brownschidle looked at her tablet, "Your file says you were Mayor of Iron City, Tennessee?"

"Indeed! I won in a landslide victory. I got one vote and my opponent got none."

"How is that even possible."

"I threw a party on election day."

"I don't understand."

"When a Montopolis throws a party in Iron City, Tennessee, everybody shows up."

"And this kept them from voting?"

"Hell, they were so drunk they completely forgot about the election. I walked over to the library, cast my ballot and won."

"But, you left for Bravo Colony shortly after taking office. Why did you do that?"

Ricky fidgeted, "I don't want to talk about it."

"You don't want to talk about the dead hooker?"

"I swear she drowned."

THE TRIALS OF JACK KEMPER

The group was enjoying a nice breakfast when Dr. Brownschidle walked into the room and stopped at the end of the table. The genetic enhancers had made quick work of Darrel's injuries over the past two weeks and having him back in the fold added to the general sense of cheerfulness among them.

Jack asked, "More testing today, doctor?"

"You'll be happy to hear that I've finished with my evaluations."

There were cheers all around with an impromptu raise of their water glasses in a toast. "Praise Vesta!"

"All of your medical screenings have come back clear." she paused as she looked directly at Ricky with a smirk on her face, "Well, as clear as can be expected."

"Does this mean we're finally getting out of here?" Sarah asked, "I could really use some different scenery."

"It does." she replied.

Jim stood up and walked over to the cabinets along the wall. He retrieved the bottle of Glenfiddich and returned to the table. There were smiles all around. He looked at the now almost empty bottle and sighed, "This may be the last bottle of this fine scotch in the entire world, but I can't think of a better way to finish it off." He picked up a glass, poured a finger's worth into it and handed it to the doctor, "I won't take no for an answer this time Dr. Brownschidle."

The doctor accepted the glass, resigning herself to Jim's offering. She couldn't help but get caught up in the levity of the moment. She lifted the glass to her lips and tilted it back, finishing off the smooth, aged, scotch in one gulp.

Everyone at the table sat there silent, astonished at what they had just witnessed. Ricky was the first to break the silence, "That's a helluva way to drink that down, doc!"

"Damn right!" agreed Marie. "Don't be stingy with that bottle, Jim," she said as she held her glass out for her share of the bottle. The glass was quickly joined by five others and Jim, ever the professional, filled them without a drop spilled between them.

The group stood in line at the exit hatch waiting to exit the quarantine area. Jack couldn't wait to see the rest of the ship. He had heard rumors of its technology while on Bravo Colony. He turned back to give Dr. Brownschidle one last look, "Thanks for taking care of us, doctor."

"You're welcome, Mr. Kemper." she replied.

A red light above the hatch began to strobe and an alarm sounded. A few seconds later the hatch slid open. Jack was quick to exit. Ricky and Darrel followed closely behind him. Of course, Marie had her arm around Darrel. She wasn't about to let go.

Jim had just gone through the hatch when PO Daniels voice came over the communicator of Dr. Brownschidle, "Doctor, we have your new arrival."

"Mr. Tang?" she replied.

"Yep, fresh off the beach."

Malinda was just about through the hatch when she heard the name. She turned to Dr. Brownschidle,

THE TRIALS OF JACK KEMPER

"Harry Tang?"

The doctor looked down at her tablet, "Yes, he's the latest Bravo Colony survivor to be picked up."

Malinda looked at Sam, "That's not possible!" and began to run down the hallway toward the intake hatch. Sam bolted after her.

Dr. Brownschidle found this all quite alarming and quickly went after them, "Excuse me, you can't.." she stopped as they got out of earshot.

Malinda and Sam were standing at the intake hatch when Dr. Brownschidle arrived, "You two need to exit the quarantine area. If you're here when that hatch opens you'll have to remain in quarantine until we're sure you weren't exposed to any new pathogens."

The mist in the disinfection chamber subsided. Malinda could see an asian man inside, but she couldn't make out who it was. The hatch began to slide open and Malinda raised her fist. If it was Harry Tang, which it couldn't have been, she was going to drop him straight away.

As the hatch slid open it quickly became apparent that the man standing before them was not, in fact, Harry Tang. She didn't know who it was, but, Sam sure knew. He shouted, "Seng!" and promptly lunged toward the naked man.

Dr. Brownschidle had no idea what was happening. Although, she knew they'd be in quarantine a bit longer, "Sam Dillinger, stop that right now!" she ordered.

Sam was having none of it. He wrestled Commander Seng to the floor, climbed on top of him and began raining down punches while shouting, "You evil motherfucker!"

Malinda had no idea who this man was until she heard the name. She immediately began kicking him. She didn't plan on stopping.

Malinda felt a prick on her neck which was accompanied by a hiss. The room got fuzzy. She thought it best to sit down, but she wasn't given the opportunity before she collapsed to the ground.

Sam had Commander Seng's blood splattering all over himself. It gave him great pleasure to hear the thud of his fists. Then he too felt a prick on his neck and heard the accompanying hiss. The image of Commander Seng's bloody face blurred and he noticed he could no longer feel his arms. He felt it was best to lay down and promptly did so; face first.

Jack and the others were invited to have lunch with Captain Dent the next afternoon. All they had been told is that Malinda and Sam would need to remain in quarantine for another week. They were keen to get some answers as to why.

Captain Dent stood up as the group arrived. He had laid out an impressive spread in their honor, "Good afternoon, I'm glad that you all could join me today, well, most of you anyway."

Jack shook the captain's hand but couldn't take his eyes off the table, "Are those…" he almost choked on the words, "Are those burnt ends?"

"A reasonable facsimile. We heard they were a favorite of yours. I hope that you find them to your approval."

The group all silently stared at the table. There was meat, vegetables, wine and to top it off, what looked to be a strawberry covered cheesecake.

The captain barked, "Well don't just look at it. Dig in!"

One by one they grabbed their plates and began to pile the food on. Jack filled his entire plate with burnt ends. Marie took nothing but cheesecake. Ricky could only smile.

As they filled their plates and settled in, Cpt. Dent said, "I'm sorry we have to keep your friends in quarantine a bit longer, but honestly after what they did they're lucky they're not in the brig!"

Jack swallowed what he had crammed in his mouth, washed it down with a big gulp of wine, took a breath and asked, "What exactly was it that they did?"

"They attacked a new arrival in quarantine."

Jack looked at Darrel, "That doesn't sound like something they'd do."

The captain replied, "Apparently they had good reason to do so. That's why they're not in the brig."

Jack replied, "I don't understand."

"The new arrival wasn't who he said he was."

"Who was he?"

"Commander Seng. Of the New Dawn."

Their mouths collectively dropped open. Jack was really glad his was empty. "You have got to be fucking kidding me."

Darrel turned to Jack, "How did he manage to get off of Bravo Colony?"

The captain once again answered, "He used the Presidential escape shuttle."

"Wow. And how did you not know everything about him? You knew everything about us."

"He told us he was Harry Tang. I don't know who Harry Tang is. He must have been wholly unremarkable because he didn't appear anywhere in our files."

"Ha, well that explains why Malinda isn't here. The minute she heard that name I bet her blood started to boil."

"I'm told they both had to be chemically subdued. They nearly succeeded in beating him to death."

Ricky said, "Hell yeah! I bet they did!"

"Poor Dr. Brownschidle." Darrel replied, "I bet she was wondering what the hell was going on."

"She was quite shocked by their behavior at first. But, after she learned who the man was she completely understood. We all do."

Jack asked, "So what happens now?"

"We'll take him to Liberty Island and he'll stand trial for his crimes. I expect an execution we'll be had shortly thereafter."

"Hell, just let Malinda finish him." Marie said.

Sarah agreed, "Really, she's a mean one that girl."

"He'll get what he deserves, but we're civilized. We'll give him his day in court before we carry out his sentence."

Ricky replied, "That seems like a long road to travel for a short swing on a rope."

The captain agreed, "Indeed."

Dr. Brownschidle sat in Cpt Dent's office. His office wasn't quite as warm as hers. It too was designed to be that way. He preferred that people be uncomfortable in his office. It leant to his authority.

Cpt Dent scrolled through pages on a tablet, "Some of this is quite disturbing."

"You don't need a PhD in Psychology to see that."

"At least Sam Dillinger seems, somewhat, normal."

"For the most part, sir. He does have some celery related trauma."

"Oh yeah, Cpl Lawson was kind enough to regale me with that story last week during lunch."

"That hardly seems like the appropriate time."

"I did lose my appetite." Cpt Dent put down the tablet, "Well Doctor, thanks for the analysis. I'll forward this to command along with your recommendations. I guess we'll see what happens when we dock next week."

"Indeed, sir." Dr. Brownschidle stood up, saluted the captain and quickly turned on a heel to leave.

The L.I.S. Elon descended out of the western sky towards Liberty Island. Jack and his friends stood on the observation deck staring through the window in awe as they saw the gleaming central spire of the city island.

The events of the last few weeks would forever

change them. They had been reborn out of hopelessness through cataclysm and struggle. They had persevered. And they had done it together.

Made in the USA
Middletown, DE
21 October 2022